D0614147

"IT'S A BORDELLO," WHISPERED KANE

"No," said Shasta, "it's an inn, a special place for lovers."

"Lovers?" Kane repeated skeptically. "When did we fall into the category of lovers?" He reached behind him for the doorknob and gave it a firm twist. Nothing happened.

"It's locked." Shasta smiled and took hold of his arm, leading him to the couch.

"This is crazy, Shasta. You're wasting your time and money." He laughed, but the sound was strained. "You didn't have to go to all this trouble just to get me in bed. Why the elaborate show?"

Shasta widened her eyes innocently. "Why? I told you. You need to learn how to enjoy life." She slid in beside him and placed her hand on his thigh, her dark-brown eyes melting into his. "And this is just one of the many lessons I have planned."

ABOUT THE AUTHOR

The former manager of a bookstore specializing in romance fiction, Evelyn A. Crowe is now a full-time writer. *Charade*, Evelyn's second Superromance, includes appearances by the hero and heroine of *Summer Ballad*, and in the coming months romance fans can look forward to a third spin-off. Like the others, it will be set in Houston and features the high-spirited and fun-loving characters for which Evelyn is renowned.

Books by Evelyn A. Crowe

HARLEQUIN SUPERROMANCE
112–SUMMER BALLAD
160–CHARADE

These books may be available at your local bookseller.

Don't miss any of our special offers. Write to us at the following address for information on our newest releases.

Harlequin Reader Service
P.O. Box 52040, Phoenix, AZ 85072-2040
Canadian address: P.O. Box 2800, Postal Station A,
5170 Yonge St., Willowdale, Ont. M2N 6J3

Evelyn A. Crowe

CHARADE

Harlequin Books

TORONTO • NEW YORK • LONDON
AMSTERDAM • PARIS • SYDNEY • HAMBURG
STOCKHOLM • ATHENS • TOKYO • MILAN

Published April 1985

First printing February 1985

ISBN 0-373-70160-8

Copyright © 1985 by Evelyn A. Crowe. All rights reserved.
Philippine copyright 1985. Australian copyright 1985.
Except for use in any review, the reproduction or utilization of
this work in whole or in part in any form by any electronic,
mechanical or other means, now known or hereafter invented,
including xerography, photocopying and recording, or in any
information storage or retrieval system, is forbidden without
the permission of the publisher, Harlequin Enterprises Limited,
225 Duncan Mill Road, Don Mills, Ontario, Canada M3B 3K9.

All the characters in this book have no existence outside the
imagination of the author and have no relation whatsoever to
anyone bearing the same name or names. They are not even
distantly inspired by any individual known or unknown to the
author, and all the incidents are pure invention.

The Superromance design trademark consisting of the words
HARLEQUIN SUPERROMANCE and the portrayal of a Harlequin,
and the Superromance trademark consisting of the words
HARLEQUIN SUPERROMANCE are trademarks of Harlequin
Enterprises Limited. The Superromance design trademarks
and the portrayal of a Harlequin are registered in the
United States Patent Office.

Printed in Canada

For Bill, Jane, Chris and Kellie
. . . and of course, always Mother.

CHAPTER ONE

A LUMINOUS, ENGORGED MOON hung heavily in the stormy sky, its brilliance occasionally obscured by dark clouds streaking across its surface, dappling the ground below in eerie shadows. Clouds chased one another in a frenzied rush to gain force and forge into the darkness, wreaking their vengeance across the innocent Texas landscape. As if in answer to the whispered call for destruction, the leaf-rustling breeze picked up momentum until it sounded like the gasping breath of an unknown demon.

The wind huffed stronger, and the lone female figure moved with a surefooted stride across the rooftop of the Stone estate. Dressed to blend with the night, she was a dark phantom, and only her shadow was reflected on the ground below as the clouds deigned to part, allowing the moon's brightness to peek through.

A raised arm silhouetted against the sky lifted higher, and a nylon rope snaked out, encircling the brick chimney. The figure pulled on the rope, tightened it around the chimney securely and wrapped one end around her waist. Suddenly a strong gust of wind pushed at her back, and she came dangerously close to losing her balance and plunging three stories to the ground below.

Angrily she tugged on the lines, then took a deep breath and began to back down the slanted slate roof. Her bare toes gripped the sharp edges as she continued her descent into total darkness, cursing the menacing clouds for blocking out the much-needed light. She moved by feel and touch, and when she finally reached her goal she immediately planted her heels in the wide copper gutters. As she leaned precariously backward into the night, she knew the heady feeling of a bird ready to take flight.

Another gust of wind set the taut lines vibrating. The dark figure clutched her safety line and stabilized her slipping hold, grumbling through lips turned blue from the sudden drop in temperature.

With the agility of an eel she wiggled around for a better position in front of a small, round attic window. The diamond-tipped cutter scratched the outline of the pane, and the sound it made caused her ears to ache. She returned the cutter to its case, then pulled on the rubber suction cup adhered to the center of the glass. The stubborn window wouldn't budge, and she quickly gave it a series of strong taps before the pane came free.

One jean-clad leg worked its way through the opening, and a foot came to rest on a hard surface. A leather-encased shoulder went through next, followed by a dark cap. Perched on one leg, the woman suddenly lost her balance and in a hopping, jumping movement fell through the window and landed sprawled on the dusty attic floor.

She was in! An impish grin lit her face. No one expected a *cat burglar* to strike during one of Houston's legendary gulf storms. That was the very reason she had picked this night. Who would ever guess?

Stop playing games, my girl, and get to work, she reminded herself. *You have gold to collect.* Heaving herself up and dusting off her legs, she retrieved her penlight and made for the stairs, and the master bedroom.

Once there she found her way to the bathroom and pulled open the linen closet. Leather-covered fingers felt for the hidden latch and flicked it upward, causing the shelves to swing outward. Her light shone on the complicated panel of the electronic alarm system and she hissed in surprise. The system was already turned *off*.

She stood perfectly still and counted the seconds, trying to figure out the cause of this sudden feeling of unease. Then she shrugged. So the Stones had forgotten to turn on the alarm before they left for Europe. But that wasn't likely with the new system, or was it? Had they thought they'd switched it on and actually turned it off? She shrugged again. The system wasn't her problem now. What she wanted was to get her itchy fingers on the newly installed safe downstairs and the contents inside.

Like a homing pigeon, her inner radar guided her down the wide curving stairs to the double doors of the library. The pinpoint of light that she shone before her showed her the way around the furniture to the far wall. There was just enough moonlight coming through the floral-patterned drapes to allow her to see the large oil painting that covered the safe.

Quickly she reached up and ran her fingers along the edge of the ornate gold-leaf frame, hunting for the release catch. There was a click as the painting slowly swung aside.

Shasta Masterson lovingly caressed the shiny surface of the safe, her eyes glistening with devilment and the sheer ecstasy of having reached her goal. Giving one of the big dials a spin, she began to laugh softly, only to have her merriment choked off in midchuckle as she felt cold steel pressing painfully into the back of her neck.

She listened to the deep, slightly accented male voice and stiffened.

"Make one move and you're a dead man!"

KANE STONE WAS JOLTED out of his nightmare. Though the intruding noise brought his conscious mind to an alert state, his subconscious was still reliving the loss and death of a man more like his father than his own flesh and blood one.

Sighing wearily, he lay motionless, afraid if he so much as closed his eyes again he'd see the horror of the hit-and-run accident and feel the sense of helplessness that had swept over him as he'd held that frail old body. But he did close his eyes again in exhaustion.

Before sleep could claim him, he wondered for the hundredth time what he was doing in his father's house. Memories had crowded in on one another the moment he'd stepped over the threshold. He'd looked up the darkened curved well of the staircase and the past had flashed so vividly around him that he'd cowardly turned his back. Refusing to face his demons, he'd made his bed for the night on the living-room couch. But even there the past wouldn't leave him in peace. How he'd hated this house and its owner—first with a young boy's passion and later with a grown man's strength. This hate had festered and exploded twenty-five years ago. He'd sworn then, at the tender age of twelve, never to return, and he had kept that vow—till now.

The noise came again, this time closer, and Kane pulled himself quickly up on one elbow, too quickly for his bruised ribs. He bit back a moan and eased his battered body into a more comfortable position to relieve the pressure and afford him a better view over the back of the couch.

A pinpoint of light weaved in and out of the darkness, passing so close behind the couch he could have reached out and grabbed the intruder. His fist was already on the move before he caught himself. *Not this time, you bastard,* he thought grimly. *You're not going to catch me unprepared.*

He let the light continue on its way to the far wall, then, reaching for his weapon, he followed.

"MAKE ONE MOVE and you're a dead man!"

The words tingled along Shasta's spine. Once before she had looked down the barrel of a gun, and she didn't wish to repeat the experience. She winced as the gun ground harder into her neck, then inhaled deeply to calm the pounding of her heart.

"I said, not a move. Now spread-eagle."

Time seemed to stand still as she slid her hands out and up the paneled wall. In the distance thunder rolled across the land. The wind moaned, and fat drops of rain splattered against the windows in minuscule explosions.

Using his foot as a hook, her assailant forced her feet apart and back so that the only balance she had was her forehead resting against the cold wood paneling. It was a position used by law-enforcement agencies. She made a mental note of his expertise, reminding herself to stay quiet and try to glean as much information about this burglar as possible.

Judging from the distance and sound of his voice above her, she guessed him to be somewhere between six-foot and six-foot-two. And damn him, his after-shave was driving her crazy, reminding her of summer afternoons and warm sunshine—earthy and sensual. Thieves weren't supposed to smell good, were they?

"I thought I made myself clear in Paris. Didn't your

friends relay the message to your boss? I warned him not to send his goons after me again. Maybe it's time to show him I mean what I say and teach him a little lesson in counterattack."

The husky voice stirred her hair, and a shiver seemed to slide down each vertebra, stiffening her whole body. It wasn't the soft accented voice causing the effect, but the menacing tone to his words.

"Keep still," he commanded as she twitched her shoulders, trying to relieve some of the strain.

Keeping the weapon pressed into the back of her neck, he ran his free hand around her ankles, then moved upward. Each calf was lightly touched, the outside of each thigh briefly frisked. When his fingers reached around to the inside of her thighs, she tensed and held her breath.

He stopped his search for a second, as if puzzled by something. "Scrawny thing, aren't you?" His hand wandered onward to her waist. "When did the company start hiring kids to do their dirty work? Or are you with the other group?"

Shasta knew he didn't expect an answer, and she wasn't about to open her mouth and give herself away— that would come soon enough. She grimaced as he clasped the zipper of her leather bomber jacket and yanked it down. His hand slipped inside the warm confines and quickly ran from ribs to armpit.

She heard his deep intake of breath and squeezed her eyes shut. Every muscle was tense as his fingers grazed the side of her breast then froze there.

"What the hell?" As if to confirm what he now suspected, Kane's hand cupped one nicely rounded, female breast.

"Son of a bitch." The shock didn't last long, and he

leaned over and switched on a desk lamp. "Okay, baby. Let's have a good look at you."

His words weren't an endearment. He gripped the back of her jacket in a tight fist and hauled her upright. Without allowing her time to catch her balance, he spun her around and yanked off the knit cap. Brown shoulder-length curls tumbled out, bouncing in total disarray around her face. When she reached out to push the unruly mass from her eyes, her hand was slapped away none too gently. She yelped in pain as strong fingers gathered a handful of hair and pulled her sideways, twisting her face to the light.

Shasta inwardly flinched at the thought of having to face a gun again. Resignedly she opened her eyes, only to find them level with a bare male chest. Something was terribly wrong! A tall, half-naked thief who smelled good and talked with a French accent just couldn't be true. Lowering her eyes farther, she found herself gazing down the cold, menacing barrel of the weapon he held—an empty long-necked beer bottle, imported of course.

The heat of anger flushed her cheeks a bright red. She felt like a fool. Despite the pain she jerked her head back and frowned into her captor's face, ready to burst forth with a lengthy set of questions. Instead she simply gulped and stared, absolutely stunned.

"Well, pixie, you're a surprise."

Eyes as silver as newly minted coins flashed, and Shasta wondered dazedly whether she'd see her own reflection if she gazed long enough into their depths. She gulped again for air, lost in the masculine beauty before her. And he definitely was gorgeous—and very much a male.

A loud drumming filled her ears, and she felt a short-

ness of breath. She wondered how many other women
experienced the same effects while gazing at him. He
was the most beautiful, most decadent-looking man
she'd ever seen.

It seemed a conspiracy against the female species that
any man could possess those perfectly arched eyebrows
and the double row of long, thick black lashes. Suddenly the hand in her hair tightened painfully and brought
her sharply back to reality. Here she was, faced with
possible death, and she'd been daydreaming and lusting
after a thief.

"Welcome back." He smiled and Shasta watched,
trancelike, as the chiseled lips mouthed the words, "No
you don't." He shook her head roughly. "You're not
going to fade out to never-never land on me again.
Lady, I want some answers."

Shasta wasn't dreaming any longer. She'd seen that
smile, and its resemblance to a tiger contemplating his
next meal was unnerving. She knew instinctively that
whatever she'd faced in the past was child's play com-
pared to what this man could and would do to her.
Beautiful he might be, but he exuded an air of cruelty,
and she knew that nothing would stop him from doing
exactly what he wanted. Keeping him distracted and off
balance was her only hope to get away. Her free hand
inched, unobserved, over the surface of the desk beside
her, and she asked her own questions.

"What are you doing in *my* house? Who are you?"

"Your *house*?" He snorted, then smiled again, truly
evil this time. "Do you usually sneak around your own
house dressed like a Hollywood cat burglar?"

"I'm an actress," she lied, her fingers continuing
their search. "I was getting into character."

He shook his head slowly, and Shasta was momentarily distracted by the play of lights on his blue-black hair. She was about to give up hope of finding a weapon of any sort when the tips of her fingers nudged a round object, and her hand closed over a heavy, crystal paperweight. Bracing herself, she looked directly into his steady gaze, then her eyes traveled toward the open doorway. She made her body stiffen under his hands, her eyes widened and she smiled. "Come in, Julius. As you can see we have company."

"No, lady—" his voice rumbled with laughter "—that old trick won't wash."

Shasta made a lunge, then yelled out in pain as her head was snapped back and his other hand wrapped around her throat.

"I don't like games." His eyes narrowed to silver slits. "Talk." Fingers tightened around her throat, slowly cutting off her air supply.

How was she supposed to talk when he was choking her? She struggled for one deep breath of air, certain she was going to die, when suddenly a sharp blinding flash of light filled the room, followed instantly by window-rattling thunder. That brief second, when her assailant froze, gave her the chance she needed. She swung the heavy paperweight upward with all her strength. There was a satisfying thud, then the pressure around her neck eased.

Leaning against the desk for support, she rubbed at her bruised throat, inhaling deeply, trying to calm her shattered nerves. When she regained her composure, she looked down at the supine figure at her feet and nudged his side experimentally with a bare toe. Out like a light. She grinned.

A few seconds later she had his hands and feet secured with both their belts. Only then did she sit back on her heels and relax long enough to lay her fingers to the side of his neck, checking that the pulse still beat steadily. "While you're taking a nap, friend, I'll just make a few phone calls. Maybe when you wake you'll answer some of my questions. Don't go away now," she said, chuckling, as she pushed herself up and reached for the telephone.

With the receiver in one hand, she began to punch out the numbers while her other hand idly played with a small folder. "Damn it, answer, Jeff," she growled softly, her eyes wandering back and forth between her captive and the now-open folder. As the typewritten words came into focus, she slowly dropped the instrument back into its cradle and leaned across the desk toward the lamplight. She prayed she'd been dreaming. But, no, there it was, typed neatly on the official United States passport, and if that wasn't bad enough, his signature and photograph confirmed his identification.

Shasta looked up toward heaven. "Please," she begged in a pitiful voice. "Don't do this to me. You don't realize what I've been through this week, then to be so cruel as to throw this at me now." She let her eyes drop to the open passport, and this time she read the name outloud. "Kane Maximilian du Monde Stone." Her client's son.

The passport slipped through her fingers to the carpeted floor. What now, she wondered, her glazed eyes resting on the unconscious man.

Unconscious. The word rattled her out of her stupor and sent her vaulting over the inert form and out the door. Once in the big, modern kitchen, she yanked and pulled frantically at drawers, mumbling under her breath as she searched for a dish towel and filled it with ice. She raced back to her trussed-up captive, knowing he was going to be madder than a wet hen when he woke—to say nothing of the headache he'd have.

She threw herself down on the floor, slipped a needle-point pillow from the couch under Kane's head and positioned the ice pack behind his left ear and the large lump she'd given him. Her fingers automatically went to the belt securing his hands before reason struck and she jerked back in horror. He'd never listen to what she had to say first. Shasta shook her head, recognizing Kane as the type who always came out of a corner fighting. She patted his hands gently. She wasn't going to give him any swinging room till she had thoroughly explored every possible explanation. Crossing her legs, elbows resting on her knees and hands cupping her chin, she settled down to wait for him to come to.

Kane groaned and Shasta adjusted the ice pack, her hands lingering a second longer than necessary on the springy black hair. She leaned back, intently studying the strong face, and whispered, "Well, Mr. Kane Maximilian du Monde Stone, welcome home." She reached out and lightly touched each arched eyebrow, then ran the tip of her finger back and forth over the fan of long lashes.

Lightning began to spark wildly outside, and everything faded around her as she sat on the floor, concentrating with an unnatural intensity on the man before her.

Thunder boomed overhead, but Shasta didn't feel the hammering vibrations. Rain drummed furiously against the house, bringing with it a coldness that penetrated every corner of the room, but she could only feel the heat of Kane's body.

"Do you know that you take my breath away?" Her eyes followed the path of her fingers trailing down the aquiline nose, outlining the flared nostrils. "I wonder if I'd ever have the nerve to say what I'm about to say if you were conscious?" she whispered. "From the moment you turned me around and I gazed into those soulless eyes, I knew you were mine." She caressed his square jaw with the back of her hand, smiling dreamily when the rough stubble of his cheeks tickled her sensitive skin. The clefted chin and deep lines bracketing his mouth seemed to beckon her light caress, and the tip of one finger moved to circle the sculpted lips. "You'll think I'm crazy, I know." She wondered if his lips would remain so impersonal pressed to her own. Moistening her parched lips, she said softly, "You're mine, Kane Stone," and leaned down to place her mouth on his.

Every breath he took seemed to be a sigh just for her. She allowed the tip of her tongue to trace the sharp lines of his lips before pulling back, reluctantly. For all she knew he might be married with a dozen children, but somehow she didn't think so. This man was hers, she knew it. To dispel any nagging fears, she picked up his passport from where it had fallen and flipped it open. Under "wife" there were three tiny, beautiful X's.

"So, no wife—yet." Shasta grinned wickedly. She dropped her hand to his and let her fingers travel along the map of warm veins patterning one bronzed arm. He was tall, broad shouldered, slim hipped and lean. No surplus flesh there. He had the physique of an athlete, but shadows of exhaustion belied that exterior, faint half circles of fatigue under his eyes, lines of strain that deepened the furrows between his eyebrows.

Shasta jerked her hand back from Kane's ribs as he moaned in pain. She leaned down for a better view and sucked in a hard breath. His whole side was a mass of bruises. "What happened to you, Kane?" She picked up his tied hands and inspected the scraped and swollen knuckles. "I wonder who won? Looks like you gave as good as you got though." She brought his injured hands to her lips and kissed them lightly, noticing their long, slim fingered elegance. "But, my love," she began, only to be interrupted as Kane snorted in his unconscious state. She smiled. "You don't like the endearment? No, your footloose, fancy-free spirit wouldn't, but in time you'll get used to it."

Kane twisted his head back and forth, and Shasta stroked his brow to calm his movements, then replaced the dislocated ice pack. Her eyes caressed the broad chest, lingering on the mat of black hair that tapered off to a fine line down the center of his stomach and beneath the waistband of his jeans.

The temptation was too great, the pull too strong, and gently she laid her hand on his chest, barely touching the silken hair. She followed the path of darkness to the denim barrier, and though her fingers stopped, her eyes continued a very slow, very thorough journey to his bare feet. "Yes indeed, you're mine, and you can count on that!"

Maybe she *was* crazy. She'd spent the last ten of her twenty-seven years searching for this feeling, and she wasn't about to let it slip away. She was an incurable romantic. But what did the world expect when she was surrounded by a family of happily-ever-after marriages. She always felt odd man out, because up until now she'd never experienced that special something, that instant recognition her family talked about. Her brother teased her unmercifully, saying that her unnatural nerves of steel made a shield so thick that no romantic feeling could penetrate.

She wanted to touch Kane again and reassure herself he was real. She reached out, then stopped, laughing as she noticed her trembling hand. Amazed, she shoved the other one out and watched in fascination as it shook, also. Now! Now she'd proved Jeff wrong. She was just as normal as the rest of her family. She laughed aloud again. Her nerves of iron had melted away to flesh and blood.

KANE MANAGED to lie perfectly still, though his head ached abominably and the pain around his ribs made him want to double over. His jaw clenched as pieces of what had happened began to form a clear picture. To be bested physically by a woman was bad enough, but to be outmaneuvered and manipulated by a mouse—that's what really smarted, he conceded. And his big bad burglar was exactly that—a mouse with a tangle of brown hair, big brown eyes and a small pert nose that actually twitched enchantingly.

He was jolted out of his musing by her jubilant laughter, and the muscles along his jaw knotted at the sound. There was a long pause and then she laughed again, and this time he was forced to bite the inside of his cheek because he found the delightful noise contagious. The happy sound, half laugh, half giggle, came from deep down, a gut laugh. He wondered how long it had been since he'd heard the pure joy of uninhibited laughter. Certainly not from his so-called set, who usually gave a stiff, sophisticated whinny that grated on his nerves after too long an exposure.

Opening his eyes a crack, Kane assessed the situation correctly. He was expertly tied hand and foot with no hope of slipping free till his captor deemed it so or until help arrived. His gaze shifted to the woman sitting cross-legged beside him, her chin in hand. She was staring intently at him, and the sparkle in her eyes made him extremely uncomfortable.

"You can open them the rest of the way." Shasta grinned at the frown gathering across the wide brow. "I hope your head isn't hurting you too badly to listen to an explanation?"

Kane's gaze met hers and the frown deepened—partly in self-disgust, partly in anger. He watched warily as her full, lovely mouth stretched into a heart-stopping smile. He had to concentrate hard on staying angry in order to hide his inclination to respond to her smile. "Don't tell me there's actually an explanation? I guess now you're going to hand me the old line that this is not what it appears to be?"

"Well. . . ." she drawled the word out.

"Baby, if you can come up with an explanation to convince me you're not a cat burglar, you're a better liar than I'd have suspected."

Shasta straightened, highly affronted at being referred to as a liar and being called baby. "First of all let's get a few things perfectly clear between us. You don't call me baby and I won't call you Maxie." He winced and she knew she'd hit the raw spot she'd aimed for. "Deal?"

"Deal." He couldn't help but smile this time. "If we're to have a lengthy conversation, do you think you could untie me?" He altered his expression to one of great pain. "These belts are cutting off the circulation in my hands and feet." She shook her head. "No! How about just the feet? No! Come on now, what could I possibly do with my feet?" He gave her a smile that always worked on other women, but this one only laughed and shook her head.

"You can probably do more with your feet than most men can with an active pair of hands. Sorry, Kane."

Kane looked up at her, lingering over her wide brown eyes. He forced himself to concentrate once again on the situation and his anger. "You seem to know who I am. Am I entitled to a name along with this explanation of yours?"

"Shasta Masterson." She was thinking hard and fast, trying to find the quickest and most precise way to express herself.

He waited for her to go on, and when she didn't his lip curled and his next words came out in a cutting tone. "Ahh...that explains everything. Tell me something, Shasta Masterson, how much is this going to cost my father?" He ignored her start of surprise and narrowing eyes. "I mean, doesn't a burglar turn to kidnapping and ransom when his robbery plans are thwarted and he's caught? Let me give you some advice. Neither my father nor our company will pay. That, my girl, is Texas-American Oil's policy." He paused long enough to let his words sink in. "Now, be a good girl and *untie me*!" he exploded. He calmed down, but his next words were spoken through clenched teeth. "I promise you, you'll walk out of here and we'll forget we ever met."

Shasta's eyes widened as she listened to each word, then she stopped his angry struggle to get loose by throwing her head back and laughing. When she realized he had ceased moving and was glaring at her murderously, she reached for the leather knot binding his hands. She took a deep breath. "I know you're going to find this hard to believe." She stopped what she was doing, feeling he deserved her full attention.

"Untie me!" he demanded coldly. "Now!"

"Yes, yes. But you've wiggled around so this knot is

hard to work loose.'' She continued to talk as she struggled with the stubborn strap. Her voice, usually sweet
and slow with its soft Texas drawl, began to speed up.
Words tumbled from her lips in a great rush. Syllables
tripped and stumbled over one another in her haste to
explain. While she wrestled with the belt, Kane punc-
tuated her efforts at regular intervals with the command
''Untie me.'' She looked up after her speedy speech and
noticed the blank look on Kane's face.

''What it all boils down to is I work for Masters Security. We. . . I mean my brother, Jeff, designed and installed the alarm security system for your father. It's my
job to find the flaws, and I did. The problem was, no
one was supposed to be here.'' He still looked uncon-
vinced and only held up his hands when she stopped
working. She sighed and returned to her task.

''Honestly, Kane, I'm telling the truth.''

''How did you get through the front gates? They were
locked and are ten feet of wrought iron.''

''I didn't go through them.'' She switched her gaze
from his hands to his face and wished she hadn't. The
wind-driven rain outside settled down to a steady humming noise in her ears. She felt herself wanting to drown
in his silver eyes. Like calm water they seemed to promise everything and reveal nothing of the danger lurking
within their depths. ''I. . . I went over the gate.'' She
tore her eyes away from his, her heart pounding like a
big brass drum. She wanted to say something, anything,
to break the silent hold he had on her. ''Kane.''

''Woman,'' he roared. ''Would you finish untying
me before my fingers and toes fall off?'' The belt finally
fell away and Kane sat up, pushed Shasta aside and
began rubbing his hands together briskly before he
reached down and expertly released his bound feet.

He turned the blaze of silver on her. "If what you say is true and you were running a test on the alarm system—" his mouth tightened "—what were you doing at the wall safe?"

Shasta smiled confidently. "We installed that, too."

Silence hung between them with only the flicker of lightning and the ominous rolling of thunder breaking the quiet. "I don't know whether to believe you or not? But I'll hand you this, lady, you're a cool one." Lightning split the sky again, lighting the room in an eye-blinking brilliance. Kane moved before Shasta knew what was happening. "Let's just see how calm and cool you really are?"

Before the thunder had time to follow the streaking light, Shasta found herself stretched out on the carpeted floor beneath Kane's full weight. Their eyes clashed and held for a moment, then his head came to rest in the curve of her neck and a low moan escaped his lips. Catching his breath, he raised his head. His eyes had turned the color of pewter and held a residue of pain. "What in the name of hell did you hit me with?"

She opened her lips to answer but was cut off by the pressure of his mouth on hers. Her first instinct was to fight, give him a good whack in his already sore ribs. She couldn't hurt him again, though, so she lay there unresponding. But, oh God, how she wanted to open her lips for him.

When Kane raised his head and looked down, the shutter of cruelty had left his face and been replaced with a hint of humor. "Well, I see you really are a cool lady. A shame I'd have—"

Shasta reached up, gathered a handful of his hair and pulled his mouth down to hers. This time her warm pliant lips met his, and as quick as a butterfly her tongue slipped between his parted lips. She felt him stiffen. Then, not to be mastered by a woman again, he took command and threaded his fingers through the shoulder-length curls, adding his own expertise to her kiss.

Shasta had thought to teach him a quick lesson in fair play between the sexes, but she realized this was no game, and though she wanted him and intended to have him, now was not the time to expose all her cards.

She opened her eyes and moved her head back, breaking contact. Thunder crashed overhead and the electricity blinked out, but the lightning highlighted Kane's features, casting his eyes into shadows. She gazed into them and felt herself succumb to their power. They pulled her like a leaf into a whirlpool of swirling silver water. Hypnotically she closed her eyes and gave herself up once again to the beauty of his mouth, savoring the firmness of his lips, the hardness of his teeth, the feeling of his warm breath blending with hers. They broke apart as the lightning struck once more, this time with all its fury, then it seemed to give up the fight and slip away into the night, the thunder reverberating in its wake, leaving them in total darkness.

"Hell...." Kane swallowed the rest of his comment, not sure if the heart-stopping sensation was from the kiss or this latest display from mother nature. He smoothed the springy curls back from her fevered brow and smiled into the darkness. She might be small, but she packed a most desirable punch.

"I don't think the lights are going to come on again," she breathed against his lips, allowing herself the luxury of teasing the corners of his mouth with the tip of her tongue.

"No," he whispered, his hand playing in the silken

curls. "I guess there's nothing left to do but go to bed."
He felt her stiffen. "Be reasonable. You wouldn't get
one block on this street before your car was door deep in
water. Besides—" his voice hardened "—I'm not one
hundred percent sure I believe your story. I'd rather
have you close by till I've checked you out. Okay?"

"I guess," she sighed. She knew only too well what
happened to Houston's streets in a flash flood. Kane
moved away and she followed him, her hand in his. She
trailed behind him as he gave instructions where to turn,
when to lift her feet to climb stairs, when to walk
straight. Finally she felt the firm, high bed.

Kane turned back the covers, then touched her arm to
signal her to climb in. Snuggling down, she pulled the
blanket to her chin. "Good night, Kane." She heard his
movements and assumed he was making his way to the
door, but when the other side of the bed sank with his
weight, she demanded, "What do you think you're doing?"

She felt a hand run the length of her leg and sat up.
"Listen, Kane Stone—" She stopped, stunned speechless as something soft was tied firmly around her ankle.
"What the hell...?" She tried to yank her foot away,
but he held it firm as he tied the sash of joined neckties
to the bedpost.

"Be still, damn it." His voice floated out of the darkness. "I'm making sure I get to check out your story.
Cats have a way of sneaking off in the middle of the
night. Just be thankful your tethers are silk and not
leather."

The bed gave a few bounces before she settled down.
"Well I'll be damned."

"We are both more than likely damned already."
Why did he have an uneasy feeling in the pit of his stom-

ach? He was attracted to her, though he hadn't figured out why. She certainly wasn't his type. Maybe that was the answer. He was tired of experienced, sophisticated women. Maybe for the next few weeks, while he searched for the information he'd come back for, he'd entertain himself and play with a mouse who went disguised as a cat burglar. He smiled. Things might not be as boring as he had anticipated. He was aware of her wiggling around, trying to find a comfortable position, and it irritated him to feel the tightening in his loins. "Keep still or you'll cut off the circulation in your foot," he said gruffly. "Go to sleep. I promise I won't take advantage of you during the night."

Shasta knew he was leaving. "Where are you going?" She hissed into the darkness, tugging frantically at her securely tied ankle. "Don't leave me alone like this."

"Afraid! You?" The sound of his laughter lingered long after he'd left the room.

Shasta wondered at the rusty rasp she'd heard—as if he'd forgotten how to really laugh. She certainly had her work cut out for her. Lying back, her arms folded behind her head, she decided she'd rest her eyes awhile and throw him off guard. Then she'd work herself free and follow him downstairs. Her eyes became heavier and a dreamy smile touched her lips as she thought of all the fun she could have teaching Kane how to enjoy life.

CHAPTER TWO

SHASTA OPENED HER EYES to an unfamiliar peach-colored ceiling. She wondered briefly why she was torturing her body by sleeping on her back, then tried to flip over onto her side. One leg seemed to be twisted at an odd angle, refusing to budge. She yanked it sharply toward her, then sat bolt upright with a yelp as pain shot through her ankle.

Once her befuddled brain was elevated she realized she was in a strange room, in a strange bed, and fully clothed. Gradually the previous night came back into focus, which wasn't easy at such an ungodly hour of the morning. Giving her foot an experimental tug, she leaned forward and in a few seconds was struggling grimly with a series of intricate knots. Reluctantly she grinned at Kane's sense of humor.

She persisted working at the taut silk, but with each pull the line of knots seemed to shrink. Frustrated, her fingers sore, she bellowed, "Kane!" and waited.

When he didn't answer, she propped her chin in her hand and contemplated the situation. She studied the length of silk, judging the amount of give at both looped ends—one around her ankle, the other around the bedpost—and the row of knots in between. As the seconds ticked by, she began to smile. Though short in stature, she was blessed with long legs and, as her grandfather put it, was "as limber as a double-jointed snake."

Shasta loosened the loop secured around the wood post so it could slide. Then, standing on her untethered leg, she did a slow split, working her foot up inch by inch until at last she slid the loop over the top of the tall post.

She collapsed amid a tangle of covers, then leaped off the bed. In a whirlwind of sheets, bedspread and trailing blankets, she bounded out of the room and down the stairs. Catching the scent of freshly brewed coffee, she marched into the kitchen, stopped in the doorway and yelled at the man calmly ensconced behind the morning paper. "That was a damn dirty trick, Kane Stone." Her nose crinkled in disgust when her words brought no response. She tried again. "You're a mean, vindictive man. You heard me calling you. What if I had needed to go to the bathroom?"

The paper vibrated a second, then lowered only as far as the bridge of Kane's nose. "Did you?"

"No," she snapped, sliding into the nearest chair and reaching for the coffeepot. She was more frustrated than she'd like to admit. His roving eyes had taken in everything from her bare feet, wrinkled and twisted clothes to her unruly hair before he slowly raised his paper shield.

"I'd like two eggs, scrambled. Bacon, crisp and blotted. Four slices of toast, crust trimmed and lightly buttered."

"So would I," she grumbled under her breath, her stomach jumping at each item he called off. Then she realized he was speaking to *her*. But just to be quite sure a cook wasn't lurking about, she searched out every corner of the kitchen before her vivid eyes flashed him a scorching look that should have melted him on the spot. Of all the nerve! She gently set the coffeepot down and leaned across the thick glass table. With both hands at the top of his morning paper, she pleated the sheets down to his lap. Their eyes met levelly. "I, Mr. Stone, can't cook."

"Figures." He shook both ends of the paper and folded it neatly.

She looked up into shimmering silver eyes, a deceptively sweet smile on her lips, and watched him struggle to keep his expression stern.

"You know, Kane, God won't strike you dead if you laugh out loud," she whispered, then pushed back from the table and left the room. She wondered what had happened to make him afraid to feel or show any emotion. Even his anger the night before, though loudly vocal at one point, had still been under rigid control. She was going to have her work cut out for her, and she still hadn't figured out a way to see him again after today.

Moving quickly across the hall to the living room, she winced at the sound of chair legs scraping on Spanish tile and ignored the heavy fall of footsteps behind her. She picked up her leather jacket from the floor, pulled a stethoscope out of an inside zippered pocket and inserted the rubber ends into her ears.

Kane leaned against the doorframe, watching as she walked to the huge painting on the wall. He smiled as she went up on tiptoe, her fingers searching for the hidden latch. Releasing the catch, she swung the ornate frame out, placed metal to metal and began to work the round cylinder dials slowly. His smile widened at her serious expression. Did she really think she was good enough to break the combination? He'd seen the trademark on that safe and knew the company's reputation. Besides, only two people in the world knew the magic numbers—his father and the German manufacturer.

The smooth tumbling clicks soothed her raw nerves.

A smile twitched her lips as she recalled her brother's taunting words. "This time we gotcha, my girl. No one, but no one, can open the Stones' new safe."

Jeff and their cousin Daniel had spent weeks in conference calls between the German company and their New York representative to obtain this special locking system. They were so pompously sure of themselves they had laid a hefty bet that Shasta couldn't break the combination. They had even talked J. T. Masterson, her grandfather, into entering their so-called fun. Shasta knew heads were likely to roll in all directions tomorrow. If there was one thing J.T. hated worse than losing an argument, it was losing a sure-thing bet.

She couldn't restrain a soft chuckle. What none of her family of supersnoops had yet to discover was that she had designed the new lock system and sold her plans to the German company. It was the only way she could afford to indulge in her passion for fast, deadly, little sports cars.

Shasta purred with pleasure as she heard the last tumble of oiled metal. She reached up and pulled the handle, but before she could swing the round steel door open, Kane's hand clamped down on hers. In her total absorption she'd completely forgotten about him. She looked over her shoulder, meeting the renewed suspicion in his eyes.

"Kane, the only things in this safe are three Krugerrands and they're mine." She tugged on the handle, but he applied pressure to still her efforts.

He studied her expressive face. The big brown eyes were honest, yet there was a hard intelligence and perceptiveness in their depths that surprised him. For some unknown reason he wanted desperately to trust her, but he hesitated. The ease with which she'd opened the safe bothered him; she'd handled the whole operation so professionally. He knew it took a lifetime of experience to attain that self-assurance, and she didn't have the years, unless she'd started learning her trade from the cradle.

"Before you open the door why don't you tell me why three of your Krugerrands would be in this safe?"

A frown marred Shasta's brow. She had wanted him to believe her without proof, to take her word as the truth. Now she could see that it wasn't going to be that easy. She sensed his lack of trust for anything female and wondered what kind of woman had inflicted such deep scars.

She tilted her head and glared up at him, angry with herself for expecting so much so soon. Quickly she related the terms of the bet without adding any of the funnier sides of the story. She fell silent and waited for his reaction. The mask shuttering his face remained stonily fixed, his eyes mirror hard. Then, making up his mind about her, he smiled and dropped his hand.

Shasta didn't move—couldn't move if she'd wanted to. Her eyes were glued to his face, mesmerized by the power of his smile. Then, in response to the dazzling effect he was having on her, she slowly answered his smile with one of her own. She couldn't recall how long she stood there grinning like an idiot before she came to life at the touch of his finger caressing her cheek.

"Come back to me, Shasta."

"Yes," she breathed, and mentally gave herself a hard kick in the rear end. This just had to stop, she admonished herself. She was a woman of twenty-seven, not a love-struck kid. Spinning around, she pulled the safe door open and reached in for her winnings.

Her thoughts weren't on her victory but on the desire

she'd seen in Kane's eyes and her own body's response. Her blood had warmed to that spark of life, and there was no doubt he knew exactly the effect he was having on her. She hoped she'd never have to drive him anywhere, because if she wandered off to dreamland she'd end up killing them both.

Shasta turned around reluctantly, keeping her eyes on the three big coins she juggled in the palm of her hand. "What time is it?" When no answer came she was forced to look up and meet his steady gaze.

"You really are quite lovely," he mused out loud, as if the realization was something of a shock.

"What time is it?" She tried again, her voice a hoarse whisper.

"About nine o'clock. Did you know your nose crinkles enchantingly when you smile?" His fingers traced her pert nose from the bridge to the tip, where he paused to tap the end tenderly.

"I have to go." Shasta fought for breath wanting to pull away from his touch, knowing he was deliberately baiting her, playing with her like a big cat teasing a tiny mouse before he pounces. She spun around, and marched away, picking up her jacket on her way to the front door. Kane Stone didn't play the game fairly. And that's just what this was to him at the moment—a game. He made his own rules as he went; and she'd have to stay one step ahead of him if she planned to accomplish her goal and stay alive.

She pulled open the door and stopped, staring blindly out over the wreckage of the front lawn. How was she going to stay one step ahead of him if she never saw him again?

She turned quickly and was jolted backward as she bumped into the solid wall of Kane's chest. "Well, I

guess this is goodbye?'' she said awkwardly, and held out
her hand. Immediately she wished she hadn't as he took
her fingers, lifted them to his mouth and lightly kissed
them, his eyes twinkling knowingly down at her. Damn,
she wished he'd say something. ''Kane?''

''Yes.'' His smile widened.

''I'll have one of our men come out and replace the attic window.'' And she'd come along to supervise the job.

''Don't worry about it.''

''No, no. We can't leave it like that.'' She turned
away, her cheeks stained red. She felt like a fool standing
there waiting for him to ask her out. Giving up, she spun
around and stomped down the wide stone steps to the
graveled drive.

Kane followed slowly, laughter twitching at the tight
corners of his mouth. She was so damn adorable he
wanted to grab her and give her a big hug. He watched the
angry switch of her hips, the determined bounce in her
walk, then hurried his own steps. When the object of his
intense gaze came to an abrupt halt, he suddenly became
aware of his surroundings. The storm with its high winds
and torrents of rain had made a quagmire of the perfectly
manicured lawns. He may never have liked his home
when he was young, but he did appreciate its beauty.
Now, all was in ruins.

As if on the same mental wavelength, Shasta looked
back at the house and grounds and shook her head. The
Stone estate sprawled over more than an acre of thickly
wooded land in the older, wealthier section of Houston's
Memorial area. The large brick Tudor house had sat like
a jeweled crown amid the emerald-green vegetation and
brilliantly colored flowers. Now several big trees and a
multitude of shrubs had been uprooted and strewed
across the grounds. The once-green lawn was covered

with broken branches and a blanket of leaves and crushed flower petals.

Shasta was shocked. She hadn't realized the storm had wreaked such destruction. Remembering the rain and knowing Houston's streets were prone to flooding in record time, she set off at a run to the front gates, praying that the company van parked on the side street hadn't floated away. She was halfway up the wrought-iron gates when she was unceremoniously hauled down by strong hands gripping the waistband of her jeans.

"Are you trying to kill yourself, woman?" Kane yelled, settling her in his arms before he allowed her to slide down the length of his body to the ground. She'd been up that high gate before he knew what was happening, and when he saw her he felt as if someone had punched him in the gut. Why the hell should he care anyway? None too gently he set her aside, pulled out a key and unlocked the gate. "There, now you can walk out of here like a civilized human being." The thought of relieving his boredom with her company died a fast death. He'd be damned if he'd ask her out. She was nothing but a five-foot-four-inch, one-hundred-five-pound bundle of trouble. He'd had enough problems lately to last a lifetime. This was one temptation he could live without.

SHASTA COULDN'T SAY later what had happened. One minute she was on her way over the gate, the next she was hustled into the van and driving down the street, viewing Kane through the side mirrors and trying to figure out what had angered him so. Guiltily she realized she hadn't given a thought to her family and their concern about what had happened to her. She picked up the van's mobile phone and punched out the office number. When he received a busy signal on all the rotating lines, she tried her brother's house and then, out of desperation, her own home. All lines gave the same irritating signal. She sighed with relief, knowing that the phone lines were downed.

Two hours later Shasta parked the van in the parking lot adjacent to the tall office building that housed Masters Security. She stepped out, relieved to be on solid ground. The drive from the Stone estate to the Galleria area would normally have taken about fifteen minutes, thirty in rush-hour traffic, but this morning had been sheer chaos. She'd dodged downed power lines, driven around fallen trees, avoided flooded streets when she could and forged on.

She gazed up at the twelve-story glass-and-steel structure with pleasure. DeSalva's was as neat and sleek as its owners, who occupied ten of the twelve top floors and dealt with electronics in the oil industry, a highly competitive and secretive field. They felt fortunate that Masters Security was the tenant of the remaining two floors and an underground suite, and had put the company in charge of DeSalva's security.

Shasta grinned as she entered the building, showed her pass to the elderly guard and waited for him to sign her in.

"Everyone's about to pull their hair out trying to find you, Miss Masterson. You better hurry up."

"Thanks, Frank," Shasta said over her shoulder as she made for the row of elevators.

"You'll have to take the stairs," Frank called out. "Electricity's back on, but it keeps playing funny flickering games, so Mr. Brandon closed down the elevators."

Shasta waved and headed for the stairway, smiling. She could just imagine Brandon DeSalva trying to take over. He was the company's corporate attorney and a dream to look at, but he didn't take anything seriously in life except law and his older brother, Lucas. At times she wondered if law and Lucas were one and the same, the way everybody bowed at Lucas's feet. Though their many dealings had been all business, she had not missed the interest in his eyes. Lucas DeSalva with his rugged good looks was not her type. He seemed to have come to the same conclusion, because his interest had never developed further than that gleam in his eyes.

Shasta pushed open the big double glass doors to Masters and stepped into a madhouse. She paused a moment, listening to the three people arguing vociferously about the next step they would take to locate her.

"You can stop worrying. I'm here safe and sound, if a little wet." She grinned apologetically to the three angry faces now turned in her direction.

"Just where the hell have you been?" Jeff demanded. "Rena and I have been up all night trying to find you." He draped a long protective arm around his wife and glared at his sister for once again disrupting his well-ordered life.

"Sorry, but I couldn't call from where I was. You see—"

"And where was that?" Rena interrupted, a smile hovering around the corners of her mouth.

Shasta saw the twinkle in Rena's green eyes. Her sister-in-law's looks were deceptive. She resembled the classic cold blond goddess, but in fact she was one of the warmest and most tenderhearted people Shasta had ever met. And Rena further endeared herself by keeping the family off Shasta's back when one of her harebrained ideas backfired.

Shasta couldn't hold back her smile, and as her lips

turned up and her dark-brown eyes began to sparkle, she
pulled her hand from her jacket pocket and held her palm
open toward her brother.

Jeff gazed at the gold coins in disbelief and then
groaned in defeat. "I should have guessed," he said
tiredly, rubbing his hand wearily across his red-rimmed
eyes.

Shasta wasn't fooled by his easy capitulation; she
knew her brother too well. Every member of the Masterson clan carried one strong trait, they hated to admit
defeat or give up. Jeff accepted the fact that he'd lost the
bet, but he wasn't going to allow her to get off scot-free.
She could see it coming—he was about to spring a guilt
trip on her that would have her groveling for at least three
or four days.

A mug of hot fragrant coffee was shoved into her free
hand. She turned and nodded to Masters's top sergeant
and peacemaker—Margret Sellers, their stylish, sixty-
five-year-old executive secretary. "Thanks, Margret."
She caught the woman's knowing look and went on
meaningfully, "You're a lifesaver."

"Yes." Margret's lips barely moved as she lowered her
voice. "You're more trouble than you're worth, young
lady. When J.T. hears about this he'll have your hide."

"Now, Meg," Shasta wheedled softly. "What pappy
doesn't know won't hurt him." She smiled brightly,
knowing her grandfather's watchdog wouldn't tell on
her.

Shasta also knew Jeff would never say anything no
matter how mad he got. The Houston office of Masters,
though two years in operation, was still on J. T. Masterson's "not sure" list. Shasta, Jeff and Rena had wanted
to branch out on their own—Jeff and Rena because of
Rena's parents' constant interference in their marriage,

and Shasta because she figured it was time for a change. She'd been stuck at the head office in Dallas long enough, and the time was right to move on. It had taken the three of them months of long business discussions and involved meetings with J.T., and still they'd been forced to resort to pleadings and dire threats till their dear old tyrant agreed.

"Shasta," Jeff roared, making her spill her coffee. "I want to talk to you." He seized her arm and marched her into her office. When she smoothly slipped away, slid behind her desk and sat down, taking command, he realized his mistake. Frowning, he tried to shift the authority back to himself. "Shasta, you've pulled some stupid stunts before, but this takes the cake. Of all the—"

"Shut up, Jeff dear." She looked toward the open doorway and the two grinning women. "You two might as well come in. I have work for you."

"Work!" Jeff exploded. "You leave yesterday afternoon to check the security on the Stone estate, then waltz in here eighteen hours later...." He took a deep breath. "And—and you have the nerve to start throwing around orders without the least explanation as to where you've been all this time?"

"Hush, Jeff," Rena cautioned her husband as she perched on the arm of his chair, her fingers automatically going to the blond curls at the nape of his neck and stroking them soothingly. "Let your sister talk."

Shasta looked at the two of them and sighed enviously. They both had inherited their families' Nordic good looks, and she felt like the ugly duckling in a flock of swans. The entire Masterson family, from her seventy-two-year-old grandfather, who looked like an aging Cary Grant, to her mother, father, two older brothers and sisters, were all tall, beautiful and very fair. She couldn't figure it out. She'd come into this world short, with a curly tangle of brown hair and equally dark eyes, and had never attained the color and grace characteristic of the rest of the family.

"Jeff." Shasta picked up a pencil and twirled it between her fingers as she began relating all that had happened last night. From beginning to end she told her story, leaving out only her newfound feelings for Kane. She tried to be detached and impersonal, but an image of silver eyes and a smile that could melt the devil's own heart kept intruding and she would lapse into silence until Rena gently prompted her.

"Jeff, dear," said Rena, "when was the last time you saw that dreamy expression on your sister's face?" Three pairs of eyes studied Shasta.

Jeff was quiet for a moment, then smiled. "When I took her to the Black's Kennels to pick out a nice *little* dog for companionship and she fell absolutely head over heels in love with a mammoth puppy that grew into a full-grown monster. Why?"

"Ahh, yes. Head over heels, did you say?" Jeff nodded and Rena reached across the desk, snatched up the pad Shasta had been writing on and shoved it under her husband's nose.

Jeff craned his neck backward to read the squiggling lines, which turned out to be Kane's name written repeatedly. "Don't tell me she's in love?"

Shasta lunged and grabbed the paper back. "Wait till you see him."

"Sexy?" Margret asked, her eyes twinkling.

Shasta leaned back and gazed up at the ceiling. "Sexy is entirely too tame a word for Kane." She mentally shook herself and glared at her grinning sister-in-law. Their interest made her nervous, and she squirmed uncomfortably in her chair. She wasn't ready to discuss her feelings just yet. "Listen, you three. Stay out of my personal life. I mean it!" Their smiles grew, and she tried to ignore them by going on with her tale.

"What I've told you sounds all very logical, right?" They agreed. "But something's wrong. One—Mr. Stone knew we were going to run a test on the alarm system while he was in Europe. So why didn't the old man tell us of his son's arrival? Two—somewhere along the way someone tried to beat the hell out of Kane." She stopped talking and let her eyes follow the tip of her pencil across the fresh sheet of paper, but she wasn't seeing what she was writing. She was seeing instead the long, ugly dark bruises on Kane's side and his grazed knuckles.

"Did you question him about his condition?" Margret asked softly.

"No, I was in a rather precarious position to be interrogating *him*. Besides, I don't think Kane's the type to reveal anything till he's ready. Damn!" She threw down the pencil. "Something's not right. Jeff, why would a man, a seemingly ordinary man, know how to do a professional body search? Believe me, he didn't miss a thing." Her cheeks turned pink, but her audience didn't interrupt. Jeff knew Shasta and her steel-trap mind, knew she was capable of sensing things the average person wouldn't detect, so he kept his questions to himself.

Shasta glared unseeingly at her brother. "Why would this man use words like agency, boss, goons, fieldwork and counterattack?" Again she picked up her pencil and began to doodle. "Those aren't everyday words he was throwing around."

There were other things that bothered her, but she wasn't ready to reveal them. Kane seemed to be expecting another attack. Why? From his conversation while he searched her, it appeared he believed there could be more than one group after him. Why? And how could a man in perfect physical condition maintain such a jaded demeanor? It almost seemed to be an act. Why?

The pencil snapped between her fingers. She tossed the two halves down and looked at her brother. "I want you to put that whiz of a computer and your brain to work and find out everything you can about one Kane Maximilian du Monde Stone. Go through any agency you have to. If you run into trouble use our clearance codes, and if for some reason you're blocked there, call pappy." She and Jeff stared at each other in complete understanding. They were on to something big, and they could feel it in their bones. "I want to know everything there is to know about Kane."

"From birth?" Jeff's voice was tinged with excitement. His first love was his beloved computers; even Rena knew this and accepted it in good grace.

"From the womb, brother mine. Kane's in some sort of trouble, and I want to know what. After all," she said logically, "we are employed by his father and must look after *his* interest. Now get out of my office, all of you. I have a report to write up for pappy."

Jeff groaned and stood up. "By the way, sis, you neglected to tell me how you managed to breach my system."

Shasta grinned wickedly, her chin resting on her folded hands and her brown eyes dancing, enjoying his discomfort. "Through the attic window."

"That's not fair, you're so damnably small," he protested.

"Jeff, Jeff." She tried to interrupt his curses, then laughed. "Jeff," she shouted. "I hate to tell you this, but professional burglars don't come in stock sizes. Now, don't you think it's time you called pappy to tell him he lost his sure-thing bet, and your new system has some bugs to work out?''

Rena led a shaken Jeff to the door. "Darling, how does she get away with calling your grandfather pappy when everyone else in the family has to call him J.T.?''

"Damned if I know, Rena. You've been in this family for three years. Why the hell are you asking me this now?''

Shasta listened to them arguing all the way out of her office and smiled. Rena had a way of taking Jeff's mind off his troubles. She was of the old school, believing you could lead a man around by his zipper, and if by some small chance that didn't keep his attention, you totally confused him with meaningless chatter. It usually worked on Jeff, one way or the other. She tried to visualize the same tactics working on Kane and chuckled out loud. Kane was not the type to be led anywhere, and she pitied anyone who had the gall to try.

"Kane must be some man from that dreamy expression you're wearing. What are your chances?''

The question made Shasta jump, as if she'd been shot. She hadn't realized Margret was still in the room. "Not good, Meg. I think Kane has a connoisseur's taste. He's had everything that's beautiful, the crème de la crème. What would he want with me—yesterday's leftovers?'' She dropped her chin into her small cupped hands and frowned.

"Shasta Masterson!'' Margret yelled scornfully. "I can't believe you said that.'' She walked around the desk and pulled a surprised Shasta out of her chair, marched her through a side door and into a small washroom, where she positioned her before the mirror over the lavatory. "That, my dear, is an enchanting face.''

"You're just prejudiced, Meg," Shasta shot back, but there was a hopeful note in the belligerent comeback.

"Listen to me, Shasta, you're no stunning picture-perfect beauty like the rest of your family, but you are pretty, and that loveliness also glows from the inside. You're small, yes, and you'd better quit moaning because there's not a darn thing you can do about it. And don't ever let anyone tell you men aren't attracted to small women because they are. It brings out their protective instincts."

Shasta opened her mouth and quickly snapped it shut as Margret went on. "Your hair is a shiny mass of curls, your eyes are big and round, and you've been blessed with thick lashes. Your skin's clear and healthy and you have a knockout figure for your size. And when you take the time with your makeup you're a head turner. So stop this self-pity. There's not a man alive who could resist you if you set your mind to it. My heavens, girl! Look how you twist J.T. and your father around your finger. That's no mean feat, even if they are family." Margret stopped her tirade and cocked her neat gray head in the direction of the ringing phones. "You think about what I've said," she ordered, and left the washroom.

Margret was right. She wasn't plain. But Margret's view was a woman's view, and she wondered what men really saw when they looked at her. Impatiently she combed her hair with stiff fingers. She was a mess and needed a bath and a change of clothes. From now on, she vowed, she'd take the time to give mother nature some help.

She grinned impishly into the mirror, showing all her small pearly teeth. Maybe, just maybe she had a better chance than she thought. After all, she'd caught the look of desire in Kane's eyes and that was a good starting place. She just had to figure out how she was going to see him again.

"The telephones are back to working and you have a call."

Jolted out of her musing, Shasta refocused her eyes on the older woman's reflection. "What did you say?"

Margret chuckled and snapped her fingers in front of Shasta's eyes. "A phone call." She stepped aside to allow Shasta by, then followed her out. "From Maximilian Stone in London."

AN HOUR LATER, Shasta emerged from her office to face the waiting threesome.

"Well?" They chorused in unison.

She struggled hard not to dance a little jig, as she'd done before she'd opened her door. She didn't want them to see just how ecstatic she was. "Mr. Stone has hired us for another job. It seems he's just been informed by the French Sûreté that his son was beaten up before he left Paris. He wants us to supply Kane with around-the-clock bodyguards till his business is complete in the States."

Jeff frowned, but it was Rena who asked the next question. "Did he know why Kane was attacked?"

Shasta sat on the edge of Margret's desk. "He said he didn't, but I don't believe him. I gave him an edited account of how I met Kane and touched on a few of my suspicions. He didn't sound shocked or surprised, nor did he offer any suggestions. For a man who's worried about his son's safety, he's shown a shocking lack of knowledge of Kane's troubles. He wasn't forthcoming with any answers to my direct questions, said I'd have to ask Kane." She jumped off the desk and began to pace the length of the reception area. "Jeff, is dad's old friend still with the French police?" She didn't wait for an answer and continued to pace.

"Who are you going to assign as Kane's bodyguard?" Rena opened a desk drawer and pulled out a manila folder. "Harry's free."

"No, Mr. Stone asked that I take care of this one personally," she lied. Shasta stopped her pacing, letting their vocal disapproval wash over her as she studied the Samantha Grey painting hanging in its solitary splendor on the Chinese-red wall. A small hunting party of Indian braves were mounted on their painted horses, but instead of the proud posture usually associated with them, their expressions reflected desolation, a pain that caught the onlooker's eye and held it for a long moment, till the gaze shifted and followed the Indians' line of vision. It took only a second to realize that the wide expanse of open plains was covered in the bleached bones of a great herd of dead buffalo and not melting patches of snow. The painting was appropriately titled *The Beginning of the End*.

Shasta shook her head in amazement. Who would have thought to have such a painting in an office decorated solely in an ultramodern decor. But Rena, who had done the decorating, had a flare for the unusual.

"Shasta. Shasta!"

She jumped, startled out of her thoughts, and answered, "There's no use arguing, Jeff. Mr. Stone was determined that I handle this." She didn't meet her brother and Rena's probing looks. Instead she caught Margret's narrowed glance and winked.

Margret smiled. "How do you think Kane's going to take your interference?"

Shasta's eyes danced with suppressed laughter. "Like a tomcat to water."

CHAPTER THREE

SHASTA SAT QUIETLY in the small confines of her recently acquired Porsche, oblivious to the purr of the engine and the sounds of the overworked air conditioner as it struggled gallantly to offset the rising temperature outside.

Houston weather never ceased to amaze her. One moment it could storm, threatening to wash the entire metropolis into the Gulf of Mexico and leave you praying for an ark. Then the sun, hot and bright, would pop out from behind angry clouds. The humidity would then rise far above its usual steaminess to a tropical swelter.

Shasta rested her chin on the top of the steering wheel, her attention on the open gate across the street. For the past hour, as she waited for the glazier's truck to leave the estate, she'd curiously examined the best way to break the news to Kane that he'd acquired a bodyguard. She'd let her imagination run free with possibilities and had come up with stories even she had to laugh at. But this seemed to be one time that a tall tale wouldn't suit. Only the truth would suffice, and she had a feeling that Kane wasn't going to take kindly to being watched and told what to do, especially by a woman.

She was roused from her thoughts by the sound of the old repair truck backfiring as it rumbled down the graveled drive and out onto the street. Shasta shifted gears and with a flick of the wheel sent the gleaming lit-

tle black car across the street and up the drive, pulling to
a stop before the front steps. Without hesitation she
jumped out, dragging the suitcase with her. She bounded up the steps and punched the bell confidently. When
nothing happened, she pushed briskly again, then nodded as she heard the chimes from within and the distant
sound of footsteps on hardwood floors.

The heavy door swung sluggishly inward, and like a
magnet automatically pointing north, her eyes were
drawn slowly up the tall body.

"Did you forget something?" Kane drawled.

His tone set Shasta's teeth on edge, and as incon-
spicuously as possible she placed the toe of her shoe on
the edge of the suitcase and nudged it an inch or two
through the doorway. "No, actually I'm here because
of my job." She smiled, the corners of her wide mouth
turning up and freezing in place as her eyes roamed over
him. He looked even better in the light of day, and the
fact that he was fully dressed didn't hurt the dream. The
casual elegance of dark-gray slacks with pleated front,
immaculate white shirt opened at the collar and with
sleeves rolled up only added to his male beauty. Kane
wore his clothes with an easy nonchalance, and even
dressed in rags he would have looked just as magnificent.

Shasta was keenly aware of her own neat appearance
as she watched Kane's eyes run appreciatively over the
length of her severely tailored suit, contradicting the softness beneath. She'd taken special care with her makeup,
adding to the roundness of her velvet brown eyes and
touching her lips and cheeks with color. She was glad
she'd taken heed to Julie's teachings as she saw the
renewed desire in Kane's steady gaze. Her foot pushed at
the suitcase, moving it an inch farther.

"I know this is going to be a shock to you, Kane." She paused and extended her foot, shoving the case once more till it met an obstacle—Kane's outstretched shoe. They both looked down at the intruder crossing the threshold, then their gazes lifted and locked. Shasta tugged at the lapels of her jacket and straightened the pale-yellow silk tie at her throat. "May I come in and explain?"

"It rather looks as if you've come to stay." He raised an inquisitive eyebrow at the case on the floor, and when he received only a strained smile in reply, he stood back and waved her in. She was entirely too professional and sure of herself.

Before Shasta could get past Kane, he reached out and caught her shoulders, turning her to face him. Ready with a quick answer to any questions he might fire at her, she was startled to feel his fingers work at the waistband of her skirt and shift it slightly.

"Your seams were twisted. Lady cat burglars should always be neat," he said gently, his deep voice rumbling with suppressed laughter.

With that one deliberate act he had totally blown her cool composure and efficiency. Shasta slapped at his still-helpful hands, her cheeks flushed bright red, and she stepped back, picked up her suitcase and marched into the living room.

Devious, mocking devil. She dropped her case with a thud and whirled around. "Your father has hired me as your bodyguard. He seems to think you're in some sort of trouble. Are you?"

She waited in the suspended silence for the explosion, and when the long string of expletives eventually ran down to dire mutterings, she smiled in satisfaction.

"You can wipe that cat-and-cream grin off your

face." His frown deepened. "I neither need nor want a bodyguard. You're fired."

"Can't!" She shot back, the bewitching grin spreading over her entire face, enhancing the mischievous sparkle in her dark eyes.

"What do you mean, can't. I can do anything I damn well please." He wished her nose wouldn't crinkle up like that when she smiled; it distracted his train of thought.

"Your father employed me. He's the only one who can fire me."

"Listen to me carefully, Miss Masterson. My father does not run my life."

Kane's eyes narrowed dangerously and his voice had sounded contemptuous, making Shasta wonder at the relationship between father and son.

"Now, I would suggest you pick up your case and go home."

Shasta shrugged helplessly. "I can't do that, Kane. Your father is one of our best clients. The security system for this house—" she waved an impatient hand around the luxurious room "—is just a small part of what Masters handles for your father."

"I don't give a damn—"

"But I do," she interrupted, her voice as hard as his had been. They fell silent, each assessing the situation.

"If it's money," Kane offered, "I'll double what he's paying you."

She shook her head vigorously, loosening the combs that anchored her hair away from her face. Her task was going to be harder than she had imagined.

"You can't get rid of me, because all I'll do is change tactics, and instead of acting as a bodyguard I'll set up a round-the-clock, close surveillance. I'm afraid you're stuck with me till you leave the country."

''The hell you say,'' Kane muttered under his breath, deciding to take a new tact. ''Tell me something, Shasta, has my father ever seen you?''

She was idly roaming the room, striving to appear as self-possessed as possible, but his question caught her off guard. She spun around, nearly dropping the Lalique seagull she was examining. ''I don't think so, why?'' Her heart did a series of crazy beats as she gazed at him standing across the room. With his head thrown back and his silver eyes gleaming wickedly, he reminded her of an eighteenth-century pirate. All he needed to complete the illusion were the clothes and a flashing rapier. She could almost hear his *en garde* challenge. Shasta pushed aside her fanciful thoughts and carefully returned the fragile work of art to its resting place. Looking up, she asked, ''Does it make a difference that your father and I have never met face to face?''

''My dear girl, if he'd ever seen you as you are now, he would have had a spasm at the thought of you passing yourself off as anyone's bodyguard.'' His eyes roamed disdainfully over her diminutive figure, taking in the wide eyes, the soft full mouth and the stubborn chin, now thrust out a little farther than before. ''You're about as menacing and threatening as a dormouse.''

Kane clenched his teeth hard. His long-buried conscience suddenly emerged, and he hadn't the heart to continue lashing out at her. She need never say a word to chastise him; all she had to do was cast those big eyes his way and he was lost. He turned his back on her, his mind rapidly going over other ways to rid himself of this watchdog when he felt the clamp of surprisingly strong fingers on his arm.

''You listen to me, you arrogant bastard. I might be small, but I'm as competent as any trained bodyguard in this country." She swung him around with little effort. "Would you like some references?" Her usually gentle temper rose with each word. Placing her hands on her hips, she inadvertently pushed her jacket open, revealing a dainty shoulder holster and the deadly compact twenty-caliber Beretta that snuggled securely under her left arm.

Kane spotted the weapon, his eyes widening in astonishment. "My God, an armed mouse," he choked out, then seeing the humor of the situation threw back his head and laughed uproariously.

Shasta's stillness should have warned him, but he was so caught up in the picture of an armed mouse with big expressive eyes that when he suddenly found himself lying stretched out full-length on the carpeted floor with Shasta sitting sideways on his chest, he could only continue to chuckle while gasping for breath. "Sor... sorry," he managed as a spasm of pain twisted his laughter to a moan.

Remembering his bruised and battered ribs, Shasta slid onto the floor beside him, but kept a firm hold on his arm. "Company policy, Mr. Stone. Bodyguards are armed at all times." When his lips moved to speak, she applied pressure, watching with a ruthless detachment as he flinched and snapped his mouth shut. She saw understanding dawn in the darkened eyes at her application of the art of pressure points. She smiled. "Yes, we *mice* must learn to fight dirty. Now, as for references...." She pressed her fingers a little to make sure she had his full attention. "Are you with me, Mr. Stone?"

"Oh, yes, madam," Kane growled, the muscles along his jaw knotting in anger. "Please, do go on. Believe me, you have my undivided attention." He noticed the fleeting softening in her glaring stare and relaxed.

"I hold a master's degree in criminology and am a licensed private detective, as is everyone with Masters."

"You mean you're not just another pretty face?" he drawled.

She pressed again, harder this time, and was momentarily pacified to hear the hiss of his indrawn breath. "Masters is not a second-rate security agency, Kane. We specialize in corporate and executive protection. We do security analysis and sensitive investigations and develop countermeasures to deter criminals. The security alarm system in this house is a minute part of our work. I don't spend my days just breaking into private homes."

"What do you do?" He moved his arm from beneath her slack fingers and placed both hands behind his head.

"I've delivered documents and merchandise around the world, trained executives who might be targets for terrorists or kidnappers, acted as bodyguards to a few rock stars, politicians, industrialists and the occasional high-ranking military bigwig."

Kane listened in astonishment as Shasta quickly listed her credits. He knew that she was downplaying some of her responsibilities and wondered at the chances she took. But the fact was, this pixie did a job that many men dreamed of but could never handle. For some inexplicable reason he wanted details of her work. He felt compelled to know what kind of chances she took, what kind of jeopardy she put herself in, and most of all he needed to figure out why a woman would want to involve herself in the hazards and dangers of the job. He'd never met anyone quite like her, and the change from dewy-eyed seductress to hard-eyed career woman intrigued him. What was really amazing, he realized, was the fact that in the last eight hours or so he'd laughed more than he had in months. And oh, what a delight she was. His mouse had a temper.

Kane reached out and fondled a silk curl that had slipped the confines of the tortoiseshell comb and now lay enticingly at her temple. He twisted the end around his finger and tugged lightly. When he met no resistance he continued to guide her head down till their breaths mingled and their lips barely grazed one another. "Who was the military man you acted as bodyguard for?" he whispered against her mouth.

What had happened to all her anger? Shasta felt the tip of his tongue slide across her lower lip and fought to think clearly. "General Howiser," she answered dreamily, "when he was stationed in Italy." She tasted and nibbled at his mouth, and finding the flavor of warm moist skin to her liking, she parted her lips invitingly for the kiss that never came.

"General George P. Howiser? My dear mouse! General Howiser was kidnapped over ten months ago, and the United States is still negotiating with the Italian terrorist for his release."

Shasta gazed down into his silver eyes and said innocently, "Ah, but Kane, I wasn't the general's bodyguard ten months ago. I was fired!" Stretched out beside him, her arms crossed over his chest, she settled her chin on her folded hands and waited for Kane to gain control over his laughter.

"Fired!" he choked out. "Dare I ask why?"

"For some reason the general got it into his head that I was supposed to do more to his body than guard it. We had a mild disagreement, and the general didn't care for my manner of refusal, so he fired me. One week later the terrorist grabbed him."

Mindful of his injured side, Kane cautiously tumbled

Shasta onto her back. With an impatient flick, he removed the combs from her hair and tangled his fingers in the thick waves. "You certainly pack a powerful punch for such a. . . ." He stopped, knowing any adjective he used to describe her stature would be taken as a jest and only serve to inflame her temper once again.

Lulled in quiescence by the fathomless depths of his voice, Shasta grinned like a half-wit and nodded, heedless of the warning bells ringing in her head. Fascinated by the movement of his lips, she couldn't seem to drag her eyes from them. She almost sighed out loud with bliss as he lowered his mouth to hers. But instead of his earlier teasing kisses, this one was deep and long, edged with passion and feeding a newborn hunger in both of them. Kane was the first to break away, and Shasta wanted to cry at the loss.

"You know, Shasta," Kane breathed into her ear, sending a bone-jarring shiver through her body, "if you want to stay with me a couple of nights while I'm here, that's fine with me. But, sweetheart, I really don't need a bodyguard." Before Shasta could collect her thoughts he went on. "You have a sexy little body." One confident hand left her hair and moved slowly to her rounded breast.

Kane's voice dropped to a smooth hypnotic timbre, and Shasta squeezed her eyes shut, frantically trying to think of her job. But her mind seemed to go blank as his fingers loosened the silk tie and the buttons of her shirt magically fell open with a mere touch.

"Your skin is like satin." Warm lips slid leisurely down the column of her neck to her collarbone, and he nipped along the ridge lightly, sending a hard jolt of desire through her. "Think of all the fun we can have. You can forget about your job and just enjoy yourself."

"Job? Job. . .job!" She kept repeating the word, whispering it till it finally sank in. Shasta's eyes popped open and she glared at her seducer. "Very clever," she grated, and rolled out of his reach. Coming to her knees, she quickly straightened her clothes, buttoned her blouse, and hopped to her feet. Where were her shoes? She didn't even remember kicking them off, but there were a lot of things that had eluded her in the past half hour. She looked up into Kane's mocking gaze and frowned. "You don't play fair."

"I wasn't aware this was a game," he warned ominously. "Shasta, I don't want a bodyguard, and I especially don't want a female hanging around my neck all day." Kane watched her closely as she searched for her shoes. "Come here," he ordered, and was surprised to see her grinning. She was up to something. He could tell by the odd sparkle in her eyes.

Shasta stood before him. "Would you be more at ease if we had a chaperon?"

As he studied her smug expression, he wondered what trap he was falling into, but it really didn't matter. All his determination to fight seemed to have dissolved. He unbuttoned and rebuttoned her blouse correctly while she stood docilely waiting for him to finish. Then he leaned down, pulled the absurdly high, high heels from under the couch, and one by one fitted them on her dainty feet.

"Okay, mouse." He tapped her nose lightly. "We'll try it your way for a while. I just hope this chaperon gets here soon and she brings food—I'm starving."

Shasta smiled agreeably. "Oh, Julie always comes prepared. But why don't we go out to eat now? I'm hungry myself." She turned to pick up her purse, then stopped. "What did you call me?" she demanded indignantly.

"What?"

"Just a second ago." She glared at his amused expression. "It sounded suspiciously like mouse—again."

"It did? I don't remember. Maybe you're hearing things." He began to move purposely toward her with a hungry look she immediately recognized, one that had nothing whatever to do with food.

She backed away, then spun around. "Come on, I'll treat you to a real Southern meal that will have your epicurean taste buds crying for more." She threw the words over her shoulder and headed for the front door, one hand groping in the depths of her purse in search of her keys.

Kane followed, stopping only long enough to pick up his jacket from the back of a chair. They walked out into a hot, muggy night, though the sky was clear and the stars gleamed brightly around a fat luminous moon.

Shasta heard Kane's footsteps crunching behind her as she rounded the back of her car. Even though he appeared world-weary, he was still gentleman enough to open a lady's door. As the car door swung open, she stepped forward and collided with his broad shoulders. "Hey," she all but shouted. "What . . . ?" Seeing what he was up to, she used her smaller size to advantage. She slipped under his arm and stood barring his entrance to her car.

"I'll drive." He held out his hand and snapped his fingers impatiently.

Shasta clutched her car keys to her heart. "Drive my car?" she squeaked. "No!"

"Come on, sweetheart, I don't like to be driven by anyone."

"Tough! And if you do that with your fingers one more time, I'll give you these keys where you least expect them." She slid into the seat and started the powerful engine with an angry roar. "If you're hungry I suggest you hop in or I'll leave you to fend for yourself." She stuck her head out, looked up and smiled impishly. "I promise you I'm an expert driver." With that she pulled the door shut with a force that squelched any thoughts he might have of bullying her into changing her mind.

She waited patiently as Kane buckled his safety belt before sending the car careering down the drive with a squeal of rubber. As she turned onto the street, she glanced down at Kane's white knuckles, which threatened to pop off his kneecaps, and bit back a laugh.

"How long did you say you've had your driver's license?"

"I'll have you know I rated highest in evasive-driving techniques."

"Well for God's sake, slow down. We're not trying to lose anyone now. I'd appreciate it if me and my stomach arrived at the restaurant at the same time."

"Oh, but this car was made for speed."

"On speedways, not city streets."

As Kane grumbled on about drivers, Shasta quickly glanced in the rearview mirror. She had that peculiar tingling in the back of her neck, an instinctive warning she'd learned to pay close attention to. "Have you ever had chicken-fried steak?" Figuring Kane was more European than American and certainly not Texan, she didn't give him time to answer but went on to describe the state's culinary trademark. "They use a cut of beef called round steak and beat it till it's tender." The blue car behind them was slowing for the stop sign, carefully maintaining a safe distance.

Shasta pushed the indicator for a left turn, checked the oncoming traffic and turned right. The car behind them was now pulling up to the stop sign with its left-turn signal blinking, but it also turned right.

"Then you batter it like you would chicken and deep-fry it till it's golden brown." Accelerating, she shifted and expertly negotiated a hairpin curve that led to a shadowy tree-lined street. The trailing car picked up speed in an effort to keep up. Not very professional, she thought, then returned to her description of their upcoming meal, hoping to keep Kane distracted so he wouldn't notice they were being followed.

"They absolutely drown the steak in thick gravy and it tastes like heaven." The blue car was now far enough back that she could carry out her next maneuver.

"The mashed potatoes are light and fluffy, and the fried okra are gilded nuggets of ambrosia." Speeding up, she hooked a sharp right turn and headed down a back street.

"But the pièce de résistance is the hot peach cobbler topped with a huge scoop of vanilla ice cream." She out-maneuvered her followers and pulled up behind them, tailing them till they realized they'd been set up and sped away—but not before she'd memorized the license number and made note of the two male occupants. There wasn't any doubt Kane was their target. But why was he under surveillance and by whom?

There was a rustle of movement beside her, and Shasta looked sideways, her forced smile dissolving slowly as she met Kane's remote gaze. Quickly she returned her attention to the road ahead, and they continued their drive to the restaurant in brooding silence. She wondered dismally if dinner was going to be as strained as the atmosphere in the car.

DINNER WASN'T AS BAD as she had anticipated. Apparently the food not only appeased Kane's appetite but helped change his mood. Shasta took the long way back to the Stone estate, and the companionable silence was broken only by Kane's questions about her career and the history of Masters Security.

Slouched down in his seat, Kane leaned his head back and closed his eyes. "Your grandfather must be quite a man to have started a business from a one-man detective agency and built it into the dynasty it is today." He rolled his head back and forth on the leather headrest, fighting to keep his eyes open.

"Oh, J.T.'s a very determined man." Shasta adjusted the temperature of the air conditioner and slowly eased to a stop. "My father wanted to go into the diplomatic service, but J.T. wouldn't hear of it. He decided the only way to hold dad was to get him a wife. He had the young woman all picked out—a Southern belle from Kentucky with a long pedigree and an influential U.S. senator for a father. It seems the senator was being blackmailed for something in his past and had privately hired Masters. So, instead of going himself, J.T. talked dad into taking the job. Well, you can guess what happened. Dad met mom and they did exactly what J.T. knew they would, fell in love on sight." She didn't want to tell Kane just yet that it was almost a tradition among her family to fall in love at first sight, usually in the most unconventional places and circumstances.

A snort of disbelief came from the passenger side and Shasta smiled. She put the car into gear and pulled away from the stop sign. "I take it by that disgusting sound that your opinion of love at first sight leaves a lot to be desired?"

"You could say that."

"Or is it love you distrust?" She waited for an answer, and when only silence greeted her question, her shoulders sagged in disappointment. She should have realized it was going to take more than the ability to

make him laugh to capture this man. He didn't dislike
women; on the contrary, he appeared to be a man who
enjoyed women to the fullest but didn't respect or trust
their motives.

They reached the open gates of the estate, and Shasta
pulled to a respectable stop in front of the house without making Kane grab for the dashboard. As he moved
to open the car door, Shasta's fingers pressed urgently
into his arm.

"Kane, did you switch on the burglar alarm before
you shut the front door?" She felt a familiar tingling at
the nape of her neck.

Kane followed her gaze, his eyes mere slits as he took
in the heavy carved door, flung wide open. "Looks as if
I forgot, doesn't it? But I did close and lock the door.
Stay put."

He was out of the car in a flash, but Shasta was faster
and paced him as he vaulted up the stone steps. Silently
she cursed her stupidity as she dug around in the depths
of her purse for her gun. If she hadn't given in to his
fierce refusal to sit down to dinner with a woman pack-
ing a gun, she wouldn't have been scrounging around
for her weapon like a fool.

They reached the open door at the same time and
both stopped, alertly surveying the situation. "You
stupid woman," muttered Kane. "Get back in the car."

Shasta took immediate exception to his remark. "I'm
your bodyguard," she replied sharply. "I go in first."
She stepped in front of him, but a hand of steel clamped
down on her shoulder.

"Have you totally lost what few brains you have?
Someone could still be in there," he whispered angrily,
trying to pull her back. He was rewarded for his efforts
by his arm going completely numb.

Shasta lost all her composure and yelled at him at the top of her voice. "I have the gun, you fool." Never in all her years had she met a more pigheaded man who seemed bent on having his way no matter what the cost. Couldn't he see that she knew what she was doing and wasn't some helpless female?

"Then give it to me and stay out," Kane barked. "And if you ever disable me like that again I'll strangle you. Now," he bellowed, "give me that damn gun!"

Shasta snarled at his outstretched hand and slipped through the yawning doorway and into the dark hole of the living room. Her back to the wall, she moved, inch by inch, her hand out in front of her feeling for the light switch. With a quick flick of the switch, the overhead chandelier bloomed into a soft glow. Down on one knee, her arms extended, Shasta swept the gun from side to side, ready for the intruder to pop up. She felt Kane's presence behind her and whirled around, her back to the shambles of the room. "Don't you *ever* interfere with my job again." She glared at him, her eyes as cold as winter leaves. "I'm a trained professional and know how to handle situations like this. I don't need some fool playing macho man. You're a civilian and don't know how to handle yourself."

Kane growled something under his breath and stomped out, heading for the stairs, hiding the smile that would have caused her temper to explode like a bomb had she seen it. Oh, but his mouse had a fine roar.

"Where do you think you're going?" she demanded, following him up the stairs at a run.

"To see what damage they've made of my things."

The entire house was a wreck. Every drawer from the bathroom to kitchen had been emptied onto the floor. Furniture had been toppled and slashed, and stuffing was scattered everywhere. But the Renoirs and Degas were still hanging in place, and the statues and other pieces of art had been left untouched. Shasta checked the rooms carefully, remembering the insurance list that Masters had inventoried. Whoever had ransacked this house, she mused, was a professional looking for something special and definitely in a hurry.

Shasta found Kane sitting at the kitchen table calmly drinking a cup of coffee. She poured a cup for herself and sat down across from him. "I've called the police." He nodded, his face contorting before he lowered his head into his hands and began to laugh.

She glared at him, sipping her coffee till he had stopped. "You find the sight of your father's house turned into a garbage pile funny?"

"No, but I find the sight of us arguing and yelling at the front door while the burglars were sneaking out the back rather amusing. It reminded me of one of those old B-movies."

A tiny smile struggled to turn up the edges of her mouth, but the seriousness of the situation won out. "Do you want to tell me anything before the police arrive?"

Kane's eyes glimmered like the surface of a newly polished mirror. "What's to tell?"

"I thought you might like to explain a few things."

He picked up his cup and studied the contents before looking directly at her. "I have nothing to say."

Shasta was about to contradict him when the doorbell chimed. Angrily shoving her chair back, she left the kitchen, mentally cursing Kane's stubbornness. She suspected he knew exactly what the intruders were looking for and it all tied in with Paris, his beating and the blue car following them. Stepping over strewed papers in the entrance, she yanked open the door and faced three uniformed policemen and a detective. "Hello, Bill, I thought you'd quit smoking?"

Bill Davidson removed the half-smoked cigarette from the corner of his mouth and flipped the glowing ember into the night. "I thought so, too, till we got your call." His smile belied his gruff tone. "Why is it, Shasta, that every time I hear from you there's always trouble?"

She returned his smile and stepped aside to let the others enter. "Could be the line of business you're in, Bill." Tall and lanky, Bill was a former basketball player who'd been on the force too long and seen too much. She was pleased to notice that his recent transfer from homicide to burglary had taken some of the tension and strain from his face.

Shasta spotted Kane leaning nonchalantly against the living-room doorway. She introduced the two men, then disappeared into the room, shadowing the three policemen as they checked the doors and windows for signs of forced entry.

As they searched, Shasta hurriedly gave Bill a rundown on all that had happened earlier, including their uninvited escort.

Bill made copious notes in a small spiral book while Shasta talked. When she finished he pulled out a cigarette from his shirt pocket and stuck it in the corner of his mouth. "Don't frown, it'll make ugly lines." He tapped the end of the unlit cigarette. "I've had my quota for the day. This is just a pacifier." His eyes bore into hers. "Is there anything else you've neglected to tell me?"

Shasta hesitated, then gave him the blue car's license number.

"Withholding, Shasta?"

"No, just a feeling that the number isn't going to do you any good. Besides, Jeff will have a rundown on the car before you can get back to the station and put it through your computers."

"True." Bill shrugged helplessly. "Are you trying to tell me that the men dogging you and Mr. Stone weren't the same who broke in here?"

"Oh, I'm ninety-nine percent sure they're one and the same. It's just too pat for them not to be."

An hour later they found the burglars' means of entry—the housekeeper's rooms off the kitchen. A windowpane had been cut and removed to allow access to the lock. As the police questioned Kane, Shasta listened grudgingly, admiring his ability to talk about everything, answer all their questions and still tell them absolutely nothing. She was so deeply absorbed in his mastery of evasion and prevarication that she nearly jumped out of her skin when the telephone blared beside her. Yanking the receiver up, she shouted, "Hello!"

"Shasta!" Jeff Masterson sighed with relief. "Where the hell have you been? Rena and I have been trying to reach you for hours."

Shasta matched her brother's sigh. Sometimes family could be the worst possible pain in the backside. "Kane and I went to dinner, Jeff. Now what's wrong?"

"Shasta, I know sometimes you think I'm a worry-wart, but please listen to me very carefully." Shasta leaned against the wall and waited for the long harangue she knew was coming.

"Do I have your full attention?"

"Yes, Jeff."

"Okay. I want you to get out of that house—now." He waited for his words to sink in before continuing. "We'll send Julie over till we can assign someone else.

But not you, sis. This one's rotten to the core, and I'd rather not have you exposed to the stench."

"Jeff, what are you rattling on about?" She straightened up and gripped the phone hard in anticipation.

"Don't go thickheaded on me now, sis. I've just scratched the surface on Kane's background. He's a....." Jeff searched for adequate words to describe Kane, and finding none, he tried again. "He has a reputation that would curl the devil's toes."

"Ahh, come on, Jeff," Shasta said scornfully, and relaxed. "What wealthy, single man doesn't have a reputation? Even you had one, and that was laughable." Her eyes followed Kane around the room: the ease with which he moved; the haughty way his head would tilt; the insolence in the curve of his lip; the intelligence in his unusual eyes.

"Damn it, sis. I checked some old articles about him, then called that society barracuda, Hanna McCoy. Shasta, the man's rolling in money, his friends are the European jet-set crowd. You know the kind. The ones that have no aim in life but to abuse and destroy everything they touch. She told me of Kane's parties and women, of gambling in Monte Carlo for sums of money that would even raise J.T.'s eyebrows." Jeff stopped long enough to catch his breath but not long enough for Shasta to interrupt. "There were skiing jaunts to St. Moritz and that Chilean resort in the high Andes. Hanna told me outrageous stories of barbarian acts in every sun spot in Europe. And women, Shasta, always women—world beauties who run as wild as he does. He's—"

"Jeff, what Kane appears to be and what he is are two different things." She turned her back on the room and spoke quietly into the receiver. "You've always trusted my instincts before, why not now?" She explained about the car following them and repeated the license number to be traced. Then she told him of the break-in at the Stone house. "Collate the new developments with what we already know, and I think we'll find another piece to the puzzle and maybe what kind of trouble Kane's in." As for his past escapades, she dismissed them flippantly and chuckled when she heard her brother's teeth grind together in frustration. His interest was piqued, though, and he was fighting an internal tug of war. "Call Julie—explain that I'm taking Kane to my house."

She turned and found Kane standing behind her. Startled, she jumped back, bumping her head against the wall in the process. "How long have you been there?" she demanded, ignoring Jeff's confused mumbles as the receiver slipped from her hand.

"Not long." Kane reached out to rub the back of his knuckles against her cheek, and his eyes locked with hers. "The police are through and want to know where they can reach me. I told them that was up to my bodyguard." He'd expected an outbreak of laughter at his words and was surprised that the men had taken them seriously.

"My home. Bill knows the address." She smiled, wanting to drown in the invitation in his eyes. Her smile widened as he tapped the tip of her nose.

"I believe someone's trying to get your attention." Kane pointed to the telephone resting on her shoulder and walked toward the waiting men.

"Sorry, Jeff." She was still in a daze from the passion she'd seen in Kane's eyes. Maybe her chances were better than she'd thought.

"Shasta! I don't like this setup," Jeff grumbled over the phone. "Just remember one thing. Kane Stone is not one of those injured animals you're always dragging home...sis, he's already rabid."

CHAPTER FOUR

THE DRIVE ACROSS TOWN to Shasta's home was accomplished in record time, even with the detours caused by the storm's havoc. Shasta kept quiet, realizing the man slouched comfortably beside her was deep in thought. She hoped his self-absorption would eventually lead to him answering some of her questions.

Periodically, she checked her rearview mirror to verify they were still being followed. This time she didn't even attempt to lose their escort. Jeff would trace the license number, and she'd soon find out who was so interested in Kane's movements.

The street signs changed colors, announcing that she was now out of Houston's city limits and in her own neighborhood of West University, a small well-established community completely independent from the big city that surrounded its perimeters. Enormous trees formed a green leafy canopy over narrow streets, casting bypassers in a shower of shadows and bespeckled sunlight. Old homes, which until a few years earlier had begun to deteriorate, had been restored and now showed off their graceful lines in proud homage to past architectural fancies.

J. T. Masterson insisted that all his grandchildren invest in real estate, and Shasta had begrudgingly followed his orders. It wasn't the investment she minded, but the fact that owning a home had a stigma of permanence, another step in keeping her tied down to family and job. And even though each year she planned her escape from the restraint on her life the noose seemed to tighten.

She wheeled the car up the driveway of her home and wondered if she'd ever be able to break away and live the life she had envisioned years ago. Was it all just a dream? Sighing, she flipped off the ignition and returned her attention to the man climbing out of the car. What were his thoughts about the night's events? She slammed her door and turned, meeting that shuttered look once again.

"You're sure this Julie won't mind picking up my luggage on her way here?"

"Julie's used to running errands." She worked the key into the lock, and because the door was old and tended to stick in wet weather, she went through her usual ritual to open it. She kicked the bottom left corner three times, pounded above the lock twice then applied her shoulder with a good push. The stubborn door swung open amid Kane's chuckles and he followed her in, his eyes everywhere. In a brief flash Shasta wondered what he thought of her home. There was no opulence here, only warm colors and a homey comfort.

While Shasta quickly began to pick up scattered magazines, Kane inspected the living room with interest, pleased to see that the room reflected her personality. A woman with a softness and sweetness, yet strong and capable. All the furniture from the couch to the chairs seemed to invite his tired body to collapse; the pale-coral and green prints were a soothing balm, and the over-stuffed couch a beacon to his sore muscles. Healthy greenery sprouted from gleaming copper pots, and fine pieces of glass sculpture—Steuben and Lalique—picked up the light and reflected a multitude of bright colors over the surface of the hardwood tables.

He studied one corner of the room a long time before he realized what was hiding among the profusion of a leafy schefflera and lacy ferns. Two antique wooden carousel horses were cleverly placed among the small forest. Their once colorful bodies were now pale and blotched, enhancing their camouflage. He smiled at the whimsical setting, and his smile grew as he realized one of the animals was a unicorn.

Kane's abused body and tense muscles began to relax. He was feeling a certain serenity when a low growl from the open doorway caught his attention and he went perfectly still. A huge black-and-brown Rottweiler lumbered toward him slowly, its head down, teeth bared and a low menacing rumble coming from its throat. Kane felt the hairs stand up on the back of his neck as he gazed into bottomless black eyes that were glued to his, their intent clear. He was about to become dinner for this one-hundred-eighty-pound monster.

"Baskerville, behave," Shasta called out quietly, and Kane watched the pony-size dog turn immediately into a cavorting puppy, jumping and hopping around Shasta in ecstasy at having his master home. Shasta introduced man and beast, and Kane couldn't decide who was more leery. He held out his hand for Baskerville to sniff and prayed that those jaws would never decide to clamp down on him.

Still watching Baskerville take his measure, Kane asked, "Why is it that little women always have huge dogs?"

Baskerville, having judged Kane safe, trotted over to Shasta, wagged his docked tail and whined pitifully.

Looking down irritably, she scolded, "No, Baskerville, you know you can't. You go lie down and behave yourself." Another whine followed this order, but

Baskerville picked himself up and padded to his favorite place before the fireplace, a place that allowed him full view of his master. Shasta was watching the dog's play for attention with amusement when she remembered Kane's question. "Maybe the reason small women have big dogs is to keep men with free hands at bay."

Kane still eyed Baskerville apprehensively. The dog was still making faint growling noises deep within his throat. "Is that why you got him? Men trouble? And where did you come up with the name Baskerville?"

Shasta finished straightening the room, then went behind the bar. She rested her elbows on the hardwood surface, chin in hands, and smiled. "I picked him out because he was the runt of the litter and I felt sorry for him. I named him after an old novel that I must have read a thousand times, *The Hound of the Baskervilles* by Doyle." She began to pull out liquor bottles from behind the bar. "What would you like to drink?" When he hesitated she tried a little cajoling. "I'm going to have one, please join me." Ever since they had left the Stone estate, Shasta had been toying with an idea. Maybe she could get him drunk, she mused, and get some answers to her questions.

"Scotch, if you have it." He settled down on the feather-soft couch, and it felt so good that he kicked off his shoes and stretched out, something he would never have done anywhere but here. With that thought he frowned. Now why, he wondered, did he feel at home here? But he didn't get a chance to think of an answer, because at that moment a cold glass was pushed into his hand. He took a hefty swallow and nearly choked. The drink was practically three-fourths liquor. His eyes narrowed as he watched Shasta sit down across from him, her drink suspiciously light in color. He had a sudden feeling it was going to be a long night.

"How did you get those bruises, Kane?" She didn't look at him as she sipped her diluted drink.

"I fell down a flight of stairs?" He closed his eyes wearily, the alcohol warming his insides.

"I'll believe that only if you can convince me that those skinned knuckles happened when you grabbed on to a ninety-year-old woman who was tumbling head over heels beside you."

"What woman?"

"Exactly!"

Kane opened one eye and stared at her smug expression. He sighed, drained his glass and leaned his head back. "Listen, Shasta. How I got my bruises has nothing to do with you."

"Don't they, Kane? I'm your bodyguard now." She saw his lips tighten and frowned. "I think for both our safety I have a right to know what kind of trouble you're in."

"I'm *not* in trouble!"

Exasperated, Shasta took a sip of her drink, eased her shoes off and propped her feet up on the coffee table, her toes wiggling in agitation. "Let me put this another way. If you're in danger, then as your bodyguard, you've put me in the same danger."

He didn't seem to have heard a word she'd said. "Are you awake, Kane?" When she only received a grunt for an answer, she jumped up. She was supposed to get him drunk, not put him to sleep. Music! That was the thing—loud music.

Hurriedly she flipped through her record collection in growing desperation. She didn't have any fast music; all her albums were romantic mood music. Then she came across an old Pointer Sisters album and found the ideal song. In a few seconds a trumpet blared out the beginning notes to "Boogie Woogie Bugle Boy," and she watched in wicked delight as Kane's body bounced about three inches off the couch.

"Bitch," he grumbled grumpily, but he couldn't hide his smile as she danced over to him, picked up his glass and headed for the bar. He tried to keep a stern expression as she mixed their drinks, all the while dramatically lip-syncing the words to the earsplitting music, and she looked even more comical when the music abruptly ended and her mouth was left hanging wide open.

Kane whirled around, every muscle tense, as he spotted the man standing by the stereo, his body in half shadows. As the man stepped out into the full light, Kane leaped over the back of the couch, only stopping himself from making the final lunge when he heard Shasta call out.

"Julie!"

"Julie?" Kane grabbed his injured side, his breath coming hard and fast.

Neither Shasta nor Julie had moved during Kane's aborted attack, each stunned at the speed and precision of his maneuver.

"I ain't never seen a man move that fast," Julius Bridger said admiringly, his bushy gray eyebrows working like woolly worms.

Shasta introduced the two men, and Kane shot her a look that could have melted steel. He quickly sized the old man up, but changed his mind after their handshake. Julius Bridger was not much taller than Shasta but was in amazing condition for a man his age, an age Kane determined must be somewhere between sixty and sixty-five years old. His face showed his misspent youth as clearly as if someone had written it for all to see. Deep lines were etched across a wide forehead and pleated between his eyes. His nose looked as if it had been broken at least four times, judging by the number of lumps on the crooked bridge. But it was Julius's smile that robbed his round face of total ugliness, a smile so sweet that the sheer impact was enough to throw any opponent off guard.

Shasta watched in amusement as the two men eyed each other in the same manner as Baskerville and Kane had taken each other's measure. She was curious to see if Julie would take to Kane, and was rewarded by a nod as Julie left the room.

"I'll put Mr. Stone's luggage in the guest room. Then I'll make you something to nibble on."

Shasta's grin widened. Cooking was Julius's star of approval.

Julius was no sooner out the door than Kane's hands clamped around her shoulders. "You little devil. All the time you knew I thought Julie was a woman."

"Yes, but...."

"I ought to turn you over my knee, but I have a feeling I'm not the only one you've pulled that particular trick on." His hands glided to the sides of her face as if they had a mind of their own. Before he realized what he was doing, Kane leaned down and kissed her, a hard quick kiss that left her wanting more. He stepped back, away from temptation. "I take it Julie is spending the night in this house?" As an afterthought he added, "Who is he, or better still, what is he to you?"

Disappointed at the termination of his kiss, Shasta searched his face, trying to glean some reason for his hurried retreat. But the only answer was a sparkle in the depths of his eyes before he turned away from her. "Julie has the room over the garage and lives there most of the time, though sometimes he stays at Jeff and Rena's, and then there are times when he gets so fed up with us he hotfoots it back to Dallas and J.T.'s quiet household.''

"He's a servant then?"

"Julie!" She laughed. "Not Julie." As she mixed their drinks, Shasta tried to explain. But how did you describe thirty years of love and devotion to one family? How did you tell of a man who would give his life for yours, and almost had on one occasion? "First of all you'd better know that years ago Julie was an ex-convict fresh out of prison.''

Kane accepted his drink, followed her to the couch and sat down, grimacing as the strong liquor stung his throat.

"He'd been in and out of juvenile detention halls and prisons all his life, and when he got out the last time he was determined never to return. But life outside was hard and lonely." Shasta stirred her drink absently. "Julie was a first-class safecracker and cat burglar in his youth, and I guess loneliness and itchy fingers got the best of him. The only problem was, this time he picked the wrong man to rob.''

Shasta glanced over the rim of her drink and watched Kane's eyes as they roamed freely and hungrily. He looked up and their glances met.

"Go on," he said, feeling a fool at being caught.

"He tried to rob my grandfather's home and was caught," Shasta plunged on. "J.T. was so impressed with Julie's expertise he made him an offer he couldn't refuse, and hired him that very night. I don't know all the details, but Julie has never left us. He helped raise Jeff and me, but he answers to no one but grandfather.''

There was more. Kane could hear the love in her voice when she spoke of Julie. He had a feeling that Julie was a father figure and probably the only person who truly understood the workings of her mind. He made a mental note to become friends with one Julius Bridger. "Did Julius teach you his trade?" There was a note of disapproval in his voice.

Shasta frowned at his tone. She had become immune to the criticism of her job by others, but she had somehow thought that Kane would appreciate her work. "Yes, he's quite famous in his field, or he was, and—" she glared belligerently at him "—he taught me everything he knows."

The man in question blocked an argument by entering with a steaming tray of hors d'oeuvres. "Your favorite, Shasta—crab-stuffed fried wonton and rumaki." He grinned at her and, setting the silver tray down, left the room.

Shasta pushed the food toward Kane and jumped to her feet. Excusing herself, she rushed after Julie into the kitchen. "Okay, what was that look all about?"

The little man shrugged and began cleaning up his mess. "I saw the way you were drooling over him."

"I was not."

Julius turned around and stared at her, one fuzzy eyebrow climbing slowly to his hairline. When she had the grace to blush, he nodded and continued to wipe off the stove.

"Okay, okay, so I like him." Julius snorted and moved his cloth over the refrigerator door with Shasta at his heels. Changing the subject before it became too personal, she asked, "Did you search his things before you brought them in?"

"Yep."

"Well!" she demanded in exasperation.

"Nothing that wasn't supposed to be there."

"Damn."

Julius sniffed and continued his clean up with Shasta right behind him. She had a feeling of déjà vu and realized that all her life her arguments with Julie had taken place in the kitchen while she followed him around like a puppy, pleading her cause.

"Your brother's not a happy man tonight, Shasta. Not happy at all about this here setup. And I ain't too sure myself."

"Oh, Julie, honestly. It's the only way." She walked up beside him and yanked the dish towel out of his hands. "Listen to me and quit worrying. I need your help for a week, maybe a little longer." Her voice became wheedling. "I have to finish up on the Thomas case and won't be able to accompany Kane during the day, so would you be a sweetheart and stick with him?"

"Follow Kane? You gotta be kidding!" He jammed his fists on his hips and glared at her. "Have you taken a good measure of that man? He's used to doing things his way, and if he catches me he'll kill me, or worse." Whenever he was excited, Julie's sharp black eyes glittered with a diamond brightness. "Did you see the way he moves?" He shook his gray head. "You know how I hate violence."

"Please, Julie," Shasta said, pouting. "This is very important to me."

Julie was weakening. He knew he couldn't refuse her anything, but he had to have the last word. "Shasta Masterson, I've done a heap of things for you I wouldn't have done for no one. I've bathed you when you was a baby. I've cleaned up after you when you was sick. I've even chased some of those loose-handed men away. But now you're asking me to follow the devil."

Shasta gave him another pleading smile aimed straight for his heart.

"Okay, Miss Priss, but there's a limit to what I'll do. I'm telling you right now, that limit has just reached its peak."

Shasta planted a big wet kiss on his scratchy cheek and hurried back into the living room. "I'm sorry, Kane, but Julie needed to know what we wanted for dinner tomorrow night." She picked up his empty glass, fixed him a fresh drink and resumed her seat.

"Julie cooks?"

"Yes, a gourmet cook. Cordon bleu, as a matter of fact." She reached for an appetizer and stopped. The small tray was empty. "You ate all the hors d'oeuvres?"

"Some, but not all."

Shasta followed Kane's gaze to where Baskerville lay, his docked tail thumping the hardwood floor louder and louder. "You let my dog eat crab-stuffed wonton and rumaki?"

Kane chuckled. "He didn't say please, just kept growling at me, Shasta. Then he walked over and helped himself. I didn't think it prudent to argue." Kane's shoulders began to shake as he watched the nefarious hound cover his head with his paws at his beloved's disapproving looks.

"Bad dog," Shasta scolded. "I'm surprised. It's usually not food I have to watch for, but—" She broke off, calling herself all kinds of a fool. Here she was trying to pry information from a man who should be roaring drunk by now, and all she could talk about was Baskerville's problem. She leaned back, prepared to start over, only to be interrupted once more by Julie.

"I'm heading for some shut-eye, Shasta." He handed her a folded piece of paper and mumbled, "Telephone message," then left the room.

Shasta sighed. Quiet at last, she thought, and rested her head against the back of the wing chair. She unfolded Julie's note and read the spidery handwriting. "Car parked across street, two men watching house." She crumbled the paper and stuck it in her pocket. So, whoever was following Kane intended to stay on the job around the clock. It was only ten, and she wondered worriedly why Kane's tongue wasn't loosening up. But they had plenty of time—all night if that's what it took. Reaching across the table, she snatched up his drink and hurried to the bar. This time she increased the alcohol content, hoping for quicker results.

"Did you know you were being followed, Kane?" She decided to try a direct approach and see if he would be equally honest.

"Yes."

"How long have they been with you?"

Kane's eyes turned a deep pewter with anger, but he calmly picked up his drink, evading her question. "By the way, congratulations are in order. You are an expert evasive driver. Those were classic maneuvers you executed on the way to the restaurant." He took a sip of his drink, then gasped. "Are you trying to permanently damage my insides, Shasta?"

Before she could come up with an appropriate answer the telephone rang, and she cursed vigorously under her breath as she walked toward the squat instrument. Heaven was conspiring against her again. She just knew there was trouble on the other end of the line. "Hello, Jeff."

"Is he still there?"

Shasta sighed, leaned her hip against the edge of the bar for support and smiled apologetically across the room at Kane. "Yes, Jeff."

"Don't let him out of your sight." There was a long pause, then Jeff asked, "Did you hear me?"

Shasta was momentarily taken aback by his change of tune.

"Ah, yes, of course." She watched in dismay as Kane pulled himself up off the couch, picked up his shoes and moved toward her. His eyes gleamed, as if laughter lurked in their depths. "Hold on, Jeff." She dropped the receiver onto her shoulder as Kane spoke.

"You're busy and I'm tired. If you'll tell me which room is mine, I'll say good-night."

"The first on the right at the top of the stairs. But it's early, Kane!" she wailed, dropping the phone and following him out the door. At the bottom of the stairs he turned and placed his hands on her shoulders.

"I know it's early." His lips twitched at her disappointed expression. "But I really am tired, Shasta. Besides, I've had too much to drink." Kane touched his lips to her forehead and quickly slipped up the stairs.

Shasta stomped back to the living room and snatched up the telephone. "I hope you're satisfied, Jeffrey Bernard James Masterson! You just ruined my plans for the evening."

"Me? But, sis, what kind of plans?" He quickly recovered and demanded, "Is this all the thanks I get for staying at the office till midnight, hunched over this computer, neglecting my wife and child so you can yell at me?"

"It's not midnight and stop whining." Shasta picked up the phone, walked over to her chair and settled down for a lengthy conversation. "What did you find out, Jeff?"

"You know, Shasta, Rena's not very happy with me tonight. She had plans for us to go out to dinner."

Shasta apologized profusely to soothe his injured feelings. Geniuses were the pits. She cajoled him out of his bad mood and calmly demanded again what he'd found out about Kane.

"You were right about there being more to the man than there first appeared to be," he admitted grudgingly. "After I recovered from the shock of his decadent life-style, I decided just for the hell of it to search for a military record. Shasta, Kane was in the Vietnam War as a Green Beret attached to an S&D unit."

The awe and respect in her brother's voice puzzled her. "What is an S&D, Jeff?"

Jeff's tone was filled with male scorn. "S&D, sister dear, is a Search and Destroy unit that usually worked directly under the Central Intelligence Agency. Do you know what that signifies? Kane was a CIA agent and more than likely still is."

"But, Jeff, that was during the war, and the war was over years ago."

"Come on, Shasta. You know better than that. Once an agent, always an agent. They don't like to let go of their trained men. But listen to this. When I tried to check further, I was blocked by a high-priority code. We have the clearance, but I didn't want to use it till I discussed it with you." Jeff was quiet for a while as he let this information sink in. "Oh, and sis, that license number you gave me, it was a rental car, issued to a Jess K. Raco, an employee of High Tech Offshore Exploration."

Shasta could hear a shuffling of papers and smiled at her brother's disorder. She picked up a pencil and pad and wrote down the names he'd just given her. At her brother's next words she sat upright.

"There's something funny here, though. High Tech

Offshore is only a small subsidiary of another company.'' Jeff groaned into the receiver. "Do you know how long it took to run down the parent company? I'll tell you—two hours. But listen to this. High Tech is just one in a long list belonging to one man—'' He paused, deliberately dragging out the suspense.

"Jeff!"

"Tramble Carter Baldwin, Jr., 'Old Tram' to his friends. The president and chairman of the board of U.S.A. Oil. And, Shasta, our Mr. Raco's name also appears on their payroll. Quite a coincidence, wouldn't you say?"

"Yes." Shasta felt a growing dread. If Kane was mixed up with U.S.A. Oil, then the trouble was about as serious and dangerous as you could get. Oil companies didn't fool around being nice guys. Damn, Kane. He should have known that since his father owned Tex-Am Oil. Another thought struck her. "Jeff, does Kane have any stock in his father's business, and if so, how much?" She waited while Jeff noisily shuffled papers again.

"Yeah, sis. He inherited twenty-five percent of Tex-Am stock from his grandfather. I know what you're thinking. Baldwin's trying to force Kane into selling him his shares and then he'll initiate a takeover. But you're wrong. There was a clause in the old man's will stipulating that Kane can't sell his shares to anyone but his father. From past gossip, that's been a bone of contention between father and son over the years.

"Kane wanted to sell?" Shasta asked.

"No! That's just it. Max has harassed his son for years to sell out to him, but Kane wouldn't. It's not a money issue, either. Kane's grandfather left him his entire fortune, and that must stick in Max's craw. That same gossip has it that Kane wasn't Max's son but the old man's. Now don't get all upset, it's just hearsay and you know how that goes.''

"None of this makes sense, Jeff. I think we're starting at the wrong point. Kane was assaulted in Paris. Wrap up your search here and begin at that end.'' She absently said good-night and hung up. What had Kane done to make oil-company goons trail after him? No answers came as she sat there gazing off into the darkness. Baskerville, sensing her agitation, laid his big head on her knee and whined sympathetically. Shasta automatically scratched behind his ears as she tried to fit together the pieces of the puzzle. But she didn't have all the parts and was left frustrated. Kane was not what he appeared to be, and she wondered how many layers she'd have to peel away before she reached the real man. Then she realized it didn't make any difference who or what he was, she wanted him just the same.

Shasta shooed Baskerville away, turned off the lights and climbed upstairs. Outside her bedroom she stopped and stared longingly at the closed door across the hall. Were his thoughts of her this night? She'd seen the masked desire in his eyes throughout the evening and wondered if, alone and warm in his bed, he was dreaming of her.

KANE LAY IN THE DARKNESS, his hands behind his head, listening to Shasta's light footsteps on the stairs and down the hall. When they stopped momentarily, his pulse increased its tempo and his breath was caught in the back of his throat. He didn't need that kind of involvement, but, damn, she was hard to resist.

The fact was, he'd thought over her earlier words about his danger becoming hers and realized she was right. By allowing Shasta to continue her job he was placing her right in the middle of his problems. When he'd given in to her bullying about his father's orders, he'd thought it would be a way to pass a few boring nights. The problem was, he hadn't expected her to be so professional and thorough in her work. His boredom wasn't worth her life—or his piece of mind.

Kane closed his eyes, straining to hear any movements from the other room. He could barely make out the sounds of running water and took a deep breath as erotic pictures ran rampant through his mind. He'd have to get rid of her. But how? And there in the night an idea formed and took root. The only way to keep her out of danger was to force her to quit. A smile, sharp and conniving, curved his mouth. After he got through with her she'd be so exhausted she'd beg to quit.

CHAPTER FIVE

IN THE EARLY HOURS of the morning, before the sun harnessed the night and rode the moon down, a strange wailing pierced the dark. Shasta shot bolt upright and cocked her head, listening again to the unearthly howling. As a child the sound had driven Shasta under her covers for safety, but now it sent her leaping from bed and flying down the stairs.

Panting for breath, she arrived at the kitchen door, shoved it open and skidded to a stop as a giggle escaped her lips. Kane stood in the center of the room, frozen in motion, a sandwich in one hand and an open bottle of beer in the other. Baskerville was planted directly in front of him, his massive head thrown back, jaws wide open and long white teeth gleaming in the light from the open refrigerator door. The ungodly sound he was producing was guaranteed to give anyone who heard it nightmares for days.

Shasta erupted with giggles as she watched. Kane, still shocked, moved only his eyes and Shasta marveled at how menacing he looked in his thigh-length robe, which revealed a tantalizing amount of chest and muscular, well-shaped legs. His steady stare threatened her early demise if she didn't call off her dog.

"Do something before he decides it's me he's going to eat instead of this sandwich."

Galvanized into action by the desperation in Kane's

voice, she swallowed her laughter. "It's not food he's after." Snatching the bottle of beer from his hand, she walked over and filled Baskerville's bowl. The happy dog lapped loudly, his tail wagging so fast it defied detection. "You were drinking Baskerville's beer and he takes exception to thieves." She turned around in time to see Kane reach for a chair and sit. He threw back his head and laughed uproariously.

Shasta joined him at the table. "It's true. Baskerville's drinking problem is the deep, dark family secret around here." She pulled out a chair and sat down, fascinated by the sight of Kane's shattered composure. "If you had opened two beers, that would have been a different matter. Baskerville would have been delighted to share with you." She clucked her tongue at his ignorance. "But to insult him by just opening one was unforgivable. You could have saved us all that infernal racket he made."

Her words broke the last thread that held Kane together, and he groaned loudly. "Please, no more. My ribs can't take it."

Baskerville joined them, heading directly for his newfound buddy. He licked a bare knee in heartful thanks, then padded off to bed, a loud belch sounding over his shoulder.

Shasta's eyes followed the retreating dog with amusement. "When I first brought Baskerville home he was a skinny runt. Unfortunately my father was here on a visit and told me to give my poor pup a bottle of beer to improve his appetite." She sighed. "That was my first mistake. I believed him. My second was in doing it! So now I have a dog who loves beer and has to be watched carefully."

She stood up and flipped on the overhead light. Picking up the mangled sandwich from the floor, she asked, "Would you like me to make you another one?" Kane shook his head and continued to watch her as she cleaned up.

When she began to wipe off the table, Kane reached out and ran one finger around the short hem of her nightshirt. Shasta looked down in surprise, realizing by his touch that she'd forgotten a robe. The only thing that saved the cotton nightshirt from being completely transparent was its peacock-blue color.

"That's an intriguing little number." Kane would have continued his finger's exploration, but Shasta stepped back and out of his reach.

"What are you doing awake in the middle of the night?" Self-consciously she crossed her arms under her breasts, which only added to Kane's pleasure as the material pulled tight across her chest, unveiling a fascinating shadow of dark nipples. Shasta followed the path of his eyes and dropped her arms.

Kane's gaze lifted slowly to her face, his eyes heavy with desire, his mouth pulled taut at the corners as thoughts spun around in his head. "To tell the truth, I'm not used to going to bed quite so early." His gaze returned to roam her body freely. "Besides, all that alcohol you tried to force down my throat only succeeded in keeping me awake."

Shasta's cheeks flushed a bright red. "Well . . ." she hedged, then grinned. "I tried. You must have a great capacity for alcohol?"

"I do."

"You're good at keeping your mouth shut, too, aren't you?"

"I am."

"I'll bet you'll even deny that the men who are follow-

ing us and those who ransacked your father's house are
one and the same?''

"Right.''

"And you're not going to tell me why those two men
would want to put an around-the-clock tail on you, are
you?''

"No, love.''

She sighed, her shoulders slumping dejectedly. "I
didn't think so.'' She slipped into the chair across from
him. "You know of course that we'll find out *everything*,
Kane? It would make things much easier if you'd just tell
me.''

Kane shook his head. "I can't do that, Shasta.''

"Why?'' she demanded. "Is someone threatening
you? Who are you trying to protect, Kane? Your father?'' Her voice trailed off as she looked at him closely.
Kane was trying to smile, but Shasta could see additional
lines of strain bracketing his mouth. Her gaze dropped to
his side, and she saw how firmly he was holding his ribs.
"You've hurt yourself again.'' She moved to his chair,
her hand on his arm to aid him in getting up. "Come on,
I've got something that will help.''

Kane, in pain, didn't argue but allowed her to assist
him out of the kitchen. They were passing the entrance to
the living room when she stopped, her arms easing their
hold on his waist. The snoring from within caused Kane's
lips to twitch and Shasta frowned at both man and beast.
"Bad dog!'' she yelled, and Baskerville whined but
didn't come fully awake. "Some fine watchdog,'' she
grumbled as she guided Kane up the stairs.

"Shasta, stop!'' Kane's shoulders shook as he slowly
mounted the steps, his hand clamped on the banister. The
woman was going to be the death of him if he stayed
around her for long.

A few moments later, seated on a dainty, spindly legged vanity stool in Shasta's bedroom, Kane looked around in puzzlement. The room, for some reason, was a shock. He'd expected the same homey comfort as the rest of the house, but here in her domain were ruffles and lace, colors of old ivory and the palest yellow. The room was romantic and feminine, and it made him uneasy.

Kane tried to relax and take some of the pressure off his side. Despite his pain he was thoroughly enjoying watching Shasta. The show she was unconsciously putting on was better than any strip show he'd ever seen, and he followed her with his eyes as she bent, stooped and reached, searching through a linen closet that had been turned into a medical supply cabinet. "Are you a hypochondriac?" he asked, eyeing the impressive array of articles.

Her answer came muffled from the depths of the closet. "Of course not. It's just my line of work tends to attract injuries."

Kane wasn't listening. His eyes were glued to the flash of smooth white flesh that beckoned and titillated his senses till he questioned his sanity in wanting to rid himself of this tasty morsel. She had captivated and aroused his interest more than any woman he'd ever met, but there was a gleam in her eyes that threatened his freedom. He knew he should leave with the next strong wind, and yet she held him with her sparkling smile.

Kane raked his fingers through his hair, forcing himself from the outrageous path his thoughts had taken. He had no intention of staying around long enough to get involved, he told himself scornfully. He'd come to get information—to find a murderer—then return to Europe and his old way of life. He wasn't about to let an enchanting pixie sway him from his goal, and he certainly wasn't going to permit her to become so involved in his troubles that she could get hurt.

"Here it is!" Shasta spun around, a wide, thick roll of elastic bandage in her hand. "Take off your robe and stand up," she ordered. When he remained seated, staring at her, she demanded impatiently, "Did you hear me?"

Kane stood slowly. "I heard, but think you're—"

"Now don't be childish, Kane," she broke in. "I'm not going to hurt you. I'm just going to wrap your ribs to relieve the pressure. Now drop the robe."

Without further comment Kane did as she ordered. Untying the looped belt, he shrugged the robe off his shoulders, his eyes sparkling.

Shasta blinked rapidly at the sight of Kane's naked body in all its beauty.

"Someday maybe you'll let me finish what I started to say." Kane's teeth flashed brighter than a beacon at the color staining Shasta's cheeks.

Spinning around, Shasta yanked a large warm towel from the heating rack. "The sight of a nude man does not shock me, Kane." But her hands shook as she held the towel out to him. Forcing her eyes to remain on his face, she silently cursed his slowness, wondering if it was deliberate or from pain. When he at last secured the towel with a final tuck, she allowed her eyes to meet his and frowned. He was having entirely too much fun at her expense. "Hold up your arms." She placed the end of the wrap in the center of his chest. "Now hold these ends in place."

Kane mutely did as he was told, and the next few minutes stretched into eternity. His fists clenched, and a fine sheen of perspiration popped out on his forehead as she bandaged him, but it wasn't the vicelike wrapping that was causing him such discomfort. It was the touch of her hands on his body; the brush of a breast against his arm; the feel of her arms reaching around his back and bringing her body within a fraction of an inch from his that was driving him mad. "Are you through?" he growled, exhaling slowly, his breath stirring her fragrant hair.

"I'm just about finished." Shasta lowered her head and coughed. She had always been taught to fight fire with fire, but now she began to doubt the soundness of that advice. The firm bulge beneath the towel was evidence of her revenge. The only problem was, her game had backfired. In the process she'd managed to become equally excited from touching Kane, and now she tried hard to mask her own heavy breathing by humming softly to herself. Hurriedly she fastened the metal clamps and spun away, only to have her shoulders caught in a firm grip and whirled around.

"Oh, no, mouse. You'll damn well finish what you started."

She gazed up at him, her velvet brown eyes wide and round and full of innocence. "I don't know what you're talking about." Her chin quivered slightly as the tips of his thumbs traced the bones along her shoulders to the base of her neck.

"You love to tease and play games, don't you?" He pulled her close. "But this time it got out of hand." Her body was touching his. "I saw the look in your eyes." His breath fanned her cheek as he leaned down to whisper in her ear, and a shiver raced across her skin like a gentle breeze. "I can read your body's message to me. No, don't say a word." He placed a finger firmly against her lips to stop the flow of denials he saw in her darkened eyes. But she couldn't hide the pounding of her heart as he touched the pulsing artery in her neck.

Shasta swallowed painfully. His deep rumbling voice with its pronounced French accent and his mirror-bright gaze were as hypnotic as a pendulum. Kane's charm was dangerous. He was a man accustomed to getting what he wanted with a minimum of effort. He'd been waited on hand and foot since a baby and denied nothing. Shasta sensed all these things about him and grimly realized that she wasn't capable of resisting or breaking his record of conquests. She could no more turn him away than any other woman. Knowing this, she snuggled into his embrace, as trusting as a newborn lamb.

Kane's mouth claimed hers. He pulled her against his waiting body, the hunger of her response answering his desire. With an expert movement he shifted her body sideways and his nimble fingers deftly released the buttons of her nightshirt.

Shasta stood naked before him as his eyes savored her softly rounded body. Without a word she turned and walked to the edge of the bed, grasped a handful of bedcovers and yanked them to the footboard. She felt the heat of Kane's body close behind her and relaxed, knowing instinctively that his hands were already reaching for her. Like a young willow bending in an untamed wind, she leaned into his warm flesh and snuggled back into arms that cradled her small frame in strength and security. If there was love only in *her* mind, that was all right, too. This was her man, and she was about to receive him into her body and be as close to him as any human could.

Both hands covered her rounded breasts, his palms rubbing the pert nipples to flowering peaks. "You're so damn tiny. I'm not going to hurt you, am I?"

Shasta's mind, heavy with desire, took a long second to register his question. "No, Kane. You could never hurt me." A husky chuckle sounded above her head and she looked up, only to be locked against his chest.

"I don't know whether to take that as an insult or a compliment." His hands pressed her hips to his own hardness, and her sleepy brown eyes widened.

"Oh, I. . . ." Her words were lost in the dark cavern of his mouth as he eased her onto the bed. She rolled onto her side, facing him and tried again. "You know—" But his mouth claimed hers in a deep kiss that touched off a singing in her ears. She savored his warm velvet tongue with her own, and her hands kneaded the flesh of his shoulders. Lost in the feel and touch of him, she fought to regroup her thoughts and pulled away from his kiss. The mischievous lights in her eyes should have warned him. "I promise to respect you in the morning."

"What?" She'd completely disoriented him again.

"Well, we've only known each other a short while, but I can keep my mouth shut. I mean, I don't kiss and tell."

"Oh, God, no Shasta. Not in bed—not now! Please, don't make me laugh."

"But, Kane—" she pouted as her fingers traveled down his spine, over the bandage that strapped his abused ribs, to the firm muscles of his buttocks "—making love should be spiced with laughter." Before she could slip her searching fingers around his hips to his stomach, he captured her hand in a steel grip.

The pressure was released as he pulled her hand to his lips and smiled into her eyes. He inserted her fingers, one by one, deeply into his mouth, where he gently sucked on each, then pulled it out slowly. While he played his erotic game he watched her changing expression. "Is that something to laugh at?" She shook her head, and he listened carefully to the sharp intake of breath as his other hand worked its own special brand of magic between her thighs. His touch was gentle, yet there was a firmness in each caress, each stroke; a sureness and expertise.

Shasta planted tiny kisses along his jaw to the strong brown column of his neck, then to his chest, where her tongue played temptingly around a hardened nipple. Kane's chest ceased to move, and the rhythm of his breathing was suspended. Quickly capturing her face, he guided her mouth up to his.

Concerned about his ribs, Shasta rolled Kane to his side, but he edged back. She gave up agonizing over his injuries and lost herself in the soundless world of their lovemaking.

Kane gathered Shasta's hands in his and held them above her head. He lowered his mouth, taking hers in a quick kiss before his lips began a journey designed to drive her to a world of exploding light.

"No, Kane." Her voice came out a breathless plea, and she wondered if he heard her halfhearted denial.

"Oh, yes, mouse." His teeth nipped lightly along the sensitive skin on the inside of her thigh. "Did you think I wouldn't want *all* of you?" The trail of his words left a brand on her flesh that she knew she would never be able to erase or forget.

Kane raised his head, and Shasta looked into eyes that promised heaven. She shivered in anticipation as his head dipped again and his lips teased and tantalized, driving her crazy. He took the breath from her lungs and the beat from her heart, and she called his name in a hoarse voice that sounded as though it belonged to another human being.

Later, as she lay in his arms, Kane smiled, then slipped between her legs, filling her, burying himself in her body. Her eyes opened lethargically and her mouth curved sweetly. "You're going to hurt yourself. Why don't we change places?" she murmured softly.

Kane lowered himself fully onto her, his thrusts slow and deep. "Not necessary, love." His own breath came fast as he maintained the pace till Shasta groaned and wrapped her legs around his hips, increasing their rhythm. Kane followed her movements, matching the tempo till both froze in time and space, then collapsed in a tangle of arms and legs.

Shasta lay deathly still, a forearm thrown across her eyes, as dawn's light slipped between the slightly parted curtains and spilled across their naked forms like an eager voyeur. Her breathing was placid and unbroken, as if her body slept but her mind refused to surrender. *Why,* an inner voice screamed over and over again. *What had gone wrong?* The feel of cool air drifting across their damp skin brought Shasta back to reality. Without thinking she reached down, caught the edge of the sheet and pulled it over them. Kane shifted his weight and she began to move away. He cuddled her close, his lips grazing her ear with light kisses.

"Please, Kane. Not again." She ground her teeth together at the sound of his muffled chuckle.

"Did my lovemaking wear you out, baby?"

She'd always despised being called baby, she'd even made an issue of it on their first meeting. But she couldn't bring herself to call him Maxie in retaliation. The name just didn't fit. Besides, Kane was too sexy to insult with that wimpy nickname, and somehow his French accent took away the sting of insult.

"Don't call me baby," she muttered weakly. "And

no, Kane, you didn't, as you so crudely put it, wear me out." The bite in her voice brought his head up off her neck with a jerk. "I wouldn't call what you did making love. Sex, yes, but there were no finer feelings there. I sincerely doubt that you're capable of anything so deep."

His silver eyes darkened ominously and he leaned across her, his body holding her immobile.

"You're playing a dangerous game, lady. Don't lie there and taunt me." He brought his face a breath away from hers. "I satisfied you, love, and if you try to deny it, I'll do it again and again. Only this time you'll wish I hadn't."

"I would never try to repute your prowess, Kane. You're a considerate lover. An expert in the arts of making a woman feel alive in every nerve of her body. You know all the right buttons to push. There probably isn't a man alive who could surpass your expertise." Shasta watched his brows come together with each compliment, and after a brief pause she went on. "It's just a crying shame that you feel nothing in return. You watched, gauged and analyzed my every response, each move choreographed and staged as if you were programmed like some robot."

Kane rolled onto his back and laughed at the lace canopy above him. "I've never heard such rot in all my life. What the hell do you want from me?" Raising himself up on his elbow, he reached out and grabbed her chin. "You got exactly what you've been asking for from the moment we met."

"Did I?" Shasta flinched inwardly at his tone but refused to back down. She had to make him understand. "I expected to have a warm giving man, not a stranger who dictated each move. Where was the spontaneity, the adventure and the fun? You're inhuman."

"And you're crazy." Kane shoved the covers back and lunged out of the bed. As he straightened, he grabbed his side and inhaled deeply.

"Am I crazy, Kane?" Quickly she moved in front of him and blocked his retreat. She reached out to place her hand on his chest but was stopped as Kane's fingers curled around her wrist. "Why don't you want to be touched?" His grasp tightened, and Shasta stood her ground, lowering her voice to a pain-laced whisper. "Every time I wanted to stroke or caress you, you intercepted me. Why? Why did your eyes never change color with your desire or the intensity of the moment?" Her heart ached for him. "Because you had to be in total control—master of your emotions."

Kane released her wrist as if he'd been holding a red-hot iron. "Stop it, Shasta! You don't know what you're talking about."

"Oh, I think I do. What happened to you, Kane? Where did your passion and capacity for love go?"

"Love!" he snarled, and caught her by the shoulders. "For years I watched that overrated word tear my mother apart. You see, she loves *all* men. And passion, Shasta—what does passion get you but obsession. My father's ruling passion is Texas-American Oil. Passion and love tore them apart. It destroyed my mother and will more than likely be the final weapon to kill my father." He pulled her close and stared down into her eyes. "Don't confuse love with lust or sex. I've been around a lot longer than you have. I'm older and have seen and experienced what people do in the name of love. They lie, cheat, steal, do unspeakable things to each other and, yes, even kill—all for love!"

Kane let go of her shoulders, but instead of stepping away, he rubbed her arms briskly to return the circulation. "Hell, I didn't mean to blow up like that. But, mouse, you could drive a man to murder with your pushing. Fair warning, don't do it again."

The golden sparkle returned to Shasta's eyes. "Kane Stone, I don't know what sort of people you've been around, but it's obvious that they, and you, know nothing about life." She laughed. "Strange how, with all your sophistication and intelligence, you could be so ignorant. And since you're going to be in town for a while and we'll be *so* close, I just might take you in hand and teach you how to be a human being—human enough to want to feel again and enjoy life."

"If I had about a hundred years you might have some luck." His fingers trailed lightly across her collarbone to the base of her neck, then dropped to brush the tops of her breasts and slowly circle her nipples. "I think I'll let you start right now."

"No!"

"Hmm."

"The next time you and I end up in bed I intend to have Kane the man, not a mechanical clone."

"You're joking?" Kane's hands moved over her stomach in an erotic pattern and Shasta stepped out of his reach.

"You needn't give me that look, either. I won't change my mind." She whirled around, picked up his robe, handed it to him and guided him to the door.

A second later Kane stood in the cold hallway wearing only gooseflesh and carrying his robe. The loud click of the lock on Shasta's door brought him out of his stupor and sent him hurrying to his bed. He lay there on his back, his head cradled in his hands and a frown etched across his forehead. It seemed to him that for every step he took forward in his plan to rid himself of Shasta, he was forced three steps backward.

Shasta was also wide awake. She glanced at the bedside clock and groaned. In two hours she'd have to get up and go to work. She reached over and snatched up Kane's pillow, hugging it to her breast. She sighed. There would be no self-recrimination for this night, she decided. What did disturb her, though, was knowing what she had to do. Changing Kane's perception of life wasn't going to be a piece of cake. She snuggled down farther into the warm covers. But, by heaven, she vowed, she was going to change his outlook on love—she had to for both their sakes. Whether she would win in the end remained to be seen, but Kane had a right to walk in light and love; he'd lived in darkness long enough.

Her eyelids began to droop in exhaustion and a tiny smile turned one corner of her mouth upward as a thought slipped across her mind. Despite his many faults, Kane *was* a wonderful lover, and she'd listened to the unspoken desires of his heart and body and willingly succumbed to them. There was a lot to be said for his methods.

CHAPTER SIX

"MIRROR, MIRROR ON THE BATHROOM WALL, who's going to tell the devil he's in for a fall?"

Shasta grinned at her reflection and dabbed on additional makeup to cover the faint shadows under her eyes. Squaring her shoulders, she straightened her poppy-red silk blouse and checked to make sure she'd completed tucking the shirttail inside her white linen pants. She readjusted the white lizard-skin Judith Leiber belt, centering the large gold buckle, then picked up the matching handbag and marched out of her room.

She paused outside Kane's closed door, her hand raised hesitantly as she listened for any signs of awakening life. Hearing only the quiet of the house and the familiar sounds of Julius cooking breakfast, she dropped her fist and hurried on, the smell of freshly ground coffee drawing her like a parched person to water.

Shasta stopped in the open doorway of the kitchen and leaned against the frame, smiling. The air was filled with the delicious fragrance of hot croissants, thick sliced ham frying in butter and a spicy omelet guaranteed to open sleepy eyes. Julie was in his element in the kitchen and worked efficiently, his hands quick and sure as he and Kane discussed the merits of cooking with truffles.

Still unnoticed, she shifted her attention to Kane, who

was propped nonchalantly against the center cooking island, sipping his coffee. Dressed in a multistriped polo shirt, snug-fitting white shorts and clean tennis shoes, he made a devastating sight for any woman. She hadn't had time to appraise his body last night, but as she eyed his beautifully shaped legs and enticing derriere, she remembered that his stomach muscles had been hard as a washboard. His wasn't the body of a decadent playboy. Kane was a man who, for whatever reason, kept himself in top physical condition at all times.

Baskerville barked, announcing her arrival and bringing her lustful thoughts to an end. She looked down at her faithful dog planted firmly at Kane's feet. "Traitor," she scolded, and received another playful bark as if to confirm her accusation. "That's fine, Baskerville, but who are you going to butter up to when Kane leaves?" Baskerville's clipped ears perked up, and he cocked his head thoughtfully, then lumbered over to give her hand a wet apologetic kiss. She patted his head. "That's it, monster, keep all your options open." Accepting a cup of coffee from Julie, she nodded at Kane.

"Good morning." He eyed her over the rim of his mug, eyes alight with devilment.

"Morning," she mumbled in return. "I hope you slept well?"

"I did, and you?"

"Like a log."

They were both lying. Neither had had any peace of mind during the remainder of the early-morning hours.

"Shasta," Julie interrupted their silent clash, "wash your hands, breakfast is ready." He shoved his fist on his hips as he demanded, "And tell this overgrown drunkard to get out of my kitchen. Every time I open the refrigerator he's got his head inside breathing on my food and hunting for his bottle before I can stop him.''

Baskerville knew he was being talked about and sat quietly, his massive head swinging from Julie to Shasta. Realizing he was in for another scolding from his master, he curled his lips in a mock snarl, growled at everyone in the room, then padded out, his head high and his docked tail pointed toward heaven.

Shasta sighed. "Another normal morning," she said to Kane, and smiled. "They love each other, really they do." Setting down her cup, she stepped to the sink to wash her hands. "Did Julie tell you that I have to go to the office this morning, so he'll stay with you till I can wrap up the case I'm on?" She reached for the tap, but Kane stopped her by taking her hands in his.

"He told me, and I informed him it wasn't necessary for him to hang around here all day." Kane quickly buttoned her cuffs, which she'd left undone, turned on the water and handed her a towel to dry her hands with. "I'm just going to laze around and give my ribs a chance to heal."

Shasta eyed his casual attire suspiciously.

"Believe me, Shasta, I'm quite capable of keeping myself entertained. Besides, I noticed you have the new Robert Ludlum novel, and I'd like to read it."

WHY DIDN'T SHE TRUST HIM? Later, at the office, she asked herself that question again, remembering his bland, innocent expression as they'd parted. Kane Stone hadn't seen innocence since he'd passed his first birthday. She picked up the telephone and quickly dialed her number. When the ringing went unanswered, she slammed down the instrument. She'd been duped. Her only consolation was in knowing Julie was trailing Kane. Julie on a job was like a bulldog with a bone.

"Well, well. What's put the bloom in your cheeks, or should I say whom?"

Shasta glared at her sister-in-law lounging gracefully against the doorframe. "I thought you were going to take Lizzie to the zoo? By the way, how is my angel of a niece?"

Rena straightened slowly and glided across the room to perch on the corner of Shasta's desk. "You won't distract me from my purpose, you know. But since my husband's so engrossed in this Kane project, I'll indulge you. Lizzie's fine, if you consider going through the terrible two's with a vengeance fine. And the reason we're not at the zoo is because last night the poor angel got bored and decided to change the color of her hair like mommy does. Do you remember when I wanted Jeff to take me to the Virgin Islands two months ago and he wouldn't?" Shasta nodded. "Do you also remember I threatened to dye my hair bright red if he didn't?" Shasta nodded again. "Well, your little angel found the red coloring and dipped her pigtails. She's now the youngest punk-rock kid in Houston."

"You could have it cut, Rena," Shasta suggested, laughing.

Rena picked up a pencil from Shasta's desk and expertly wove it between each finger with amazing dexterity. "Ah...now that's where you're wrong. You see, the reason for the aborted zoo excursion is that Lizzie likes her new hair color. She keeps dragging me to the television and pointing out those groups on the rock videos. Tell me something. How can you argue with a two-year-old who's been raised watching and believing what she sees on television? I mean, really, Shasta, 'Sesame Street' and Big Bird would never steer her wrong. I told the little monster, no haircut, no zoo."

Shasta cleared her throat. "Has Jeff seen her yet?"

Rena eyed her sister-in-law, displeasure stamped on her beautiful features. "My dear Shasta, your brother— you notice I stressed *your*—spent the night here waiting for J.T.'s friend, Monsieur Duval of the French Sûreté, to return his call." Rena slipped off the edge of the desk and pulled the nearest chair closer for an intimate chat. "Now that we're off my problems—" she leaned forward eagerly "—what's he like?"

At that moment Jeff stormed into the office, saving Shasta from Rena's probing questions. Clothes crumpled and wrinkled, his blond hair standing out in all directions, Jeff looked every inch the absentminded professor. He waved the wad of papers in his hand and tripped over a loose shoelace. Rena jumped up and grabbed his arm, rescuing her husband from total destruction.

"Sis, you're not going to believe this!" He flopped his long body down in the chair Rena had just vacated. There was excitement in his voice, the eagerness of a hunter who, after days of tracking, has finally caught a glimpse of his prey. "While I waited for Duval's call last night, I decided to go ahead and use some of our government access codes."

Jeff tried unsuccessfully to press out the creases and frayed edges of the roll of papers on his lap. "Do you recall me telling you I hit a dead end searching Kane's military background? He wasn't discharged, and payroll still shows his salary being deposited in a Paris account, yet his service record doesn't show any order assignment."

"Jeff, that was years ago. What does all this have to do with now?"

Jeff frowned and said absently, "There's still those three blank years." He scratched his head thoughtfully as Shasta's question finally penetrated. "Oh, it's important. Are you ready for this? After busting my buns trying to trace Kane for that missing three-year span, I'll be damned if I didn't just happen to fall onto his name on another government list. Would you believe Kane Stone is registered as a diplomatic envoy attached to the United States government?" Jeff's blue eyes, though red rimmed and shadowed, sparkled with triumph.

Distraught, Shasta raked her fingers through her hair, destroying what little order she had achieved that morning, and yelled in total confusion and frustration, "None of this makes sense. If Kane's a diplomat, why are oil-company goons making a shambles of his father's home and following his every move?" She stared at her brother and braced herself for more. Jeff had that smug expression she recognized only too well. He was about to drop another bomb, and he wanted to make sure everyone felt the fallout.

Rena studied her husband and snuggled beside him, her arm thrown around his shoulders and her hand patting his arm encouragingly.

Shasta exhaled loudly, resigned to wait out the suspense in a calm ladylike manner. She folded her hands on the desk top, gritted her teeth and smiled sweetly at her brother. "What else?"

Jeff made a show of shuffling his papers, and she realized he would have continued getting his own back for the trouble she'd caused him, but his excitement over the new find was too great.

"Mr. Duval with the French Sûreté returned my call about an hour ago. We had a delightful chat. By the way, he said to be sure and remind grandfather that he still owes him two hundred francs."

"Jeff, so help me!" she said threateningly.

"Duval was familiar with Kane's name. As a matter of fact, the French police would like another interview with him concerning the murder of an American professor named Melvin Kimble."

"Murder!" Shasta breathed. "Kane! They want to talk to Kane about murder?"

Jeff's voice grew serious. "Yeah, seems this professor was killed in a hit and run, and Kane was in someway connected with the old man."

"They don't think Kane was the driver, do they?"

"No! Kane was with this Kimble fellow when he was hit." Jeff scratched his head again thoughtfully. "Or at least he was near him. I didn't get all that down."

Shasta's heart resumed its normal beat, and she exhaled the breath she'd been unconsciously holding. "It seems the deeper we dig into Kane's past the more confusing and involved it gets."

"I hate to burst your bubble of excitement, but has anyone thought of just *asking* the man himself what's going on?" Rena's lips tightened as two pairs of eyes damned her as an ogre determined to ruin their fun. She jumped up and glared at them. "Okay, so I don't understand the thrill you two get out of mysteries and puzzles." She looked down her perfectly sculptured nose at them. "I keep forgetting I'm the normal one around here." Throwing up her hands in defeat, she gave her grinning husband one more scorching look, laced with a sensuous invitation, and stomped out. "I'll just go home and see if Lizzie's changed her mind."

Shasta hid her smile as Jeff hastily gathered up his papers from his lap and the floor and followed Rena out the door, a bright gleam in his tired eyes. She picked up the telephone and dialed her number, slamming the instrument down after the tenth ring. It would have been to her advantage, she realized, if she had taught Baskerville to answer the telephone. Rena's words came back suddenly about enjoying the thrill of excitement, and she realized her sister-in-law was right. She tried her number again, and as the ringing continued, she prayed that no matter where Kane was, Julie was not far behind.

KANE STROLLED THE SIDEWALKS of downtown Houston with familiarity, though it seemed to him that the skyline had changed. New towers of glass and steel in unique shapes and sizes sprouted out of the concrete like tenderly nurtured plants. The sun's rays bounced and flashed off miles of tinted glass and polished steel, washing the milling lunch-hour crowd in a shower of brilliance.

Kane glanced over his shoulder and searched a knot of people for anyone showing an unusual interest in his movements. He'd been walking the streets for an hour, getting his bearings before making his move. Now he picked up speed, his long-legged stride eating up the distance between him and his followers. Crossing the street with the crowd, he entered the mammoth bronze portals of The Park, a new covered shopping mall in the heart of the city. The mall was the hub of a series of above-street walkways connecting numerous office towers and creating a shopper's delight. Kane passed specialty shops and restaurants without slowing his pace and exited at a side entrance, crossed the street and calmly stepped into the lobby of the Four Seasons Hotel. Again, without slowing down, he left the hotel through another door. On the street once more, he began another series of twists and turns through department stores and restaurants. Checking over his shoulder, he smiled. He'd lost the two men who had been tailing him, but there was still one more. With a wicked gleam in his eyes he speeded up his steps and entered a crowd of pedestrians waiting for a light to change. When the surge of people stepped off the curb, Kane quickly moved to one side, then headed down another street, where he turned the corner and stopped, waiting.

Julius Bridger, his breath coming fast, trotted around the same corner after Kane and ran straight into a solid chest.

"You following me, Julie?"

"That's right." Julius dusted off his vest and pulled at his jacket fastidiously, checking to make sure his pocket watch hadn't been lifted—a habit left over from his youth and one he had never been able to break.

Kane pushed up the sleeves of his navy linen sports jacket to his elbows, slipped his hands into his pants pockets and leaned against a granite wall, regarding the dapper little man insolently. "Want to tell me why?"

"Shasta's orders."

"I see."

"I don't think so."

"How's that, Julie?" Kane stared coldly at him, demanding the truth.

Julius studied the toe of one shoe distastefully, then rubbed it behind the opposite pant leg to remove the spot marring his spit shine. "She's got a bee in her bonnet that you're in danger and being followed."

Kane smiled wryly. "Just between you and me, Julie, she's right."

"I seen them." Julius smiled, his bushy gray eyebrows wiggling. "You done a real fine job of losing them. I doubled back to see what they was up to and seen them heading for their car. Do you know who they are?"

"I think so." Kane pushed away from the wall and started down the street, his pace slower so the little man beside him could keep up. "How about a drink? I'm sure you're thirsty after that long morning stroll."

"You said it." Julius rubbed his hands together. "I could do with a cold beer. There's no peace at Shasta's to enjoy one with that hound of hers kicking up a fuss and drooling all over you."

Kane paused under a cool, green canopy that covered an unusual set of double doors. A sculptured picture in hammered brass, copper and silver depicting a long line of charging bull elephants spread from the door down one entire outside wall. The magnificent work of art brought a wry twist to Kane's lips as he reached for the thick brass elephant tusks that served as door pulls.

"You ever been in Harry's Kenya, Julie? No? Then you're in for a treat." He held the heavy door open and waved the other man into the world of African safaris. The wall around the bar area was lined with stuffed animal heads that made the patrons feel as if they were sitting in a restaurant deep in the heart of Africa. Kane ordered a martini for himself and a beer for Julie, then settled back in his chair. "Tell me about Shasta and her family."

Julius took a hefty swallow of cold beer and studied Kane for a long second. Then, as if deciding to trust him, he said, "Got to you has she?"

"You could say that," Kane ruefully replied.

Julius sipped his beer, his expression thoughtful. "First of all, you have to know that Shasta is the baby of the family and was a big surprise." He lifted his gaze to Kane's. "There's only ten months between Shasta and Jeff, and there are the two older children. John's thirty-nine and Virginia's thirty-seven. See, Jeff was planned and Shasta was a slip up.'' Julius crossed his arms on the table and leaned forward. ''Jeff was real sick as a baby and Shasta's parents had their hands full, so Shasta was left to her grandfather, a nanny and me. We raised that kid till she got old enough to take care of herself.''

Kane snorted disbelievingly.

''You listen here, mister,'' admonished Julius, ''if you think she can't take care of herself, you're a big fool and in for a shock. I ain't seen nothing she can't do.'' He was quiet for a second then chuckled, '' 'Cept those woman things.'' Julius caught a glimpse of Kane's interest and leaned forward conspiratorially. ''She never learned to cook, doesn't like to clean house and has no taste in clothes or style. Why, hell, half the time either me or Rena does her shopping. She don't even carry her own charge cards, I do.'' Suddenly Julius clamped his lips together. ''I'd be in your debt if you'd forget what I just told you,'' he said stiffly. ''Shasta'll kill me if she knew.''

Kane laughed and agreed, but continued to probe. ''Do all the Mastersons work in the company?''

''Everyone down to second cousins.''

''No black sheep?''

Julius threw back his head and laughed. ''Black sheep. I guess that's as good a description as any.'' He saw Kane's puzzled expression and explained. ''Shasta's the family black sheep, troublemaker or whatever you want to hang on her. She's the only one in the entire family with the dark coloring. All Mastersons are tall, blue-eyed blondes, and it's been the bane of her life. She's also the only one who wanted to work outside the company. That caused a row, I can tell you. But she's the apple of her grandfather's eye, and if she was to be hurt...." Julius's forehead pleated and his eyebrows dived inward. "Well, I wouldn't give the man any odds on staying alive long."

The two men stared at each other in perfect understanding—one giving warning, the other accepting.

Kane sighed in defeat. He'd been trying to find an avenue of escape. Now he realized he'd have to handle this affair carefully, or he'd end up with the entire Masterson family on his back. "Julie, I need your help. What I've come to Houston to do could get dangerous. I don't want anyone to get hurt, so how do I persuade Shasta to give up this bodyguard business, or better yet, make her quit?"

Julius smiled. "Can't! She senses danger and that's all it takes. You ain't very smart, are you? You haven't figured her out yet. She thrives on adventure and excitement and, mister, you reek of danger and mystery. She's on to you till she's tired of the game, or she's done what she has to do. Either way, you ain't going to shake her till she's good and ready to be shook."

Kane cursed long and low, shoved his chair back and stood up. "Let's get out of here." He threw down a twenty-dollar bill, and they walked out of the cool dimly lit room into a searing, humid afternoon. Julie was about to flag down a taxi when Kane stopped him, informing him he needed to pick up some dress shirts.

The two men returned to Shasta's house hours later laden with boxes and bags. Julius, finding himself amid the elegance of Sakowitz, talked a reluctant Kane into helping him choose a dress for Shasta. After the first show of distaste, Kane plunged into the world of silks, chiffons and sequins. Julius, pushed aside in favor of Kane's European taste, could only stand back and think of the hell this little shopping expedition was going to cause. If Shasta ever found out—he gulped—the fur was going to fly.

As THE SKY GLOWED with a scarlet sunset, Shasta pulled up to a red light and stopped. Picking up the mobile phone mounted on the dashboard, she punched out her home number. Busy! For the past two hours she'd received the same signal and wondered who Kane was talking to. The light changed, and she shifted gears with a grinding noise that expressed her mood. At least, she thought, she now knew that Kane and Julie were home. Turning down her street, she gunned the deadly little car into her driveway and squealed to a stop. Flinging the door open, she was out of the car and through the back door in a shot. "Where the hell was everybody today?"

Standing at the kitchen sink peeling shrimp and arranging them artfully around an iced bowl, Julius waved her to silence. He pointed to the living room, explaining that Kane was on the phone, then proceeded to tell her about their day—omitting the shopping spree and the fact that three new day dresses and four evening dresses now hung half hidden in her closet, not to mention the shoes and accessories he'd tucked away.

"Who's he been on the telephone with for so long?"

"I ain't got the foggiest idea, but it's not just one person. He has his little black book open."

"Black book indeed!" She snorted in disgust. "Julie, where's that satin thing Rena gave me last Christmas?" She stormed out of the kitchen and headed for the stairs, Julie right behind her.

He grabbed her arm to stop her. "Shasta Masterson, never tell me you're going to wear that to dinner?"

Her eyes were filled with determination as she met Julie's scandalized gaze. "'Fight fire with fire,'" she quoted one of his famous sayings. "Julie, I'll be damned if he's going to make dates and have me follow them along as his bodyguard. If Kane Stone goes anywhere, it's me he'll take."

Julius studied her for a long second. "If you're serious about this, then for heaven's sake wear the robe that goes with it." He frowned furiously, showing his disapproval in every stiff line of his body as he turned and walked away. But as the kitchen door closed behind him, he cackled out in gleeful joy and rubbed his hands together. Baskerville trotted in from outside, his nose busy following his mistress's trail. Julius smiled and patted the dog's head. "You best stay out of the living room tonight, beast, cause Shasta Masterson is about to meet her match."

Upstairs, water splashed onto a tiled floor as Shasta angrily finished her bath. She quickly dried off, dabbed Joy everywhere a pulse beat and some places it didn't. There would be no repeat of last night, but she would keep his interest high just in case he had other ideas. She held out a delicate porcelain-pink floor-length slip before her. Without further thought she slipped it over her head and stood before the full-length mirror. Her fingers touched the pale gray lace that barely veiled the tops of her nipples then dived to a plunging vee. She picked up the matching wrap robe, trying to arrange its folds to cover her slinky outline. But the clinging material only seemed to add emphasis to her slim, shapely body. A woman could get herself into real trouble in an item like this, she conceded warily, then wondered at her sanity in wearing it for Kane. Swallowing her nervousness, she quickly ran a brush through her tangle of soft loose curls, slid her feet into pink high-heeled slippers, hiked up her gown to her knees and marched out the door and down the stairs.

Shasta stood in the living room, her heart skipping a beat as she watched Kane's eyes lift at her entrance. With pure pleasure she observed the heavy droop of his eyelids as his conversation broke off in midsentence. She had definitely made an impression.

"I'll call you back, Boston." He hung up, then stood, his gaze glued to the petite vision gliding across the room toward him.

Shasta lowered her voice to a husky whisper. "Would you fix me one of those?" She tapped the rim of his crystal glass, which was still suspended halfway to his mouth.

With a jolt, Kane came to full attention. His mouth tightened. "What game are you playing now? After last night I'd have thought you would—"

"No game, Kane," she interrupted. "I just wanted to get into something more comfortable before dinner." Her cheeks flushed at the lie and the look in his eyes, and she hoped the dim lighting covered her uneasiness. She followed him slowly to the bar and leaned her elbows on the hard counter, affording Kane a tempting view.

"You know, Shasta, you can't ignore talking about last night or pretend it never happened just because it didn't go the way you wanted. And, goddamn it, if you don't straighten up I'll take you here and now on the floor."

Shasta jerked upright, then stepped back as Kane reached across the counter, a paring knife in his hand. She watched as fascinated as a bird before a cobra as he snipped off something from her sleeve then handed it to her. Shasta looked down to find a price tag lying across her palm and her eyebrows rose at the figures stamped on it. "Rena's totally out of her mind paying this for a few pieces of fabric stitched together," she mumbled, turning to Kane, her eyes glistening with laughter. "Should I leave and come in again?"

"No, mouse," Kane said with a chuckle. "You've done enough damage to my libido for one night." He guided her to a chair, handed her a martini, then plopped a boiled shrimp in her mouth before she could think of a comeback.

"I wish you wouldn't call me mouse." She scowled at him. "I've had to deal with nicknames all my life. I hate them, really I do, Kane."

"Sorry, but this one you'll have to get used to."

"It's not very complimentary."

"To me it is."

She leaned back in her chair and sipped her drink. "Did you have a nice restful day? How are your ribs, by the way?"

Kane grinned. "My ribs are fine, thank you, and you know I went downtown today."

"Why?"

Still standing beside her chair, Kane leaned down and gave her lips a hard kiss. "What an inquisitive little hardhead you are," he murmured, and was saved from further questions by Julie's timely arrival announcing dinner.

Through mushroom bisque to lobster thermidor, Shasta kept him totally fascinated with her chatter, regaling him with stories of Jeff's computer genius and Rena's new troubles with Lizzie. He was completely captivated and genuinely surprised when Julie placed a large wedge of chocolate-chip cheesecake and a cup of coffee before him. And he, who didn't care for lobster, now ruefully remembered he'd cleaned his plate, never realizing what he'd eaten.

"Who were you talking to on the telephone for so long?" Shasta watched the curtain fall across his features. Why, she wondered, did she have the feeling that those phone calls had something to do with her, and she didn't think they were full of goodwill.

Kane took a bite of cheesecake, his hard gaze fixed on her puzzled expression. "The calls were to some old friends letting them know I was in town. By the way, bodyguard, I hope you're free at night because I'm going to be renewing some friendships."

"What about the men following you?"

"What about them? I guess they'll have some long hours, now won't they?"

SHASTA WOKE in the middle of the night to the feel of a cold wet nose nudging her bare arm. A soft persistent whine penetrated her sleep-fogged mind. She opened one eye and stared at Baskerville. He whined again, then bumped her arm, his toenails clicking urgently on the hardwood floor.

"What's the matter, boy?"

Baskerville growled this time, his feet working like pistons even though he remained in the same position. Shasta threw back the covers, yanked open the bedside drawer and pulled out her gun. She flipped off the safety and checked the clip to make sure the gun was sufficiently loaded. Baskerville might be a clown with a drinking problem, but he was also a trained guard dog and every inch of him was screaming trouble. This was no stray cat or dog intruding into his territory, but a human he didn't know.

Her adrenaline pumping, Shasta ran down the stairs and was at the back door in a flash. She slid the lock aside, eased the door partway open and motioned the now-bristling dog to be quiet as she listened. When no unfamiliar sounds were forthcoming, she studied Baskerville's aggressive stance. "You're sure, boy?"

A low angry growl answered her whispered question. Then she heard the noise and froze, her body still as the night as the first faint sounds of someone tampering with her locked back gate reached her. Baskerville tried to push her away from the door, but Shasta again waved him away. "Let's wait till they're all the way in so. . . ." She trailed off, her heart pounding with excitement as she heard the squeak of a rusty hinge.

Counting slowly to ten, she opened the door wide and gave Baskerville the silent hand order to attack. One hundred eighty pounds of killer bounded soundlessly out the door. Unlike some guard dogs, Baskerville was more menacing because he was trained never to let his victim hear him. An intruder would turn on stealthy feet and find himself staring into a snarling face that nightmares were born of.

Shasta brought her gun up to the ready position in both hands, ready to step outside and follow Baskerville before he tore his captive apart. Suddenly her perfect night vision was blinded by the brilliant blooming of the overhead light. She blinked and spun around, her temper rising as she spotted Kane standing in the kitchen doorway, his hand suspended on the light switch. Confusion reigned as a scream, growls and loud cursing flooded the backyard. Kane sprinted across the room, making a grab for the gun.

In a quick reflex motion, Shasta chopped his hand down and out of the way. "What do you think you're doing?" she yelled as they collided into each other. She didn't wait for an answer as Baskerville, caught off guard by the commotion in the house and his master's angry voice, gave a loud yelp.

Tangled in Kane's arms, Shasta squirmed to be free, and without thinking she elbowed him in the side, delighting at his grunt of pain. But he held her struggling body till Baskerville came charging up the steps, eyeing Kane and growling deep in his throat, his jaws still clamped around a strip of a man's pant leg.

"You damn fool woman!" Kane let her go and stepped back, shaking his numbed hand up and down. "I wonder why I'm forever leaving myself unprepared for your tricks? You'd think I'd have learned by now, wouldn't you?"

Shasta glared up at him as she knelt to check Baskerville. "I don't have anything to say to you right now," she ground out between clenched teeth. Baskerville yelped as Shasta found and touched a large lump on the top of his head. She wrapped her arms around his thick neck and talked baby talk to him while he whined even more pitifully for sympathy. "See what you and your Machiavellian secrets have done. Baskerville has a knot on his head the size of a baseball, and our burglar got away." She pushed Kane out of the way and yanked open the refrigerator door as Baskerville whined even louder.

"Damn it, Shasta—"

"Don't talk to me. Not yet—not till I've calmed down. Of all the macho, stupid, asinine...the nerve of rushing me when I have a loaded gun in my hand. I would have thought with your training you'd have known better."

She didn't notice Kane's steely expression or the shutter that seemed to fall in place over his eyes. Retrieving a bottle of beer, she tucked the cold container under her arm and pulled out a handful of ice cubes. Baskerville, spying the beloved brown bottle, moaned and limped slowly after her. "You faker, it's your head that's hurt, not your leg." She yanked out a dish towel from a drawer, dumped the ice in the center and rolled it up. Opening the beer, she knelt down in front of her dog and tied the towel around his massive head, positioning the ice on the swelling knot. Baskerville sat patiently as she completed her task, his tongue hanging out in greedy anticipation.

Shasta poured his beer, gave him another hug and picked up the strip of torn pants, inspecting it closely before she pitched it into the trash. She faced Kane and frowned, furious all over again at his interference. "Why can't you let me handle things my way?"

"God only knows!" Kane declared coldly. "You've proved you don't need my help."

Shasta pulled out a chair and sat down. "Kane, this has gone on long enough. You're going to have to tell me who's after you and why."

"No, and after tonight I think I'd better go to a hotel." He joined her at the table.

Shasta's stomach twisted at the thought of his leaving, and her gaze traveled over the broad shoulders under the smooth material of his robe. She wished she had handled last night's fiasco better, realizing now that she had cut off her nose to spite her own face. She was the one missing his touch. Cold and unemotional as she had accused him of being, she could still enjoy being held in the warmth of his arms. He was looking at her with amusement, and she tried to bring her thoughts back to the present.

"Will leaving here stop whoever is after you?" She scowled at him fiercely, and his lips twitched involuntarily. "I'm your bodyguard whether you like it or not. You can leave my house right now, but it won't change things or solve the problem. If I have to, Kane, I'll just set up a twenty-four-hour surveillance. Besides," she said, grinning, "you seem to be so protective of me now, just think what you'll feel knowing that I'm sitting on some dark street—alone—watching you."

Kane sighed in defeat. "You are without a doubt the most hardheaded woman I've ever had the misfortune to meet."

"Yes, I know." She folded her hands over one of his. "Kane, it's time you told me what's happening and how dangerous it's going to be."

Kane pulled his hand free and brought her palm to his lips. "This is not a case of the more you know the safer you'll be, mouse. Those men out there want something they think I have. But more important, I want something I know they have, and I intend to get it. So, if your mind is made up and you insist on following me around—okay. Just don't interfere in what I'm doing." He kissed the other palm, but his features had taken on that inscrutable, passive look again. He laid her hands down gently on the table, shoved his chair back and stood. "You'd better get all the sleep you can, because if you plan to keep up with me, you'll only have a speaking acquaintance with your bedroom."

Shasta bit her lip as the sardonic glint in his eyes returned. After all, she reassured herself, what harm could a few nights out on the town do? At least she'd be with him.

CHAPTER SEVEN

WHAT HARM could a few nights out on the town do? Shasta wondered tiredly how long ago she had asked herself that question. Weeks, months ago? She felt as if she'd passed a year of sleepless nights, endless traveling and parties; a never-ending stream of smiling faces. And always they would return to Houston so she could be at work bright and early.

She pulled up the low-cut bodice of her strapless, black taffeta gown and frowned. Her closet seemed to have sprouted evening dresses lately, a development she'd have to check into when she had the time. She sighed and slumped in her chair, then straightened abruptly as she caught Kane's mocking gaze across the table. It had taken her a couple of days to finally figure out what he was up to, and when she did, her determination to keep up the pace he had set increased. She gave him a challenging smile. If he thought by dragging her all over the country he could tire her into quitting. . . .

Shooting Kane another enigmatic look, she pointed her nose in the air and gazed around the smoky room filled with people in Valentino gowns flashing twelve-carat diamonds. They all looked blissfully ignorant of life and eternally young.

Where was she? Shasta's eyes glazed over as she tried to remember. There had been so many clubs, restaurants and private parties over the past two weeks that she'd lost all track of time and place. "Dallas," she mumbled out loud, and a self-satisfied smile lifted one corner of her mouth. The Rio Room—a chic, *very* private club. She wasn't as confused as she'd imagined.

Leaning back, Shasta eyed the voluptuous redhead hanging on Kane's every word. She'd been pushed aside more times than she'd like to count. Women seemed to take root on Kane's arm. After days of trying to deal with her jealousy, a jealousy Kane spotted and played on, she soon realized that he was only paying lip service to their attentions. Kane was too busy watching *her* and sending out scowling looks to warn any interested males that she was private property and to keep their hands off.

Shasta shifted position, eased her sore feet from her shoes and picked up a glass of champagne, pretending to take a sip. Her gaze roamed the room, picking out familiar faces. Wealthy leeches, her grandfather called them, people he had little patience or time for, though he and the Masterson family could match most of them monetarily. But J.T. separated the two classes, the working rich and the parasites with eight-figure quarterly incomes from inheritances or oil royalties. Shasta shivered to think what he was going to say when he learned of her activities these past two weeks. She closed her eyes wearily and pressed her hands over her aching stomach.

Each night was a marathon in travel and food as Kane dragged her on his jaunts. Was it yesterday or last week, she wondered, that she had flown to New York in Texas-American's company jet? There Kane had hired a caravan of limousines outfitted with bars stocked with iced champagne. Their party had arrived at a white Georgian house with a black lacquer door. A private restaurant, Le Club had a regular clientele that included politicians, socialites, Wall Street turks and Hollywood sheiks.

When was it she had walked New Orleans French Quarter in the early-morning mist, breakfasted at Brennan's, lunched standing up at the long white marble bar of Acme Oyster Bar and dined that evening at the most romantic place in town, the Court of Two Sisters. *Sunday*, Shasta recalled. She had been in New Orleans on Sunday, and after a day spent in revelry she had managed to talk Kane and his friends into sitting still long enough for her to savor café au lait and hot beignets, those puffy squares of fried pastry covered with powdered sugar that New Orleans was famous for.

Shasta's stomach rebelled at the thought of food, and she dug around in her purse for another antacid tablet. She'd dined like a queen on lobster from Maine, fresh salmon from Alaska, raw oysters from the Texas Gulf, stone crabs from Florida and caviar from Russia. Her palate was well traveled; she only wished her insides would settle on firm ground.

"Are you ready to leave?"

Kane's whispered question jolted her out of her thoughts and she looked up, her eyelids heavy with fatigue. He molded her evening wrap to her shoulders and, with his arm around her waist, guided her out into the night.

Shasta inhaled deeply of the bracing air, but instead of reviving, she slumped tiredly against Kane as he led her to the waiting limousine. Before she realized it, she was comfortably secured in Kane's arms and snuggling her head against his chest. When they switched to the small jet, she nestled into his warm body and began to play lazily with the pearl studs of his ruffled tuxedo shirt. "I'm so tired I could sleep for a year."

"I know. We'll be home in about forty-five minutes."

Shasta opened her sleepy lids and looked out the round window to see the sun's brilliant colors streak the horizon in a burnt-orange glow. "I'll have about two hours before I have to dress again and go to work," she murmured. "Thank heaven I'll be through with the Thomas case today." She closed her eyes and thought about the job. Thomas Jewelers were being systematically robbed of their precious diamonds. The thefts were so cleverly committed that it had taken them four months to realize what was happening before they had called in Masters. Shasta almost chuckled out loud as she recalled the ingeniousness of the eighteen-year-old runner, a close friend of the owners, who hand delivered loose diamonds from one branch store to the other. Somewhere along the way he would stop, heat the wax seal and open the package, help himself to two or three stones and replace them with high-quality fakes. He'd then reseal the package and reharden the wax with ice.

It had taken Shasta and two of her co-workers weeks to figure out his scheme and then confront him before calling the police. Between tying up the case and Kane's marathon partying, she was exhausted.

Shasta cuddled closer to Kane and tilted her head back into the crook of his arm. "Now that I'm free, I'll be able to catch up on my sleep during the day like you've been doing." Her fingers picked a stud loose and dropped it into his breast pocket before going on to the next one. "You know, of course, that your plan is not working? I'm not giving up."

Kane's answering grin sent her blood pumping through her veins. With deft hands he quickly worked out the pins holding her hair in place. After a few seconds the floor lay strewed with the tiny pieces of metal as his hands began massaging her scalp. "I think I'll have to concede this round to you, my mouse."

"Good! Then you're not going to try to turn me into one of those women who cling to you with adoring eyes?"

Kane snorted at the thought.

"Do you truly call those people your friends, Kane? They live such a useless existence."

"So do I, Shasta."

She dropped another stud into his pocket, letting her fingers play for a brief second on the soft hair on his chest. "Do you?" Suddenly fed up with the game they were playing with each other, she began to tell him what Jeff had found out, and as she talked she felt his body go taut at each new piece of information. The more she talked, the angrier she became with his continued silence, and she began telling him things she'd never planned to, though she did have enough wits to refrain from mentioning the murder of Melvin Kimble.

Kane cursed long and vigorously. "Your brother doesn't fool around. How in the hell did he get this information?"

Shasta dropped another stud into his pocket, then slipped both hands into the opening of his shirt, loving the feel of his warm flesh beneath her hands.

Kane clasped her wrists hard and pulled her resisting hands from his body. "Back off, Shasta."

His command came out slow and precise, his accent more pronounced than she'd ever heard it. Shasta straightened slightly in his lap, realizing for the first time that Kane was magnificently drunk, that the sensuous indolence and dissipation she'd witnessed over the past two weeks was controlled drunkenness, as if that

was the only way he could endure the mindless chatter
and boredom of his so-called friends. As she moved
away, Kane grabbed her hips and pulled her back down,
making her conscious of the growing hardness beneath
her thigh.

"I asked how Jeff obtained all this material about
me?"

"Computers and codes. I told you Masters had access
to files very few are privy to." Kane's hand glided to her
shoulders, and the tips of his fingers played like a soft
breath along the tops of her breasts. She stared into his
heavy lidded eyes and shook her head. "No. You're not
human enough yet."

Kane threw his head back and laughed disbelievingly.
"Mouse, you must be numb from the waist down."

Shasta knew with the wrong word or action he would
lose control, and she'd be on the receiving end of his
temper. She snuggled against his chest. "Tell me about
your childhood—your mother and father."

Kane laughed again, but this time the sound under her
ear was harsh and grating. "I never had a childhood,
ma chérie. From the cradle I was being groomed to take
over Tex-Am Oil. I grew up watching mother and Max
yelling and fighting. Max wanted me in the business,
and because he did, mother didn't. So they each, in their
own way, used me as a pawn in their power plays. The
funny thing is, I think I would have liked to have
learned the family business and even taken it over someday. But I saw very early Max's obsession and knew he
would only let go when he was in his grave. As for
mother, she's just another vain woman afraid of growing old and losing her looks." Kane was quiet for a long
minute.

"Who's Melvin Kimble?" She slipped the question in

softly and waited. Only his even breathing met her ears, and she realized he'd fallen sound asleep.

AT FIVE TO EIGHT the next morning, Shasta straightened the pile of papers on her desk, rubbed her gritty eyes, then closed the folder of the finished Thomas report. Unable to sleep once she and Kane arrived home, she had jumped into a cold shower and headed for the quiet of the office to complete her work. Now she'd be able to give her full attention to Kane's troubles, whether he wanted her to or not.

"Hello there. You're here bright and early." Rena grinned at her from the doorway. "Want another cup of coffee?"

"Sure, and come join me, Rena, I want to ask you a question."

Shasta waited until her sister-in-law was seated, then asked, "Rena, have you ever regretted throwing over your English duke and running off with Jeff? I mean, did you truly know Jeff was the love of your life? Could you feel it in your bones?"

Rena started to make one of her witty remarks, then stopped as she saw the pain in Shasta's eyes. "Oh, dear. You've got it bad, haven't you?" Shasta nodded. "What about Kane?"

"I don't know." She looked down at her hands. How could she explain the feeling she had? Maybe she was more like her family than she'd thought. "You're going to think this is nuts, but I feel it here." She tapped her heart. "Kane *has* to love me. He just refuses to admit it." She propped her elbows on the desk top. "I'm in limbo. I don't know if I should wait or force the issue. Even though he doesn't think so, he *is* capable of love and tenderness." She shook her head and closed her eyes. "He's a stubborn man, and it's probably going to take a lifetime to bring him around. Any ideas?"

"Not offhand, but give me some time and I'll come up with something." They both fell into a thoughtful silence shattered by Jeff's entrance.

"Ah, ladies, gossiping on office time again, for shame." His neat appearance after weeks of disorder was in its own way a warning. He had exhausted every avenue in his part of the investigation and would now wait for new instructions. In the meantime he'd spend every spare second with Rena and Lizzie. He folded his long frame down beside his wife and pitched a thick folder on Shasta's desk.

"That's the rest of Kane Stone's report." He peered closer at his sister and remarked cheerfully, "You look like death warmed over. Why don't you take the rest of the day off and get some rest?"

Shasta fingered the fat file. "Summarize what's new here, *please*, Jeff."

Jeff was momentarily diverted by his wife's smile. "Oh, yeah.... There's nothing more on Kane, though I sure would like to find out about those blank three years. I checked to see if anything earthshaking was going on in our government during that time and could only come up with one item—a CIA operation involving a defected Russian laser scientist. There was a big stink over it, though. It seems our man lost him somewhere in Europe and they sent in a special agent to find him and bring him home." Jeff shrugged. "You know me!" He grinned sheepishly. "I got interested and started to check the file for more information when I was cut off, and not more than five minutes later, J.T. called raising hell. I stepped on someone's toes and they immediately informed J.T." Jeff shuddered. "I then had to explain the entire Stone case."

Shasta groaned in sympathy, knowing how thorough her grandfather could be. "Did you find out anything on this Kimble character?"

"Funny you should ask." Jeff wiggled his eyebrows in a poor imitation of Julie. "You know how strange we thought it was when Julie told us that Kane kept going downtown? Though he always ended up at Tex-Am Oil's office building, he usually made several trips by U.S.A. Oil. Well, sister dear, Professor Melvin Kimble was once employed by U.S.A. Oil in their research department. He'd been with them ten years, then suddenly one day just up and quit. And, get this, the next day he went to work for Max Stone at Tex-Am Oil." Jeff held up his hand to stop the spate of words he saw forming on Shasta's lips. "Wait. You have to hear the rest. Max Stone hustled Kimble to France and there, sister dear, we come to a dead end. It seems the professor dropped out of sight, and nothing's turned up about him until his murder in Barbizon, France, some weeks ago."

Shasta stared at her brother, her mouth hanging open. "Oil, Jeff! This is all about oil!" Her excitement dissipated, and she pressed her fingertips to her temples. "Oh, hell and damnation! I can't think straight I'm so tired. But somewhere I know there's a clue that ties all this information together." She dropped her hands and opened her eyes. "I'm going home to take a long nap, then, maybe, I can figure this out."

"Not yet, you won't," Margret said from her position by the door.

Shasta grinned. J.T.'s watchdog had slipped in unnoticed and overheard every detail.

"There's a Mr. Harold Winsome here to see you."

Shasta flipped the pages of her appointment book frantically.

"No, you won't find his name there, but he says it's urgent." Margret stood aside as Jeff and Rena left the office, then she closed the door. "He's vice-president of security at U.S.A. Oil!"

Shasta swallowed hard. Things were moving too fast, and her mind wasn't clear enough to handle it all.

"Coincidence, do you think?"

"I doubt it. Meg, have you talked to pappy?"

"This morning, and he has a message for you—'tread lightly.'" She smiled at Shasta's grimace. "Do you want me to send in Mr. Winsome?"

"Yes." Shasta closed her eyes again and sighed. "I don't know much else that could happen to surprise me in this case."

SHASTA GRIPPED THE STEERING WHEEL of her car so hard her knuckles whitened. Her words to Margret had been the understatement of the year! Of all the nerve! No, it was bald-faced gall, that's what it was. That slick Mr. Winsome in his three-piece pin-striped suit, that smooth-talking snake who had just slithered into her office and...and...." Shasta gritted her teeth together. This was all Kane's fault, she thought grimly.

She wheeled the Porsche into the driveway, slammed the door and marched in the back door. She passed Julie without a word and stomped into the living room. There she stopped, hands on hips, surveying the scene before her with angry eyes. Kane lay stretched out on her couch, a magazine covering his face as he caught up on his sleep and recovered from his hangover. And to make bad matters worse, her faithful dog lay curled up on the end of the couch, a place he knew meant severe punishment—no beer!

"I hope you're satisfied," she yelled, and both man

and dog jumped as if they'd been shot. "I have just been propositioned, offered a bribe, had my professional integrity smeared, called a liar, threatened, been accused of harboring a murderer, referred to as 'toots' by the lowest form of life, and it's all your fault."

Kane blinked and Baskerville eased off the couch and half crawled, half ran from the room. "But, mouse...."

"Don't you dare 'mouse' me," she yelled again. "This mess you're in is over some stupid synthetic-fuel formula."

Kane was off the couch and gripping her shoulders almost before the last words left her mouth. "What do you know about the formula?" he demanded.

"I know you have it, and U.S.A. Oil is willing to pay any price or do anything to gain possession. Kane, you're hurting me." She'd finally cracked the feelings he'd kept so well hidden. His usually reckless expression had been replaced by one that was cunning and dangerous. She rubbed her arms and sat down.

"I had a visit from a Harry Winsome a while ago. He offered Masters a contract to handle their worldwide security. I politely refused his offer, explaining that there would be a conflict of interest as we already represented one oil company. He then proceeded to drop not so subtle hints and insinuations of bribery. When I continued to say no, he began to get a little testy. The snake in the grass then offered me a personal bribe of an amount that took my breath away." Shasta glared at Kane. "All that was required of me was to obtain a synthetic-fuel formula now in your possession. I hadn't the faintest idea what he was talking about and told him so. That's when he got nasty, and Jeff escorted him from my office—"

Shasta paused to let the impact of her next words carry their full weight. "He said that Masters could be charged as an accessory in harboring the murderer of Melvin Kimble." She jumped up and shouted, "You, Kane," then began to pace the floor, her temper rising rapidly as she watched his smile turn into laughter.

"So, the weasels are getting nervous, are they?"

Shasta stopped, his question hitting her like a blow. "You bastard. You've been using all of us as pawns." She thumped her head with the heel of her hand. "The trips downtown, the lack of concern at being followed, the visits to Tex-Am Oil. You deliberately led them in circles while you concocted your devious plans. Damn you."

"Now, Shasta, calm down."

"Calm down? I'll calm down when you tell me what's going on and what you're up to? Well?" she demanded.

Kane was at her side in two strides, his hands caressing her arms, his voice husky with sincerity. "Will you trust me, Shasta?"

"No! Are you out of your mind? Why should I?" She tried to shrug off his hands.

"I can't tell you . . . ."

"Hah."

"Everything right now." His eyes captured hers and she quickly glanced away. "I didn't kill the professor, Shasta. You know that, don't you?" She nodded, still not looking at him. "Trust me?"

"No. Not without a good reason. Besides, Kane," she wailed, "why won't you let me help you?"

Kane sighed. "Because these men play for keeps. Masters is tops in its field, I'll grant you that, Shasta. But in all this time have you realized that we're not only being followed by people from U.S.A. Oil but by the government, as well. No, you didn't know because they're the best. And while the oil people were willing to let us fly all over and simply wait for us to return, the government men were with us every second. They never missed a city or a restaurant or a party."

Stunned, Shasta sat down and stared at Kane. "Are they after the synthetic-fuel formula, too?"

"Yes."

"Are you going to give it to them?"

"No."

"Why? They are our government men, aren't they?"

"Yes, and you needn't get that excited look. They won't make a move—not yet. Not till they see what U.S.A. Oil and I are up to. If we try to make a deal they may step in. Right now they're merely our watchdogs." He reached out, captured Shasta's stubborn chin and forced her face to his. "Shasta, the less you know about the formula, the better off you'll be."

"You do have it, don't you?" She sat back, her mind working furiously over the advantages of such a discovery. "Does it work, Kane? There've been so many different attempts."

Kane sat down across from her and picked up her hands. "It works. Better than anyone could ever imagine. But it's dangerous, Shasta." He studied her puzzled expression, then went on. "The Saudis are violently against our research. Our government would like nothing better than to have a blade to hold over the necks of the oil-producing nations. The oil companies here would like to see it destroyed. Remember that the Saudis stopped us from stockpiling oil with a firm warning. Our coal-conversion program is wildly optimistic and so is the shale extraction. The idea of synthetic fuel is more than a savings for the consumers, it has worldwide implications. But all this is not the issue here. There's already been one murder over the formula, there could be others."

"That's what I don't understand, Kane. Why kill the goose that laid the golden egg?"

"Shasta," he said scornfully. "No oil company in their right mind wants a cheap alternative to oil. That would cause a catastrophic financial disaster that would only end in bankruptcy for them. What would you do if you were wealthy beyond imagination, greedy, ruthless, and someone you couldn't buy came along and threatened your very existence?" Kane shook his head at Shasta's blank expression. "No, you couldn't contemplate murder, but there are men—and governments—who could and do."

"If what you say about the big oil companies not wanting a synthetic fuel on the market is true, then why would your father invest so much time and money in the formula's development?"

"Because what few people know is that Tex-Am Oil is in bad shape, the result of poor investments, the lowering of oil prices, cutbacks and, of course, the economic decline. Also, remember that Tex-Am is primarily a family-owned corporation without the heavy cash flow of U.S.A. Oil. Max is becoming a desperate man and will grab at any chance of recouping his losses. So he jumped at the idea of newfound wealth and power. He set up the research lab with his own money, thinking he'd discovered a way out of his problems. Now, one person is dead, and I intend to find the man responsible!"

Shasta's breath hissed through her compressed lips in horror. "You've set yourself up as bait, haven't you? Whatever it is you want, you're going to trade the formula." She jumped up and began to pace back and forth. "You can't do it."

"Shasta. Shasta!" He matched her steps for a few seconds, then laughed. "Will you stop that? It's not as bad as it sounds." She opened her mouth to contradict him, but he placed his fingers across her lips. "You're tired. Why don't you go up and rest before we go out tonight."

"And that's another thing, Kane Stone. I'm tired of being dragged all over the country and sick to death of your worthless, boring, corrupt, malicious friends."

"We're not going out of town."

"They drink too much—"

"We're going to a gallery showing."

"They're shallow and vain and sick."

"Samantha Grey."

Kane smiled as she stopped her tirade and gazed up at him, delight shining in her big eyes. He should never have come here. Every second he spent in her company he was courting danger. She'd become his Lorelei and the warmth and comfort of her home his island. She was luring him to disaster, he knew, but her small, funny face had become so dear he couldn't bare to leave just yet. Kane tossed aside his wayward thoughts. "Boston called the other day to let me know about the show."

"Boston?"

"Really, Shasta, for someone who says that Samantha is her favorite artist, you show a shocking lack of knowledge about her. Boston Grey—Samantha's husband."

"The singer Boston Grey?"

Kane grinned at the typical female reaction to Boston's name. "One and the same." He took her elbow and firmly walked her out of the living room.

They both stopped as Julie and Baskerville scrambled up from their listening positions on the bottom step. Kane frowned. Shasta sighed and said dismissingly, "You can't have any secrets around here. I don't know why I even try."

She disengaged her arm from Kane's and turned to him. "I'm not through with this formula business yet, you know. It's just that I'm too tired to argue with you and need some time to think of a plan." She poked the center of his chest with a finger. "I don't want you to think you're going to run this scam on your own." She tried valiantly to look severe, but her sparkling eyes gave away her excitement. "Besides, I don't think it's fair that you have all the fun."

SHASTA STARED INTO THE MIRROR of her vanity, batted her eyelashes and grinned. Turning her head sideways, she critically studied her makeup job and nodded, pleased with what a little sleep and a persistent hand could achieve. She checked the temperature of the heat rollers adorning her head and wondered what other women did to pass the time while their curlers cooled down. "Becoming gorgeous is such a boring job," she said to her reflection, and waited as if she expected an answer.

When a deep masculine voice said, "Yes, but it's worth every second," Shasta screamed and spun around on the stool.

Kane, as elegant as ever, sauntered over and set a frosted glass of white wine before her. "You'd better hurry, Shasta. Boston wanted us to be there early." One finger hooked itself under the fallen strap of her cream satin teddy and slowly pulled it back on her shoulder. Kane leaned down to give her a quick kiss.

But Shasta had other ideas, and her arms slipped

around his neck, her tongue invading his mouth. Then, pulling away, she turned back to the mirror and lifted her eyes to his. "I do believe you're beginning to become human. Mind you, my job is not nearly completed, but we're making headway." She began to absently undo the spiky rollers, her attention still on Kane.

"Here, let me help or we'll be all night." He contemplated the job at hand for a second, then started where Shasta should have, at the neckline working upward.

Enjoying the novelty of having the man she loved working on her hair, Shasta sat calmly, eyes closed. "You're very good at this. Have you done it before? Ouch! I take that back, you're terrible. Ouch!"

Kane chuckled, playfully slapping her hands away, and continued pulling on her hair till all the rollers had spilled onto the vanity table or rolled across the floor. "This is a first." He toyed with the soft fat curls, loving the feel of the silken strands slipping through his fingers. "Hand me your brush."

Shasta frowned at his reflection. "I put those jumbo rollers in for a reason. If you go and brush my hair to death it'll only spring back into curls. Go away. You're making me nervous."

He leaned forward, his breath tickling the back of her neck. "How nervous?" His warm lips moved behind her ear, and his hands slid from her arms to gently cover her breasts. "This nervous?" He placed tiny kisses in the curve of her shoulder. "Or this nervous?"

"Kane, I thought you said we were in a hurry?"

He threw up his hands in surrender and stepped back as she meticulously ran the brush through her hair, pushing it this way and that before she gave up.

She realized that Kane was beginning to change,

whether he ever admitted it or not. There was a peaceful-
ness about him that hadn't been there a week ago. "Are
you going to just stand there and watch me dress?" she
asked.

"I thought you might need some help." His eyes
twinkled teasingly, and Shasta caught her breath. "You
know, things like a stubborn zipper, a snap you can't
reach, or assistance with your gun and shoulder holster,
which I'm sure you're determined to wear."

Shasta giggled as she walked over to her bed and
picked up the apple-red chiffon dress lying there. Kane's
smile widened as she wiggled into it. "No, I intended carrying my weapon in my evening bag. It would ruin the
line of the outfit." She picked up the sequined bolero
jacket, slipped it on, then stepped into her shoes. "I
don't know what possessed Julie to buy red. He knows
I've never cared for this shade." She studied her reflection a long moment, still unsure. "What do you think?"
She spun around, the wisp of fabric clinging to her body
like a caress. "Do I look like a flashing traffic light?"

Kane's lips twitched. "No, the color looks great on
you. And by the way, Julie didn't pick out this little
number. I did." Shasta's mouth fell open. "You might
be shocked, but not as much as I was to find myself in
the women's clothing department, thoroughly enjoying
myself."

"You picked this out?"

"That, and a couple of others." He thought it prudent to say nothing about the other items he'd selected
for her. She'd find out about them soon enough. "Julie
said you didn't have any taste." He watched the bright
color flush her cheeks and rephrased his statement. "I
mean, he explained that you didn't have the time to
shop."

"I'll kill him. I swear I'll wring his scrawny neck."

Kane laughed and grabbed her by the shoulders, hugging her close. "Don't be angry, Shasta. I did have a good time, and besides, it's not criminal to be lacking in fashion knowledge." Her body stiffened in his arms. Still smiling, he let her go, picked up her evening bag and took her arm. "Come on, if you arrive at the art gallery with that fierce frown on your face, Samantha will think you don't like her paintings, and we don't want to upset Samantha—at least not right now."

"Why?"

"You'll see," he replied enigmatically, and marched her out the door.

CHAPTER EIGHT

THE HUNTER ART GALLERY, perched on the edge of the wealthy side of River Oaks, was teeming with art patrons and people with fat wallets. Shasta had expected a lavish elegance to the gallery and was surprised at the starkness of the decor. Then she realized that the white walls and subdued lights were designed to show off the art to advantage, enhancing the mood of each painting and highlighting every detail. Someone jostled her shoulder, and Kane wrapped a protective arm around her waist, steering her through the swarm of people.

As soon as she saw Samantha, Shasta immediately knew what Kane had meant about not unsettling her. Samantha Grey was a tall, beautiful woman with a shocking shade of poppy-red hair and freckles, who appeared to be about ten months pregnant.

Kane guided Shasta through the crowd, smiling and nodding to acquaintances, but never slowing until they reached their goal. "Samantha, you look wonderful, but what's happened to Boston? He looks about two steps from the grave!" Kane held the pregnant woman at arm's length and studied her mischievous smile and twinkling aquamarine eyes. "Ah, I see, you're driving the poor man crazy."

"Of course."

Kane gently relaxed his hold on Samantha, shook hands with Boston, then introduced Shasta, who felt like

a butterfly pinned to a board for inspection. Then
everyone spoke at once, stopped and laughed.

"Boston," said Samantha, "why don't you take
Kane and show him the painting I did for him?" As she
watched the two men walk away, she commented to
Shasta, "They're a devastating sight together, aren't
they? I bet the blood pressure in this room has risen considerably and hearts are pumping overtime."

They were indeed a sight for any woman to behold.
Walking dreams, Shasta thought. Both men were of
equal height and had that incredible blue-black hair.
But Kane's shoulders were broad, whereas Boston's
possessed a more wiry physique, a whipcord leanness.
There was also the difference in their eyes, one pair as
dark as midnight and the other as light as the silvery
moon. As the men strolled casually among the throngs
of people, Shasta saw the stares that followed them and
sighed. "Even my heart is pounding ninety to nothing."

"Kane always takes me by surprise every time I see
him," said Samantha. "He's the most beautiful man
I've ever seen, yet he's remained so totally masculine."

Shasta's grin widened. "I know, but it's extremely
hard on my ego. Do you have any idea what it's like to
walk into a restaurant and have him get all the admiring
looks and gasps—from *both* sexes?"

Samantha laughed hard, her hands holding the huge
mound in front of her. At Shasta's concerned look she
smiled and took hold of her arm. "Let's go find a place
to sit so I can rest my back, and you can tell me everything about you and Kane."

If any other woman, with the exception of Rena, had
commandeered her in such a way, Shasta would have
bristled with resentment, but from the second she met
Samantha she felt an instant rapport, an awareness of

comradeship. And most of all there was that lovely twinkle in her aquamarine eyes that tickled Shasta's fancy. Here was another woman who saw the funnier side of life and men. They were no sooner seated than Boston and Kane were beside them. Kane passed Shasta a glass of champagne and rested his hands lightly on her shoulders as he watched Boston fuss around his wife.

Exasperated, Samantha drew Boston's attention to Shasta. "Did Kane tell you that Shasta is his bodyguard?"

Boston grinned. "Honey, I'm told that all you need is red hair and you'd be Samantha's counterpart. Heaven knows that another like her would be more than the male population could stand."

Shasta wondered if Boston's words were an insult or a compliment.

"Go away, both of you," Samantha ordered. "Surely you can put yourselves to better use than standing here. Go sweet-talk some of those gawking women into decreasing the balance of their checkbooks."

Kane kissed Shasta on the forehead, flipped down her skirt, which had twisted over one knee, and grabbed a reluctant Boston, leading him away.

"We'll never get to talk with all these people around, so I asked Kane earlier if the two of you would come over for coffee afterward." Samantha frowned up at Boston. "What are you doing back?" She tried to sound fierce, but Shasta could see that she was thrilled at the attention Boston showered on her.

"I just wanted to tell Shasta that if you needed anything to signal one of your brothers to fetch it." He looked at Shasta. "I don't want her getting up and down or walking all over the place."

Shasta nodded, and Boston gave Samantha a look

that only husbands and wives understand before she, too, nodded in agreement.

"Who are your brothers?" Shasta's question was met first with blank surprise, then the two people staring at her broke into broad grins.

"Take a good look around," Boston told her, "and every time you spot an outlandish color of red hair you'll know. Samantha has six brothers and they're all here." He lovingly patted his wife on the back and left.

Shasta watched him go. She remembered all the times she'd seen him on television or lay listening to his records, fantasizing about her own dream man. She shook away her wishful thoughts. "He's very worried about you, Samantha. Is this your first?"

Samantha patted her stomach. "No. We have a two-year-old daughter named Rebecca, who looks just like her father. The reason Boston's so protective is that he's scared to death this time. But I'll tell you all that later. What I want to know is, did you really knock Kane out and tie him up at your first meeting?"

Shasta sipped her wine, refusing to meet Samantha's probing look, but when she finally raised her head, her eyes were filled with laughter. "He told you that?"

"He's told us everything about you, Shasta. Which is surprising in itself for a man as closemouthed as Kane. Though—" Samantha's searching gaze found Kane in the crowd "—I must admit I've never seen him quite so relaxed and animated before...even when he comes to the ranch." She stopped, realizing Shasta wasn't familiar with her and Boston's home. "We have a ranch out from Santa Fe, New Mexico," she explained, "and when we're in Houston we always stay at Kane's house." She saw Shasta's puzzled expression. "You did know Kane inherited his grandfather's house in River Oaks?"

"No, that's another little secret he's managed to keep from me."

"Oh, Kane's full of secrets, Shasta. Boston's known him for years. They've played around the world together, fought together, and still Boston says there's a part of Kane that remains private. I think it has a lot to do with his childhood and the fighting that went on between his mother and father. But Boston says no, that it's more to do with whatever it is Kane does." Samantha chuckled. "Heaven knows I've tried to find out, but it's useless."

They were interrupted by a steady stream of people congratulating Samantha, and by the time the well-wishers had left, Shasta spotted Kane and Boston making their way toward them.

"Now I wonder what they've been up to?" Samantha mused out loud.

"What do you mean?"

"Shasta, I know my husband like an open book, and his expression is entirely too innocent and angelic *not* to set off warning bells. If you know Kane at all, just take a look at his face and you'll know they've been up to no-good."

Indeed, Kane's expression was suspect. His smile was, too, and his eyes were darker than usual. Shasta searched his face more closely as he walked toward her, then dropped her gaze, frisking him with her eyes. Nothing!

"Don't ask questions," Kane whispered in her ear, his fingers biting into her arm as he hauled her up. "Sammy, I'm going to steal Shasta away for a minute and show her *my* painting." He gave a stubborn Shasta a nudge. "Walk."

Out of hearing distance Shasta asked, "Where have you been and what have you done?" She ground the question out between unmoving lips.

"Boston and I cornered one of the government agents following us and invited him outside to join us in a cigarette."

"You don't smoke." She glanced up and fought back laughter at his guileless expression. "And just how did you convince him to join you two? I'll bet he didn't come willingly."

"Well, no, not at first, but Boston and I convinced him it would be to his benefit to do so. Here's the painting Sammy did for me. What do you think?"

It took Shasta a minute to focus her thoughts on the painting, and when she finally did, she nearly choked on her champagne. The large oil painting depicted an Indian brave astride his horse, a blanket draped around him to protect him from the driving fury of a snowstorm, while his squaw held onto the tail of the horse and waded through deep drifts. "It's a beautiful painting, but sadly typical of man's behavior toward women. I suppose you told her exactly what you wanted?"

Kane chuckled as he guided her on to the next painting. "No, as a matter of fact, Samantha did it for me as a constant reminder that we're in the twentieth century."

"Quit changing the subject, Kane Stone. I want to know what the agent said." She tried to pull free of his hold, but Kane only tightened his grip.

"Now here's an interesting painting."

They circled the gallery, studying each work of art. Samantha's portrayal of the plight of the American Indian was beautiful but heartbreaking. Shasta wondered if the people who bought her paintings truly appreciated the passion behind each brush stroke. She sensed the rage and sorrow Samantha felt for the Indians and instinctively knew that it wasn't only Boston's Indian heritage that made her paintings so vivid but a real interest in the future of the first Americans.

Someone bumped her shoulder hard from behind, and Shasta took a quick step forward to regain her balance. As she turned to confront her clumsy assailant, she found an older woman gushing over Kane, asking about mutual friends and the painting he'd been studying. But the woman's interest wasn't in art. Her eyes devoured Kane with a greediness that both amused and revolted Shasta. She had to give him credit, though; when he wanted to snub someone he did it with finesse, and she smiled at the woman's stunned expression as he guided her away.

"One of your old loves, Kane?" she needled when he returned. Her question caught him as he took a sip of champagne, and he almost choked.

Kane took a firm grip on her elbow, but Shasta dug in her heels and forced him to look at her. Her small face was set in the stubborn expression he was becoming well acquainted with. He sighed theatrically and waited.

"Well! What did you ask the agent and what did he have to say? Come on, Kane, give."

"Not now, mouse, he's following us." She swore under her breath, and Kane shook her arm at the words he was hearing. He hugged her stiff body close to his side and bent down to whisper, "I wanted to find out which branch of the government we're dealing with. He's with the FBI. Now, does that appease your curiosity for a while? I'll tell you more later."

Shasta grudgingly nodded, her interest in his words reduced as his breath continued to tickle her ear. Teasing devil! He knew exactly what he was doing. "If you'll excuse me," she said, "I think I'll go talk to Samantha." With that she twirled away, leaving Kane to stare after her, his lips twitching and his silver eyes sparkling as he followed the swish of her hips.

Boston offered Shasta his chair beside Samantha, and as soon as he left, Samantha asked, ''Are you going to tell me what's going on, or are you going to try and protect my delicate condition with lies?''

Shasta leaned her head back against the chair and began to giggle. She looked at Samantha and replied, ''I'm sorry, Sammy, but I really can't tell you.'' Samantha's eyes sparked, and Shasta saw the anger building. ''Client confidentiality, professional ethics! Honestly, Sammy.'' She held up her hands defensively. ''I'm on a job. If Kane wants to tell you, that's all right, then we could talk about it, but otherwise I can't.''

The disbelief and anger slipped away, and Samantha's smile returned. ''I guess I'll take your word. It's just going to take me longer to get the story out of Kane and Boston than I'd like. But, make no mistake, I'll find out.''

They were interrupted as Samantha accepted more congratulations from well-wishers, and Shasta searched the diminishing crowd for Kane. When she found him, she wished she hadn't. Two vibrant brunets were hanging on either arm, raptly listening to his every word. She wondered how she would ever be able to deal with the beauties he seemed to attract.

''Shasta, Shasta!''

The repetition of her name and the jab of Samantha's elbow jarred her from her jealous thoughts.

''I want you to meet some friends of mine.'' She began to introduce them. ''JoBeth Huntley, Lucas DeSalva and....''

''Brandon DeSalva,'' the handsome blue-eyed man finished. ''We're well acquainted with Shasta, Sammy." Both brothers turned to the women with all their Texan and Spanish charm.

"Hello, pixie, how's the security business?" Lucas asked, his rugged features lighting with pleasure.

Samantha's head swiveled from the grinning men to Shasta and back again before demanding, "Explain, please."

Shasta turned to Samantha but was interrupted by the arrival of Kane and Boston. Over the commotion of renewed friendships and introductions, Shasta whispered to Samantha, "Masters handles the security for DeSalva's, and we also lease two floors of the DeSalva building."

After the arrival of the DeSalva brothers, the gallery began to clear out more swiftly. The two men bought one painting after another, leaving only those previously sold or on loan for exhibition from their owners.

Any interest Kane might have had in his adoring brunets dwindled when he overheard Brandon invite Shasta for a drink.

"Sorry, but we have other plans." He guided her swiftly away, explaining as they left the gallery, "Boston and Samantha have already gone, and I told them we would be right behind them."

Shasta inhaled deeply of the cool night air. Then she groaned, remembering the long two blocks they had to walk to the car.

"I told you to wear lower heels." Kane helped her over the high curb. In the area where the gallery was located, the streets were narrow and without sidewalks.

Shasta intertwined her fingers with Kane's as they set off down the street. "Want to tell me what else the agent had to say?" She tried to make out his expression, but the dimly lit street afforded little help. Shaking her hand free of his, she stepped in front of him and, walking backward, asked, "Does the darkness make you deaf, or are you trying to think up a good lie?" Kane gave a bark of laughter as she retired, panting, to his other side and valiantly tried to keep up with his long stride.

"Get out of the street." Kane tried to catch her arm, but she danced away, taunting him with a shapely thigh as the breeze lifted her skirt. "He said they were only ordered to observe and not interfere. They're playing their own game of wait and see, Shasta. Now get back here before someone runs over you."

As if Kane's words had conjured up a phantom, a car came careering out of the darkness like a locomotive. The headlights caught Shasta in a blinding glare, and for a moment she froze, like a startled deer before the fatal shot is fired. She didn't have time to scream a warning. As her mind cleared she dived for Kane, frantically thinking that the car would swerve toward him. And Kane, in the space of a heartbeat, extended his arms and grabbed Shasta. They collided, each trying to save the other. One of Shasta's high heels snapped and she fell to her knee, tearing the flesh on the pavement, and still the headlights bore down on them. Frantically Kane swung Shasta up against him and lunged over the high curb as the car roared by.

Tires squealed around a corner in the now-quiet night. Kane held Shasta to his chest, his heart hammering painfully against his ribs. "Bastards." He repeated the word several times as his eyes, dark and full of menace, followed the car's retreat. "Are you all right?"

Shasta mumbled against his shirtfront, shook her head free of his smothering hold and laughed. "Looks to me like you pushed too far and they shoved back."

Kane stared speechless into her dark-brown eyes. They flashed with excitement and an invitation he refused to pass up. "You're crazy, mouse. But, then, so am I." His cold lips touched hers, lightly at first, then he gathered her closer into the warmth of his arms, his mouth taking and giving, adding to the thrill of the night. Lowering her to the ground, he felt her flinch in pain. "What's the matter?"

"I scraped my knee when I fell."

Kane grabbed the torn shreds of her skirt and inspected her leg. He swallowed hard, scooped her up into his arms and took off toward the car.

"Kane, put me down. It's just a skinned knee."

"For once, Shasta, shut up and let me handle this."

She judged his temper and decided it prudent to let him have his way—this time. Before she realized how fast he could take control of a situation she was in the car and they were pulling up at a sprawling two-story, rose-brick colonial house in the center of River Oaks. Once again she was picked up, and Kane sprinted to the door.

"Ring the bell, mouse."

"Mr. Kane!" The butler's narrow face blanched with shock.

"Jones, where are Boston and Samantha?" He didn't wait for an answer but strode toward the living room with the almost soundless footsteps of the butler right behind them.

"Mr. Kane, they've brought that woman with them again. I told you the last time—"

"Not now, Jones. Please, just get me some hot water."

Shasta peered over Kane's shoulder as the ancient butler gave them a murderous glance. "Who's 'that woman'?" she inquired.

"What? Oh, Pearl is Boston's housekeeper, cook—I don't know what you'd call her. For heaven's sake, Shasta, quit asking me questions."

"Yes, dear." She received her second killing glance of the night.

Shasta was dumped on the couch, and amid concerned questions from Boston and Samantha, she leaned back and enjoyed the attention for a change.

Samantha dismissed Kane's orders and pulled up Shasta's torn skirt.

"I keep trying to tell him it's just a scrape, but he won't listen."

"It's a little worse than a scrape, Shasta. Boston, would you fix this up. I don't think Kane's capable right now."

Three pairs of eyes studied Kane's whitening features as he stared at Shasta's knee. Samantha took his arm, turned him around and led him quietly from the room.

"Well, there goes my hero!" Shasta laughed, her eyes twinkling as Boston accepted the first-aid kit and a bowl of steaming water from the haughty Jones. "Who would have thought the sight of a little blood would turn his stomach?"

Boston snipped away the leg of her panty hose below her thigh. "He's seen far worse than this, honey. I guess it's like what happened to me." He began to clean the area and Shasta hissed at the sting. "There are a lot of accidents on a ranch, and Kane and I've set our share of broken bones and doctored some nasty cuts. But not so long ago Samantha dropped a knife and sliced open the top of her foot." Boston sprayed on antiseptic, and Shasta clenched the arms of the chair. He looked up from his task, his jet-black eyes flashing with humor. "When I saw what she'd done and all that blood, I fainted—flat out on the floor. Here, hold this." He placed a large gauze pad over the wounded area and cut strips of tape. His next question took Shasta by surprise. "You know Kane's in love with you?"

Her face lit up with a bright smile. "I hope so. He's...."

Boston held up his hand, interrupting her. "He hasn't realized it yet, and when he does I think you're going to have a real fight on your hands. There." Boston positioned her foot on the low coffee table and began picking up the bits and pieces of paper he'd dropped. "I don't know how you two are going to work out your lives." He shook his head. "Believe me there are going to be difficulties. Kane's not used to answering to anyone. He's had only himself to think of, and now you've come along and complicated everything." Rocking back on his heels, he smiled at her. "He won't thank you, and don't ever say I didn't try and warn you." Boston gave her a brotherly pat on her thigh. "Now, rest that leg awhile."

"Did you really pass out?" she asked skeptically.

"Like a light."

Shasta looked at the famous singer and thought of the millions of women who would feel faint at the sight of him or the sound of his deep velvet voice, and she began to laugh.

"What's the joke?" Samantha stood aside as Boston tried to pass through the doorway.

"No joke. I was telling Shasta about the time I fainted when you cut your foot." He patted her large stomach. "Sit down, honey, you've been on your feet too long today. I'll be back in a minute. I want to have a talk with Kane."

Samantha kissed her husband, then eased her weight down on the couch beside Shasta with a weary sigh.

"Are you okay?"

"Now don't you start." Samantha rubbed her stomach. "They're just overactive tonight."

"They!" Shasta stared at Samantha's cat-and-cream smile.

"Kane didn't tell you? I'm surprised. He's done nothing but tease us since we found out. You're sure he didn't tell you?" Shasta shook her head. "There are two babies here, maybe more." Samantha laughed. "You can close your mouth. It's true."

"More than two?"

"Maybe."

Shasta spotted a bottle of Grand Marnier on the bar and hopped over, helping herself to a generous amount. "Maybe more?" she asked in awe as she sat back down.

Samantha's smile sparkled with anticipation. "That's the reason Boston's jittery and acting strange. Half the time he's so excited he can't sit still, and the other half he's so scared he can barely breathe." She settled back, folding her hands over her swollen abdomen. "Did you know Boston was an orphan? No? Well, he's always wanted a large family. Sometimes I think the only reason he married me was to be one of our clan." She was quiet for a long moment, her expression peaceful. "We planned the birth of Rebecca carefully, right down to the last second. Boston was there in the delivery room all ready to see his first child born." Samantha's face softened, then she chuckled. "I guess it got a little gruesome, because all I remember is that suddenly he was lying passed out on the floor. Now that I think of it, he got more attention from the nurses than I did. Anyway, this time he swore he'd be okay. Of course that was before we found out this was going to be more than one baby. Now he's about to jump out of his skin."

"Is it dangerous—multiple births, I mean?" Shasta asked, feeling a fool at her ignorance.

"I try not to think of the problems," Samantha said stoutly, but there was concern in the depths of her eyes. "How maudlin we're getting. What I wanted to ask you was if you'd go shopping with me tomorrow?"

"Should you?"

Samantha gave Shasta an exasperated look. "I'm not a total fool—though everyone seems to think just because I'm pregnant I've lost my senses. I'm well aware of my limitations. Besides, I'm dying to buy some new clothes for afterward, when I'm slim and trim again."

Shasta was torn between her loathing for shopping and her desire to help Samantha. Samantha won out. "I'd love to go."

"Liar!" Kane contradicted from the doorway. "You hate shopping with a passion. Hell, Sammy, she has a man named Julie buy all her clothes."

"Kane—"

"I even got hooked into one of his buying sprees and was hauled all over Sakowitz's."

"Kane—"

"She has without a doubt the worst taste in fashions I've ever seen."

"Kane Stone, you shut your mouth."

Boston and Samantha were laughing. Then Boston's expression changed and he frowned at his wife. "Sparky, I'm sorry, but I don't want you being seen with Shasta right now."

There was a gasp, and the room fell into an uneasy silence before Samantha spoke out. "What a terrible thing to say! You apologize to Shasta this minute, Boston." She struggled to get up, but gravity, weight and volume combined to make her efforts comical.

"Well, don't just stand there laughing like a couple of idiots. Help me up, gentlemen—and I use the word loosely."

"Samantha...." Shasta bit her lip to keep her voice steady. "Sammy, Boston's right. Kane's troubles have flowed over to me now." She gave Kane a speaking glance. "If I'm right, the men following Kane believe I'm important enough to be used against him. I've yet to get him to tell me everything, though that's going to change as of tonight. But from what happened this evening I'd say they've decided to escalate their plans and will use any lever they can." Samantha's unladylike snort brought a twitch to the corner of Shasta's mouth. "A pregnant woman would be an ideal target for use as a weapon against Kane."

"Well...." Samantha's lower lip protruded farther than usual as she stared pleadingly at her husband. "You'll tell me what's going on, won't you? You know how mysteries upset me." She turned her gaze back to Shasta and Kane. "Have you called the police yet?"

"No!" Both Kane and Shasta spoke in unison, but it was Kane who explained. "Samantha, there are too many people involved in this already. If the local police are called, there's a chance some nosy reporter will pick up on it and we'll really be in a hell of a mess. Besides, we've already had to call in the police about the break-in at my father's house."

Samantha was about to argue, but Kane held up his hand to stop her. "What could we tell them? We're sure it was the same blue car that's been following us, but we couldn't swear to it—everything happened so damn fast. We were too busy trying to get out of their path to take note of the license number. As for them parking outside Shasta's house and trailing us everywhere.."

Kane shook his head. "There's no law against parking on the street or following someone as long as personal contact is not made and no verbal insult is given."

Samantha frowned. "Just what sort of trouble are you in, and what do you mean there are too many people involved already?" Kane's mouth tightened stubbornly. "Damn, can't you tell me something—anything? This whole business is unsettling me, and you know I'm not supposed to be upset in my condition." She realized her ploy hadn't worked as she glanced at the closed faces around the room. Samantha's bottom lip trembled a little.

Boston looked helplessly at Kane, who only shrugged. "She's your wife. You're on your own." Quickly scooping Shasta up into his arms before she could protest, he headed toward the door. "I'll call you tomorrow, Boston."

Boston opened the front door, and both men carefully eyed the empty street. "Yeah, do that, then I'll know nothing happened to the two of you on the way home." Shasta and Kane were halfway down the steps when he called out, "Take care of him, Shasta."

Shasta snuggled her head into Kane's shoulder and smiled. Oh, she intended to take very good care of him.

CHAPTER NINE

THE DRIVE TO SHASTA'S HOUSE was accomplished in a companionable silence, though Kane thought he could feel the sharp edge of censure in the air. "I think you should start wearing your gun from now on."

"Yes," she agreed, and the word hung heavily in the cool confines of the car.

Kane gazed at the woman beside him. She might be small, but she had the heart of a lion. "We need to discuss a plan of action."

Shasta halted her wandering thoughts and shifted her position in the seat so she could watch Kane. "I hope you're not going to try and persuade me to quit this time?"

"No, that would be pointless, wouldn't it? You're in this as deep as I am." Kane stopped at the red light, his mind's eye seeing again the headlights of the car rushing toward Shasta. He saw her startled expression, then her leap as she dived for him in an effort to push him out of danger. He swallowed hard. If he hadn't been alert, and if Shasta had been a larger woman, she would have accomplished her task and more than likely been killed in the process.

Kane felt the tightness in his chest increase to a steady ache. He'd been deluding himself all the while. He realized now that he'd never had any intentions of getting rid of her, and his two weeks of partying had been a challenge to see if she could keep up with the fast pace of his life-style. The light changed, and he drove on, his thoughts a turmoil. What had happened to him? Was he going through some stage? Surely thirty-seven was too young for a midlife crisis. But no matter where his thoughts led, they kept returning to a picture of Shasta as she leaped to save his life. The tight hand in his chest squeezed harder, and Kane sucked in a sharp breath as another thought rushed at him. He needed her! But he was damned if he understood why. For one thing, she was playing games with him, and he'd never allowed a woman to get the upper hand.

Kane shifted his weight and nervously drummed his fingers against the steering wheel as he tried to figure it all out. Hell, he'd enjoyed watching her try her tricks on him. He reveled in her sparkling smile and her big brown eyes so deceptively innocent. He found himself waiting for her tinkling laugh and a glimpse of her nose as it crinkled impishly. The feel of her skin, as soft as velvet; her small breasts round and firm; her hips so sweetly curved. Kane tried to apply the brakes to his thoughts, but they kept pounding at him for an answer. He wanted her now more than he'd ever wanted any woman, yet he was loathe to make the move. Afraid to...afraid! Why had that word popped out? He'd never been afraid of anything in his life. Certainly not a woman.

"Kane, you just passed my street!"

Cursing, Kane spun the wheel and made a U-turn. The car squealed around the corner and pulled into Shasta's driveway.

She watched him carefully as he got out and slammed the door. He was in a strange mood, and as yet she hadn't figured it out. He helped her out of the car, swung her body up into his arms and paused, as if waiting for her to make some remark. She smiled instead, gazing into the reflective mirror of his eyes, and was surprised to see confusion lurking in their depths. Tightening her grip around his neck, she kissed him long and lovingly.

"What was that for?" Kane whispered against her lips, his breath mingling with hers in a warm rush.

"For saving my life tonight." She kissed away the vehement denial she saw forming on his lips. "Yes, you did."

He carried her into the house, his thoughts a conflicting whirl. Baskerville met them at the back door and stretched his thick neck up. He sniffed Shasta's wounded knee and began a combination of whimpers and growls that set Kane's already ragged nerves crawling. He frowned down at the huge animal, who was glued close to his side, hampering his every step as he navigated with Shasta up the stairs. "What's wrong with him?"

Shasta buried her head in the curve of Kane's neck, her shoulders shaking.

"Shasta, make him stop!" Kane stood in the center of her bedroom trying to decide where to deposit his armful of giggling woman, while Baskerville continued to circle them, his strange cries getting louder.

"Baskerville, hush, I'm okay," she told him, but the big dog only sat in front of them, threw his massive head back and began to howl. "Put me down, Kane, or he'll never stop."

"What's wrong with him?" He refused to lower her till she reassured him that Baskerville wasn't going to go berserk and attack them both.

"He can't make up his mind whether to sympathize with me or give in to his jealousy and take a bite out of you."

"Me!" Kane gave her a look that spoke volumes regarding her pet's sanity.

"You're carrying me, and Baskerville doesn't approve."

"That's just too bad." Kane tightened his hold on Shasta and frowned fiercely down at her pet. "Traitor. Who's been slipping you food and beer? No more, Baskerville." Kane's voice was firm, and Baskerville, as though he fully understood, stopped midhowl. Kane lowered Shasta to the side of the bed, straightened up and rubbed the back of his neck. "You know, I think I'm going crazy. I find myself talking to that dog, and what scares me is I think he understands." Shasta flopped back across her bed and began to laugh again. "Good night, Shasta."

The door wasn't exactly slammed shut, but Shasta grinned at the solid bang it made. Kane was beginning to lose his cool exterior—chip by frozen chip. She eased off the bed and patted Baskerville, reassuring him she was going to live. "What do you think, old boy, are we ready to put plan number two into operation?" Baskerville showed his teeth in a sneer and stretched out on the rug beside her bed. "Don't be a spoil sport." She hobbled to the bathroom. "I intend keeping Kane around, so you'd better make up to him." She shut the door on another show of sharp, white teeth and curled lips.

An hour later Shasta lay between cool sheets, her hands behind her head as she planned her next maneuver. It was time Kane learned to relax and have some honest fun. Time, also, for him to face the fact that there was more to a relationship than sex, time to admit the truth of his emotions. There was a knock at the door and she called out, "Come in."

"I thought some warm brandy might relax you and ease the aches and pains away." He felt his stomach tighten at the inviting sight of her freshly scrubbed face and immediately regretted his good intentions. She seemed to have an invisible rope tied to him, and when she jerked, he jumped.

Shasta sat up and reached for the warm balloon glass filled with the fragrant liquor. "That was thoughtful. Thank you, Kane." She smiled, and his agitation slipped away.

"We need to talk." His voice sounded husky even to his own ears.

"Yes, we do." She patted the side of the bed and moved over.

"That's a dangerous position, Shasta. Can I trust you to behave?" He eyed her peach satin-and-lace nightgown hungrily.

Shasta returned his look in exactly the same way. Her eyes followed his bare legs up to the edge of his thigh-length robe, then slowly upward till she met his steady gaze. "I think I can control myself." She waited till he was propped comfortably against the pillows, then said, "I take it back, I can't control myself." She leaned over and whispered what she'd like to do, then watched, fascinated by the red that stained his cheeks.

When he could speak, Kane demanded, "Where did you hear such things—a nice Southern lady like you?" He was totally captivated by the combination of her fairy-tale innocence and wanton sensuality. Taking a hefty gulp of brandy, he let the liquor burn a path down his throat.

Shasta fluffed up her pillow and lay back, thrilled by her progress. She wondered how long it had been since he'd blushed at a naughty suggestion. "Have you decid-

ed what you're going to do? This standoff is beginning
to be a bore.''

There was a long thoughtful silence before Kane
spoke. ''U.S.A. Oil wants the fuel formula, and I want
the murderer of Professor Kimble.''

Shasta bolted upright from her lounging position.
''You don't seriously think that if someone in U.S.A.
Oil is responsible for Kimble's death they're going to
come forward of their own free will, do you?''

''No. But I have a gut feeling. You see, *chérie*, I don't
believe the murder was committed without the knowledge or orders of the owner of U.S.A. Oil.'' Kane's
voice grew gruff. ''I not only want the man driving the
car, I want the man who ordered the murder.''

''So?'' she asked, still a little puzzled by his reasoning.

''If U.S.A. Oil turns over the killer in exchange for
the formula, I'll know the upper echelon of the company was ignorant of the professor's death and that
some ruthless vice-president went beyond his authority.
But if there's no trade, then we'll know the orders came
directly from the top—from Tramble Carter Baldwin,
Jr., himself. And I want his skin.''

The soft menace in his words sent a chill over Shasta's
flesh. ''If what you feel is true and there was an order to
kill the professor, then there will be no trade and they
will try to take the formula from you any way they can,
right?''

''Right.''

''They'll come after us then.'' Her eyes began to glow
with excitement. ''By the way, where is the formula,
and why did the professor give it to you?'' She met his
stony stare and tried another approach. ''The professor
was more than just a friend, wasn't he?'' Kane nodded,

and she waited for him to go on, but he remained silent. She knew he hadn't truly faced his emotional attachment to the older man he'd spent so much time with. A great wave of pity for his inability to admit he was as human as the next person washed over her. She rolled over, positioned herself across his chest and gazed into his eyes. Reaching out a hand, she let her fingers lightly play up and down his cheek. "What happens now?" she whispered.

"We wait for them to make the next move."

"I wasn't referring to the goons."

"I gathered that. Shasta, don't." He captured her hand. "Stop these games before you get hurt. I want you, and if you keep this up I'll take you." The flesh tightened across his high cheekbones, and his mouth curved mockingly. "You needn't smile like that, either." He gathered her face in his hands and brought it close to his. "I've let you play because it amused me." One hand held her head secure while the other grasped her wrist and guided her hand downward to the hardness beneath his robe. "Tonight has been filled with tension and danger, and the edge is still there. Keep on and I'll take you whether you want me to or not."

Shasta knew he was telling the truth. She wasn't offended, knowing that in his own way Kane was being more honest about his emotions than he'd ever been. She realized that with another woman and under similar circumstances he would have done exactly as he said. But he cared enough for her to warn her. She touched his face with gentle fingers. "I love you, Kane."

She waited, her ears aching from the roar within. Then came the hiss of Kane's breath.

"Oh, no, mouse, don't," he whispered hoarsely. "Don't say that." He rested his forehead against hers

for a brief second before he began to untangle himself
from her hold. The covers became ropes binding him
down. He kicked free and surged to his feet.

"Kane, loving someone is not a death sentence."

"You don't understand. I have to be free." He
cleared his throat. "Besides, I'm too old for you."

Shasta stared up at him and began to laugh at his
flimsy excuse.

"Ten years doesn't seem like much," he said, "and
normally it's not." He retied his robe, straightened the
lapels and looked directly into her eyes. "Shasta, I have
a hell of a lot more miles on me than you could ever
imagine, and they're miles you don't want to know
about."

"I know more than you think, Kane. I—"

"No." He stopped her next words. "You know
general facts about my life and a few supposed secrets,
but you don't know some of the things I've done." Suddenly Kane couldn't breathe, and he turned to leave
those sad brown eyes behind. He expected tears and
recriminations, but only the sound of Baskerville's
heavy breathing followed him to the door.

"You can't run forever from your feelings, Kane."

He stopped his hurried exit and looked back over his
shoulder. "That's where you're wrong, Shasta. Unlike
most people, I don't conform to rules or convention. I
can run as far and as long as I please."

THE NIGHT SEEMED ENDLESS. Shasta twisted and turned
till she finally gave in and swung her feet to the cold
hardwood floor. Baskerville's head jerked up and he
whimpered. "Go back to sleep, boy. I just need to think
things out." She pulled the curtain back from the window, wrapped her arms around her body and sighed de-

jectedly at the sickle moon. Shadows moved back and
forth on the street below as a gentle gulf breeze teased
the tree limbs into a slow swaying motion.

Shasta rubbed her forehead, trying to find the relationship between her dreams and something Kane had
said earlier. But each time she thought she had an
answer, it would slip away, as elusive as her dreams.
Mentally she reviewed their entire conversation, and still
nothing came. She wished she could be free of this
haunting...that was it! She grabbed the windowsill and
squeezed hard to keep from yelling. Kane had said he
needed to be *free*, and that was the problem. He thought
that loving someone meant giving up his independence.
Shasta smiled. If only she could make him see that she
cherished her freedom, too, but that didn't keep her
from loving him. Her eyes focused on the street below,
and an impish grin began to grow. With a quick turn she
was rummaging through her closet for a suitable outfit.

Ten minutes later, dressed in black shirt and jeans,
Shasta slipped into Kane's room across the hall. She'd
no sooner eased the door shut to keep Baskerville out
when a hand clamped down on her shoulder. She
jumped as if she'd been hit by lightning.

"What the hell are you doing sneaking in here in the
middle of the night?"

Shasta shrugged off his hand and aimed the penlight
into his face. "You're fast." She smiled up at him,
watching the thunderclouds ride across his forehead.
"How would you like me to show you a good time?"
She wiggled her eyebrows suggestively.

Kane couldn't help grinning as he gazed into her
flashing brown eyes. "Since you're dressed, I take it this
adventure is to take place outside?"

"Right. Come here." She led him to the window,

then paused before she pulled back the curtain. "If I let you in on *my* adventure, do you promise to follow my orders?" As her eyes adjusted to the darkness, she became aware of Kane's nudity, and her hand itched to reach out and touch his warm flesh. "What did you say?"

Kane snapped his fingers in front of her face. "Are you awake or sleepwalking?"

"Sorry, but I was distracted. Do you promise?"

"Yes."

"You'll do everything I say and not interfere?"

"I said yes, dammit."

"Good!" Kane's hand covered hers on the curtain. "No. Get dressed in some dark clothes." She watched him like a voyeur in the dark, straining to see his every move and loving each shadowed hollow she could discern.

By the time she could put a leash on her thoughts, Kane was at her side. She pulled a small gun from the waistband of her jeans and handed it to him. "Tuck that away. I didn't have another shoulder holster." Without a word he did as he was ordered. "Ready?"

Kane grasped her arm before she could take another step. "Would you mind telling me the plan?"

"Our friends are back, but this time they're driving a gray car instead of the blue. I thought it might escalate things if we repaid their greetings earlier this evening."

"How?"

"Just follow my lead and back me up."

Kane held her at his side for a long moment, feeling the trembling tension in her muscles. She was like a thoroughbred before a race. Then he nodded his head and followed her, surprised to sense the same response in himself.

They slipped down the stairs, stopping only long enough in the kitchen for Shasta to call Julie, give him some orders, then convince Baskerville that his help wasn't needed. Once out of the house and in the darkness Kane was astounded at Shasta's catlike movements. She became a creature of the night as they eased from a crouching run to stand, breathing soundlessly, behind an old oak tree. She was one and the same with the darkness. As he followed in her wake, he realized for the first time that she was truly a professional. Till now he had tried to convince himself that she was only playing at work. But watching her move with all the professionalism of a trained warrior, he felt a sudden surge of fire running like molten quicksilver through his blood. Could he have met the female counterpart of himself? Or had he simply met his match? He brushed the thought away as absurd.

They squatted behind the bumper of the gray car and Shasta touched Kane's shoulder, motioning him to take the passenger side. She leaned sideways and whispered in his ear, "When you hear my voice, show yourself." He tapped her shoulder, signaling that he agreed, and they parted, crawling beneath the opened windows on either side of the car.

"Good evening, gentlemen," Shasta said conversationally. "Nice evening, isn't it?" The burly man in the driver's seat grunted in surprise, his hand sliding to his armpit as he turned his head and looked down the short but deadly barrel of Shasta's gun. "If I were you I'd place both hands on the steering wheel." The cold steel in her voice overrode any comments the man might have made. Kane ordered the other man to grab the dashboard. Guns were removed from their shoulder holsters, and Shasta clucked her tongue in mock disappointment.

"Such fine weapons, a shame you've lost them." She stuffed the heavy gun into the waistband of her jeans. "When you explain how you were disarmed by a woman, you might tell your boss that he's made three mistakes so far. One in sending novices to do his dirty work, two in playing games with Mr. Stone here, and three—trying to run me down. Now, gentlemen, please strip!"

Kane chuckled from his side of the car as the two men blustered, then tried to reason, then began to beg. When Shasta didn't budge, but continued to glare at them menacingly, both men began rapidly shedding their clothing.

"Pitch everything in the back seat," Shasta ordered as she opened the car door. "Hand me the keys, please." The interior light flicked on, illuminating white pasty skin of the two men, but Shasta's eyes were trained on the clenched fist of the driver. "Don't even think it.... Now out!" She stepped back, affording the husky man plenty of room. When the two of them stood gleaming naked under the streetlamp, she pointed down the road. "Now, take a walk." She had to bite hard on her lip to keep from laughing at their appalled expressions. "Go on, get!"

They took off in a barefoot run down the center of the street, and Shasta sat down hard on the curb and began to giggle. She was soon joined by Kane, and they sat there following the men's retreat around a corner and out of sight.

"You little devil. I don't know when I've enjoyed myself more." Kane lay back on the damp grass and chuckled at the slender thread of a moon. Their laughter stopped at the sound of a siren in the distance. The high shrill came closer and Kane sat up. "You didn't."

"No, Julie did. I'll bet they have one hell of a time explaining to Tramble Baldwin this night's escapade, and why they were jailed for indecent exposure."

Kane wrapped an arm around Shasta's shoulder and pulled her close against his side. "You're one talented lady. But tell me something, Shasta. Why didn't you go into some form of law enforcement instead of working for Masters?"

"Originally that was my plan, but I was too small to meet the requirements of the police department, and when I talked to J.T. about the FBI or CIA, he marched me in front of a mirror and asked me if anyone would take this face seriously."

As he studied her disgusted expression, Kane had to agree with her grandfather. She was entirely too cute to look menacing, but the fact remained that she was an expert at what she did. Shasta was a confusing mixture of toughness, intelligence and femininity. Tonight she had showed him she was capable of entering his league. She had neatly turned the tables on him and proved she was more than just a pretty face. She was a woman who would be a buddy, friend and partner in adventure, as well as a lover. She'd played the game his way and on equal terms.

Shasta laid her head on his shoulder and looked up at him. "The night's still young. Why don't we make a surprise visit on these government men you say are lurking around every corner. Do you know where they are?"

Kane shook his head at her gutsy tenacity. "No, we will not interfere with their plans, and yes, I know where they are." He pointed down the street to a luxury recreation vehicle parked at the curb. "They're in there, and the week before they were in the telephone-repair truck at the other end of the street. The week before that they were in a city maintenance truck."

"But, Kane, that RV belongs to our neighbors the Parkers."

"Not now it doesn't." He stood, extended a hand and helped her up. "Our government borrowed it for the duration. We'd best get out of here before a police patrol car comes by. You might have pull at the department, but I bet we'd have some fast explaining to do as to why we're dressed like burglars and carrying an arsenal of weapons tucked in our jeans." He clamped her arm tightly as she stumbled along. "How's that knee?"

Limping beside him, she answered absently, "I'm fine, just a little stiff legged." Silently they moved down the sidewalk, their shadows cast before them from the streetlamp. Every step they took, their silhouetted images would lengthen and weave together on the cracked pavement. In an automatic reflex from her childhood, Shasta found herself avoiding the worn grooves in the cement. "Kane, are you still with the CIA?"

Unconsciously Kane fell into step with her, alternating the length of his stride to avoid the cracks. "Shasta, I haven't been connected with them since Vietnam."

"But, Jeff—"

"What your brother keeps digging up is something entirely different, and I'd advise him to stop playing gopher if I were you. He's liable to get caught in a cave-in."

"Then you do still work for some branch of the government?"

"You never give up do you? Yes! I sort of work for my country."

"How can you 'sort of work'?"

"Shasta. . . ." He was out of breath, and the cracks in the pavement stretched farther and farther apart. He found himself helping Shasta over the distances too long for her shorter legs to cover. Stopping abruptly, he gazed up at what little moon there was and called out into the night, "I must be going insane! A thirty-seven-year-old man hopping along the sidewalk at two o'clock in the morning."

Shasta coughed back a giggle at his outraged expression. "Come on, Kane!" She grabbed his arm. "It's not as if I'm a total stranger. I do have government clearance. Who do you work for?"

Kane propped his shoulder against the rough trunk of an old pecan tree and sighed. "Okay, Shasta, you win. I do some work now and then for the WSA."

The light from the streetlamp shining through the thick foliage dappled his features in sinister-looking shadows. Something warned Shasta she was pushing too fast and hard, but the waiting she had endured over the past weeks had taken its toll. "What's the WSA and what do you do?"

Kane let the cool night air clear his head, pausing so long in the process that Shasta had to touch his arm to bring him back to the present. "The WSA is the World Security Agency—and the reason you've never heard of it is that that's the way the organizers prefer it. The WSA is international and works something like a combination of Interpol, the CIA and FBI. Except their investigations are more extensive and their restrictions aren't limited."

Shasta relaxed and joined him against the tree.

"I don't know if you realize it or not, Shasta, but wealthy, bored people can be the most corrupt in the world. Always greedy for new adventures, experiences and more money, they willingly become involved in many illegal activities. Because of my background and connections, the WSA approached me after Vietnam and asked me to help them.''

He turned to face her in the darkness, his silver eyes shining eerily as a beam of light reflected off them. ''You'd be surprised how foolish people can be. Because they're on some practically deserted balcony at St. Moritz or at a Chilean resort they feel free to conduct their business openly, foolishly discounting the fact that the man at the next table could be a threat, because he's one of their set.'' Kane jammed his hands into the pockets of his jeans and hunched his shoulders. ''I resent those people making more money and getting cheap thrills off the weakness and misery of others. So I listen and report what I've heard and seen.''

''Kane, wouldn't WSA help you or ask the FBI to step in and investigate what's going on here?''

Kane's mouth curved into a sour smile. ''You're being naive. Besides, I tried that route and was told this is not a WSA concern. As for the WSA asking the FBI for help—'' Kane chuckled humorlessly ''—that would expose me as an agent of the WSA.'' He saw her question coming and headed it off. ''Yes, they know who I am and who I work for, but an open admission is not done except in high-priority cases. And you know very well that our government agencies do not necessarily share information. Trades are made, favors are granted, but when they both happen to be working on the same case they can be amazingly closemouthed. Stupid, I know, but there is a professional jealousy and fear of exposing too much and endangering their sources or having leaks to the press.'' He closed his eyes and inhaled deeply of the moist night air. "The WSA suits my purpose. The way they operate they don't have all that government red tape and bureaucracy to wade through." He opened his eyes and smiled down at Shasta. "As I said, I just have to keep my eyes open and stay alert."

"But you do more than just listen and report, don't you?" Shasta asked softly, hoping her question wouldn't distract him and bring a halt to his openness.

"Sometimes," he said absently, then gave a harsh bark of laughter. "Would you believe that I've heard people openly discussing drug drops—times and places, Shasta? They sit there as bold as brass and talk about how their yacht will meet a certain ship and pick up their merchandise. They work out the details of rendezvous to retrieve works of art they've purchased illegally. And sometimes, just sometimes, you come across a few diplomats who are stupid enough to get caught in blackmail traps and are set up to leak vital information. Those civil servants are not all from the United States, either. There's a whole network out there that passes along secrets about military installations, government satellite movements, defection attempts and a multitude of other top-secret information. "It's incredible!" He felt Shasta shiver beside him and pushed away from the tree. "Let's go in, it's getting chilly." He wrapped his arm around her shoulders and guided her across the lawn, so lost in his own thoughts that he didn't notice Shasta's silence.

Shasta was quiet, her mind furiously going over everything he'd told her. When she stumbled and he pulled her tighter to his side, she still made no comment. There was something in what he'd told her, or maybe his tone of voice, that set off bells of caution in her head. The old tingle in her spine was back, warning her that she'd stumbled onto a piece of a puzzle, but she couldn't totally connect it with what she knew. Whatever it was, she felt it was important and knew sooner or later it would come to her.

A haughty, rejected Baskerville met them at the door and lumbered at a reserved distance behind them as they climbed the stairs. "About earlier, Shasta." Kane stopped before her bedroom and clasped her shoulders lightly. "If I hurt you I'm sorry, but I think in the long run you'll see that falling in love with me would be complete folly on your part."

"Would it, Kane? I don't think so. Besides, there's not a whole lot you can do but accept it, because I'm already in love." Reaching up on tiptoe, she kissed his cheek, then slipped into her room, closing the door on his worried expression. She leaned back and sighed. It was a shame that he could see only decadence in himself. He had suppressed his compassionate side for so long he almost believed in his own image. Tomorrow, she thought, she would begin her lessons and make him admit he was worth salvaging and that he could love. Her plan, she realized, was underhanded, but she intended using his own weapons against him.

CHAPTER TEN

AT NINE O'CLOCK the next morning Shasta hung up the phone for the third time. She felt as if she'd had her ear plastered to the instrument for an eternity, talking and making plans as if her life depended on it. She refilled her coffee cup and took a hardy gulp of the hot brew, closing her eyes as the heat soothed her hoarse throat. Never in her entire life had she spent so much energy in talking, placating and downright begging. Looking across the kitchen, she checked the clock nervously, wondering what was keeping Kane, Julie and Baskerville. They'd set out more than two hours ago for their morning jog and should have been back by now.

The sound of distant, distinctive barking sent Shasta into immediate action. She pulled her chair around parallel to the table, thumped her elbow down on the writing pad, leaned back in a relaxed pose, crossed one leg over the other and began to swing a once-white tennis shoe back and forth. When the kitchen door flew open to admit three sweating, puffing males, she quickly took a generous bite of Julie's prize sweet rolls, waving her welcome as she slowly chewed.

"I thought I hid those," Julius wheezed, grabbing for the coveted rolls. But he wasn't fast enough, and Shasta encircled the plate with her arms. He flopped down in the nearest chair, Baskerville dropped with an exhausted grunt to the cool kitchen floor, and Kane casually poured himself a cup of coffee. Julius snatched up Shasta's half-empty glass of orange juice and gulped it down. "I'm too old to try and keep up with them two." He banged the glass down and glared at Shasta. "You sure J.T. ain't called and ordered me to get my tired bones back to Dallas?"

Shasta swallowed and shook her head, keeping her eyes glued to Julie's face. It wasn't concern for the older man that made her watch him so closely. She normally ran three miles a day, and he always paced her step for step. The fact was, she had had only a glimpse of Kane but figured that was enough for any red-blooded American woman to have at nine in the morning. She prided herself on her iron control. She wasn't going to gawk at him as if she'd never seen a male in jogging shorts. But her eyes slid toward the tall man against her will, drinking in the long, bare sweat-slick limbs. Her dark pupils dilated as she took in the brief shorts and wide expanse of naked chest. All the while the little voice in her head laughingly mocked her sound reasoning of the previous night. Hadn't she promised herself that she would handle her plans in a dignified manner and not fall apart like a drooling teenager at the sight of him? Shasta stuffed another big bite of sweet roll in her mouth and dragged her eyes from Kane's too-knowing gaze.

"I think I'll go shower." Kane set his cup down, but instead of leaving immediately, he squatted before Shasta and pulled her swinging foot to a stop. He tied the hanging shoelaces, checked the other shoe and retied its laces. "You're going to kill yourself one of these days." Without further comment he straightened and quietly left the room.

"You keep looking at him like you want to take a bite. Pretty soon he's going to start feeling for the missing pieces,'' Julius said, waving his hand before her eyes when she didn't respond. "Come on, kid. I ain't got all day. What have you been up to this morning? And you needn't turn them big browns on me. It ain't gonna work.''

Shasta sighed as she shook the lingering vision of a firm male derriere from her thoughts. "I talked to Jeff.'' She reached for another roll and got her hand slapped for her efforts.

"You've had enough. Save some for Kane.'' Julius flipped off the towel from around his neck and buried his face in it, wiping away the last beads of moisture rolling down his cheeks. Shasta snatched a roll from the plate and took a bite, smiling at his reproving frown as he emerged from the towel.

"Don't come crying to me when you add three pounds to your backside.''

"Julie.'' Shasta's expression turned serious. "Jeff's been driving me crazy about those three blank years in Kane's past. He's got this absurd notion that Kane's some superspy and has linked together a wild story about a Russian defector.'' Once again she felt a tingling along her spine as she related Jeff's questions to Julie. "He said you and J.T. could tell us more.''

Julius rubbed the towel through his damp gray hair. "Damned if I know what Jeff's spouting off about, but then he ain't all there, either. Russian defector?'' He shook his head again, his brow furrowed in concentration. "Wait a sec—'' He tapped his temple repeatedly as if the gesture would hammer out the information. "A couple of years back, J.T. and I met one of his army cronies. Seems this here general was in intelligence after the war, and as the evening lengthened and the drinks came faster and stronger the general developed loose lips.". Julie grinned and scratched his ear. "There wasn't any love lost between the CIA and Army Intelligence, and the general found it real funny to tell tales on his old adversary."

"The story, Julie," Shasta reminded him impatiently.

"Yeah, yeah. Hold your horse, miss. This old brain ain't what it used to be, and I got to think it out clear like." He was quiet for so long that Shasta wondered if he'd gone to sleep with his eyes open. Then he snapped his fingers with a loud crack that brought a growling Baskerville to all fours. "Stupid mutt. I remember now. All the kick up was about a Russian defector, some highfalutin scientist—did something with light."

"Lasers?" Shasta asked excitedly.

"Yeah. The CIA got him out of his country and as far as Lucerne with them commies hot on their tails. They wanted their boy back real bad. Well...now." Julius chuckled and leaned back in his chair while Shasta waited impatiently.

"Our gents lost their dove," he went on at last, shaking his head disapprovingly. "The general said every intelligence network throughout Europe was going crazy trying to find him. Anyway, Army Intelligence said they was sending in a special agent with the silliest code name I've ever heard of—Excalibur.

"Shasta, you should have seen the pure joy shining on that old man's face. He told us when the word went out of a new man in town everybody backed off but the Russians—they tripled their efforts. Seems this Excalibur was a feared troubleshooter of our government. And would you believe, in about six hours, news of spotting the defector started popping up all over Switzerland." Julie began to laugh softly.

"There were tales, Shasta, of drunken brawls and

rumors of the Russian attending parties, hobnobbin'
with the rich and famous. Sometimes there were stories
of him being in two places at once—course it ain't possible, but the old general said that was this special
agent's style, real classy. He loved to confuse and torment his enemy, and by setting the defector among well-
known celebrities and wealthy people, no one could get
close enough to nab him." By slow, stiff degrees Julius
stood and began to walk toward the back door, heading
toward his apartment over the garage.

Lightning skimmed up Shasta's spine. When Kane
had talked about diplomats and defectors the tone in his
voice had changed. Could he be? No! But why not? It
all fit. "Hey!" Shasta yelled. "What happened?"

His hand on the knob, Julius stopped and looked
back over his shoulder, his bushy eyebrows a straight
line across his brow. "Why, three days later the American embassy in France had a drunken Russian singing a
bawdy song on their doorstep."

"Whose doorstep?"

Shasta whirled around and almost sent her cup flying
across the table at Kane's question. "Nothing...no
one. Would you like some coffee?" She jumped up and
began to pour. Her back to him, she inhaled deeply and
scolded herself. Damn, she was a bundle of nerves. "I
called Samantha while you were out running." She set
the cup before him, pushed the plate of sweet rolls within his reach and handed him a napkin. Only after she sat
did she allow her eyes to meet his, then wished she
hadn't. Open suspicion was lurking in his face and she
squirmed in her chair, praying she wouldn't be forced
into giving up her secrets and plans just yet.

Kane raised his cup to his lips but stopped before taking a sip. He studied Shasta's bland expression and

knew there was trouble brewing in that charming little head. She was up to something, and it was going to put him right in the middle of the fire. "How's Samantha this morning?"

"Oh, fine—fine," she answered, relieved that he had shifted those piercing eyes elsewhere. "Last night when Boston told her we couldn't go shopping, I knew she was disappointed and probably lonely for some female companionship. So this morning I fixed it so she and Rena could meet and go shopping together." Shasta watched the frown gathering across Kane's brow and knew he was worried. "I explained to Rena about Samantha, and she promised to take care of her. She will, Kane, honestly." The words kept tumbling out of her mouth in rapid succession no matter how she tried to slow down. She ran nervous fingers through her hair and once again tried to relax, but her head was so full of plans and schemes that she couldn't remain still.

She was saved any further attempts to cover her agitated state when Julie returned and the two men began their usual bantering while Julie cooked breakfast.

It wasn't till she had spoken that she realized she'd rudely interrupted their conversation.

"What did you say?" asked Kane.

"We're going out to dinner tonight. I've already made the reservations." She clamped her mouth shut on a tight smile.

"Oh, I thought you said you never wanted to see the inside of a restaurant again, not after the past two weeks?"

"Did I say that?"

"You did."

"Funny, I don't remember. Anyway—" she waved an airy hand "—you'll enjoy this one." She could feel the heat rise in her cheeks and turned her face away from

Kane's penetrating gaze. Instead she met Julie's curious look and shot him a fierce, don't-give-the-game-away frown.

"What restaurant?"

"A Deux Inn." The name came out defiantly, and there was a jarring crash as the platter Julie was holding slipped from his hands and splintered on the floor. Baskerville yelped, jumped to his feet and staggered against the refrigerator in fright.

Kane followed the tense visual exchange between Julie and Shasta with restrained laughter, and before he gave Shasta's game away completely, he excused himself to make some forgotten telephone calls. Once in the living room he sat down in the nearest chair, trying to decide whether to laugh or cry. He'd heard of A Deux Inn, and though he'd never been there, he knew he was in for one hell of a night if he had correctly interpreted the bright gleam of determination in those big brown eyes. The pixie was out for blood—his. She had seduction on her mind, and he wondered if this time he could convince her he wasn't the right man for her? Kane rested his head in his hands and began to laugh.

Back in the kitchen Julius bent down and began to angrily throw broken pieces of china into a wastebasket. "You ain't taking Kane to *that* place. It ain't fair."

"Yes, it is—and yes I am." Shasta squatted to help, but Julie shooed her away.

"The man won't have a snowball's chance in hell of surviving. Besides, it ain't a proper place for you, either. What would your poor grandfather think if he found out?"

Shasta chuckled. "Why, you old hypocrite. J.T. would crow with glee and you know it."

"Maybe so," he grumbled reluctantly under his

breath. "But I think it's a dirty trick to pull on an unsuspecting male." He retrieved the broom from the pantry. "I wish to heaven we never did the security setup on that place—it's downright disgusting."

"Then why did you walk around with your mouth hanging open? And I saw those sly looks you kept casting toward Pandora Smith."

"Her—the owner?" Julius ducked his head and sighed. "She's a fine-looking woman, though, ain't she? All bright and buxom." He cleared his throat. "But Pan's got nothing to do with you wanting to entertain Kane at her place."

Shasta grabbed the furiously moving broom and stilled it, making Julius lift his head. "I need to put some pressure on him, Julie."

"Dammit, kid, that kind of pressure could backfire on you."

"I know, but that's a chance I'll have to take."

Julius studied her sad eyes and patted her shoulder. "I ain't never going to figure out you young people— rush, rush, rush. Everything has to be *now*. What happened to courting? You know he cares for you—give it time."

"I can't," she whispered fiercely. "I'm losing control."

"Okay, okay. Don't start the waterworks," he said gruffly, pulling a handkerchief from his back pocket and pressing it to her nose. "Blow." Shasta batted the square of white cloth away with an impatient hand. "You be careful, mind you. That place will turn a mild-mannered man into a tiger—with fangs, and you better believe it." Julie avoided her searching gaze by pushing the broom in a vigorous motion. "Don't ask! It ain't none of your business."

THE SOFT TWILIGHT sheared the edge off the day and draped the approaching night with silken colors. Kane expertly drove the Porsche south with only Shasta's directions every now and then to break the quiet of the evening. She shifted in the leather seat beside him, straightening the skirt of her white linen sundress. Kane pushed the car harder, sending it flying down the road. At the increase in speed, Shasta turned around, scanning the sparse traffic behind them.

"There's no one there," Kane told her. "I just wanted to feel some speed under me."

Shasta turned around again. "Oh, we have our escort all right. They're just keeping a safe distance behind. Julie found these." She opened her purse and brought out two tiny metal objects, one round like a button and the other a small square with a tiny wire antenna sticking out. Holding them in her palm, she showed them to Kane. "They were under the front and rear bumper."

"Are they still active?"

"Yes, indeed. I thought the goons and government men needed a nice evening drive." She rolled down the window. "Now, if you'll just pull up as close as possible to that produce truck we'll let them continue their journey in ignorance."

Kane maneuvered Shasta's car close to the ancient farm truck full of crates of peaches and tomatoes, and Shasta pitched the tiny transmitters over the side. Chuckling, Kane pushed his foot on the accelerator and the car shot forward like a bullet. They both waved to the bewildered farmer as they flew past.

Rolling up the window, Shasta began to fuss with her windblown curls, trying in vain to bring the soft strands back to order. She glanced sideways at Kane and thought how handsome he looked, casually elegant in white slacks and open-neck shirt, with a charcoal-gray sports coat. Reluctantly she focused her attention back to the road ahead, and spotting the discreet little sign announcing their destination at the next turn, she began to give directions once more.

The conditions of the dirt road forced Kane to slow down, and suddenly out of patience he demanded, "How much farther is this place? We've been driving for an hour and a half."

Shasta ignored his question. Leaning forward in her seat, she watched for the entrance. "Slower, slower," she ordered. "It's not far." Then she yelled, "Stop! Turn!"

Kane followed her directions, cursing under his breath and telling her what he thought of her navigating. He slammed on the brakes before a high steel gate surrounded by an equally high stone fence. The car's headlights illuminated the sign on the gate: A Deux Inn—An Inn For Two. A tapping sounded on the window beside him, and he turned to the guard there.

Shasta's name was checked off a list, then the guard pressed a button and waved them through the opening gates. "Have a nice evening."

Kane drove slowly, watching the gates roll smoothly shut in the rearview mirror. The sound in his head as they came together was like the clash of cymbals.

"Shasta."

"Why are we stopping?" she asked, afraid that any minute he would turn the car around and drive out—out of her plans, schemes and dreams. Out of her life. "Kane." She placed her hand lightly on his thigh, and her touch seemed to bring him out of his frozen state.

They drove down a long gravel road beneath a canopy of spreading trees that cut off the starlight. Finally they

emerged before a huge old plantation house, softly
glowing with amber lights that spilled out of the windows and open doorway. Two young men dressed in
English footmen's clothing assisted them out of the car.
They wished Shasta and Kane good-evening, then
escorted them up a multitude of wide curving steps to
the entrance. There they were met by a stately butler and
behind him the tiny, gray-haired, voluptuous owner—
Pandora Smith.

"Shasta, my dear. How wonderful to see you again."
Kane stiffened at her words, then relaxed as she added,
"I haven't seen you since you and your brother set up
our security system. And might I say again, it works absolutely beautifully." Twinkling green eyes, heavy with
mascara and fanned by laughter lines at the corners,
turned to inspect Kane from head to toe. Then Pandora
offered him her hand. "Mr. Stone, a pleasure."

Shasta watched, fascinated as Kane bowed over the
older woman's hand and saluted her with a kiss on her
fingers. They were both acting and thoroughly enjoying
themselves.

"Shasta." Pandora touched her arm. "If you'll follow me, I'd like to take you to your table now. Everything is as you requested."

They followed their hostess through a set of double
doors and down a candlelit hall with four closed doors
on either side. Stopping before one of the ornately
carved doors, Pandora inserted a card with Shasta's last
name neatly printed on it into a slot and waved them inside. "You know the procedure," she said, and quietly
shut them in.

Kane started at the hollow sound of wood meeting
wood. The brief picture of a coffin lid being fitted into
place flashed through his mind. His eyes were every-

where, taking in the red velvet hangings and overstuffed chaise longue. Tucked away in a corner was a small round table, beautifully set and surrounded by a padded high-back couch. Crystal and fine bone china winked mockingly in the candlelight. And when his ears picked up the barely audible sounds of music, one corner of his mouth lifted slightly. "It's a bordello," he whispered, loud enough for Shasta to hear.

"No, it's an inn. There's a main dining room on the other side of the house, bedrooms upstairs and cottages out back for people who wish to stay longer than one night. It's a special place for lovers."

"Lovers?" he repeated contemptuously. "When did we fall into the category of lovers? I wouldn't say one roll in the sack would qualify." Somewhere in the back of his mind he began to fully realize what Shasta had planned for him, and though the fantasy was exciting, he knew the outcome would be disastrous. He had to leave, and if insulting her wouldn't work. . . . He reached behind him for the doorknob and gave it a firm twist. Nothing happened.

"It's locked." Shasta smiled and took hold of his arm, leading him to the comfortable couch. She moved the table out and guided his unresisting body around. When he was seated she replaced the table, imprisoning him.

"This is crazy, Shasta. You're wasting your time and money." He laughed, and though he tried to inject the proper note of humor, the sound was strained. "You didn't have to go to all this trouble just to get me in bed. Good God, woman! I've been trying to get back there since the first time. Why this elaborate show?" He leaned back and stared at Shasta, a muscle ticking wildly along his jaw.

Shasta widened her eyes in all innocence and looked at

him with a wistful, almost injured air. "Why? I told you. You need to learn how to slow down and enjoy life." She slid in beside him and placed her hand on his thigh. "This is just one of the many lessons I have planned."

Kane studied her pose and relaxed. "I don't need to be taught how to enjoy life. I've been living it to the fullest for thirty-seven years. There's not a damn thing you can teach me that I don't know or haven't tried."

"Oh?" Shasta turned and pulled a three-tiered serving cart stacked with a variety of covered dishes to her side. She lifted one silver lid to reveal black caviar and transferred the iced bowl to her plate. "I wouldn't call what you've been doing living—existing, maybe, but not truly enjoying life. Don't forget, for two weeks I saw how you lived." She retrieved the plate of crisp, brown toast points and carefully scooped a generous amount of caviar onto a wooden spoon then let it drop onto the toast. "Why, just look at the changes already?"

"What changes—" He stopped, thoughtfully inspecting the table setting, then demanded, "Where in the hell is my silverware?"

"You don't get any. I'm going to feed you."

Kane shot her a strained smile. "I'm a big boy, Shasta."

She winked. "I know."

"And I can damn well feed myself."

Shasta ignored his outburst and picked up two liqueur glasses from the cart and a small carafe of chilled vodka. She set his glass before him. "Don't pout," she said, waving the delicious caviar under his nose. "It doesn't become a man of your great age and experience."

Kane snapped his teeth down on the caviar-laden toast and chewed, his silver eyes glittering dangerously in the candlelight. Then the humor of the situation struck him, and he began to chuckle. "You win, mouse. I'll do this your way—this once."

"Good. Now do as you're told and drink your vodka before it gets warm. I'm told this is the finest Pandora could find on such short notice. Do you approve?" She waited till he threw it back and nodded. She did the same with hers, finishing it in one gulp. Her voice was husky and tears filled her eyes as she gasped, "Wonderful." Picking up the wooden spoon, she fixed another piece of caviar on toast and popped it into her mouth. "You speak Russian, don't you?" Her heart began to beat erratically, and she wondered if it was the vodka warming her blood or the wary look on Kane's face. She quickly refilled their glasses.

"A little—enough to get by."

Shasta reached around and adjusted the volume of the music. She listened for a second to Boston Grey's deep voice crooning a love song, then lowered the volume to a mere whisper. She'd told Pandora she didn't want any instrumentals, but songs of passion and love. She wanted a soft background of words and phrases to entice Kane into a more eloquent state. "Does the name Excalibur mean anything to you?" Her eyes met his across the tiny expanse of the table.

Kane paled, and his face became a stark mask. "Where did you hear that name?" he asked softly, his fist clenched on the table. He forced his hand to relax and picked up the napkin from his lap and touched it to his mouth. "I asked where you heard that name?"

"Jeff was the first to put me onto it, then he told me to talk to Julie." She repeated what Julie had told her, all the while watching his carefully schooled features for any change. But he was an expert at hiding his feelings and revealed nothing. "Are you familiar with the code name?"

"Yes."

She waited, and when he was silent she started to ask the one question she'd been withholding since she'd heard the story.

But Kane stopped her, and the deadly calmness of his voice put her senses on alert. "If you want me to stay, you won't ask. On the other hand, if you want me to bust that door down and leave, then ask away."

Shasta smiled. He'd answered her question. "No more interrogations, I promise."

He returned her smile, reaching out to touch the satin curve of her cheek. "Wise woman." The tip of his finger caressed her jaw, then feathered a path to the base of her throat, where he pressed, feeling the pounding pulse under the skin. "Have I told you how lovely you look this evening?" His hand encircled her neck, his thumb tipped her head back and his lips whispered across hers, "All you need to set off that glowing face is a necklace of diamonds."

Shasta breathed in the fresh scent of his after-shave and pulled back. Whose seduction was this anyway? She clamped her teeth together and scolded herself for being easy prey where Kane was concerned. Reaching up, she removed his hand from her neck and brought it to her mouth, her tongue teasing his palm. His sharp intake of breath stirred her hair. "The only adornment a woman needs is a handsome man on her arm."

In a salute to her victory, Kane drained the small glass of fiery liquid. "Touché, mouse."

As far as Kane was concerned, the night fell apart after that one small concession. Shasta's triumph went to her head, and she laid seige to his scarred life with her love. She made him feel again, and newfound emotions surfaced, opening old hurts and wounds. He talked for what seemed like hours of his childhood and his family. He agonized over the war and the bitterness it had caused. He told her of his grandfather's love and his father's indifference. She plied him with food and alcohol in small but consistent quantities, enough to keep him talking. She whispered in his ear words that soothed the pain of remembrance, and her hands touched his body and aroused a deep passion, one he thought had been buried long ago.

"You're driving me crazy, Shasta—stop." Surprisingly she leaned back and reached for the serving cart once more. Kane winced, then shrugged. That cart was his nemesis, and like a witch she concocted a brew to keep him on the fine edge of frustration.

Shasta struck a match and brought it to the wick of a small oil lamp, then took two balloon glasses and warmed them over the flame, her fingers moving with practical grace. "My grandfather taught me this." Looking at him from under her lashes, she wondered at his thoughts and grinned. She almost had him where she wanted, just a little longer. She picked up an old bottle and poured a dark-amber measure into both glasses, setting one in front of Kane and keeping the other for herself. "Do you remember me telling you I loved you?"

Kane nodded, as fascinated by her movements as a cobra by a charmer. She opened a mahogany box, extracted a long, slim cigar and, holding it to her ear, rolled it between her palms.

"You told me not to love you. Why?" Satisfied by the freshness and age of the cigar, she took a pair of small silver pincers and snipped off the end, then held the cigar over the flame, turning it rhythmically between her fingers to warm it.

Kane raised his eyes to her face and found her watching

him. Suddenly her actions were becoming deeply erotic. "I don't want you hurt, Shasta," he answered her hoarsely, then was forced to clear his throat like a callow boy before he could go on. "And I will hurt you. Maybe not now, but sometime it will happen. I'd rather die first."

She lowered her head to the cigar and gently closed her lips over one end, rotating the other end in the flames. "You love me?"

The aroma of fine, rich tobacco drifted across the table. Her hair, alight with a life all its own, swung down and framed her face. Kane drew in a shuddering breath. Shasta picked up her glass, dipped the end of the cigar into the cognac and held it out to him. Her question burned through him, and he opened his mouth in denial, but no sound came. She smiled.

"Yes." The word came out a growl, and Shasta's smile deepened as she raised her arm, brought the cigar to his lips and gently brushed her fingertips down his cheek. His teeth clamped down on the cigar as his eyes met hers. "It won't work."

"Shh, love." She leaned forward and struck a match, bringing the hot flame to the tip of his cigar. "Puff." Shasta moved back to rest against the padded couch. His answer was all she'd hoped for, an admission of love, yet she knew this was just the beginning, her job wasn't over yet. Kicking off her shoes, she stroked his ankle caressingly, then she moved her toes slowly upward till they touched a warm hardness; there they lingered, lightly kneading.

Kane felt perspiration pop out on his forehead and fought to get himself under control, but his admission of love had cost him dearly. Now his thoughts were centered on only one thing—Shasta, and the remembered feel of her under him as he buried himself in her loving warmth. Dear God, he thought, just once didn't he deserve to let go? His hand found her foot and fondled the smooth flesh. With a gleam in his eyes, he quickly ran his fingers up her calf to her knee, then to her thigh and farther still, encountering only bare flesh. "You're buck naked under that dress!" It wasn't a question but a statement, and her mischievous smile took what little control he had left. With a groan he shoved the table out of the way, pulled her onto his lap and brought his mouth to hers.

Shasta returned the ravenous kiss and felt the strength of his embrace and the seeking hand between her thighs. "Kane, Kane." She pulled back. "Not here. I have a place."

Loath to let her go, Kane stood with her in his arms. "More of your plans, Shasta?"

"Yes, love." She felt dizzy at her triumph yet fought to keep a rein on her happiness. There were so many questions to be asked, and she knew if Kane was pushed too hard her whole evening could blow up in her face. She warned herself to go slowly, to see if Kane, now that he'd begun to realize his life was changing, would open up on his own accord. Would he trust her enough to reveal the real man she knew was lurking within that worldly facade?

CHAPTER ELEVEN

SHASTA DIRECTED KANE to a concealed door at the back
of the room, and with curses and giggles he maneuvered
her up a narrow staircase to the landing above.

"Where to now?" He stopped, feigning exhaustion at
the load in his arms, shifted her weight and fell against
the nearest wall. He laughed as her seeking lips nibbled
his earlobe. "I swear if you don't stop I'm going to throw
you down on the floor and make love to you, Shasta!"

She raised her head from the curve of his shoulder.
Loosening one arm from around his neck, she searched
the pocket of her dress and triumphantly dangled an old-
fashioned brass key before him. She squinted in the dimly lit hallway, trying to make out the number. "Room
four."

Kane's long stride carried them down the hall to their
room. He kicked the door shut behind them and with two
steps pitched her squealing on the bed.

Shasta rolled over, came to her knees and quickly
scanned the room, relieved that the heavy decor of their
dining room did not prevail there. The bedroom was
small, dominated by an oversize bed, and decorated in
soft ivory lace, which lent a romantic air.

"I think you're more trouble than you're worth, Shasta Masterson."

A rosy hue colored Shasta's cheeks and her eyes
brimmed with laughter. Jamming her hands on her hips,

she demanded, "If I'm not worth the effort, then why, may I ask, are you stripping so fast?"

"Old habits die hard?"

Bounding off the bed, she slapped his hands away from his shirtfront. "I wanted to undress you." Kane dropped his arms to his side. She wanted him so badly, but she forced herself to move slowly, drawing out every second. Her eyes on Kane's face, she stepped back, reached behind and leisurely unzipped her dress, letting it fall in a white cloud at her feet.

Kane's breath caught painfully in his chest at the lovely, inviting body. He held   his arms and without hesitation she walked into his   . Smiling down at the curly brown head, he stopped l   busy fingers on the buttons of his shirt. "I can do that a lot faster than you."

She retreated a step, watching as he disrobed, thankful that his eagerness was as obvious as hers. One by one each article of clothing was thrown aside, and when he stood before her naked, she could only stare for a second at his male beauty, the symmetry of hard muscles that defined his shape. She reached out with sensitive fingers to touch the smooth warm skin and mat of dark hair across his chest. Like a sleepwalker she moved, wanting only to wrap her arms around him, flesh against flesh, but to her dismay, Kane's hand gripped her wrist, halting her progression. Hurt shining in her eyes, she tilted her head back and met his troubled gaze.

"If I let you touch me now, mouse...."

"I love you, Kane. Don't hold back, don't think about yesterday or tomorrow—nothing matters." He slackened his iron hold and she moved quickly, wrapping her arms around his waist, her lips showering light butterfly kisses across his chest. "There's no other existence outside this room, just the two of us here and now. We have no past, no future, and the world may end at dawn. Don't throw away these precious moments." She waited for a sign from him and silently sighed as his hands slid down over her rounded buttocks, pulling her close to meet his desire.

Shasta loosened herself from his hold and began a slow silken path of kisses down his chest and across the hard muscles of his abdomen. Her knees touched the floor and Kane grabbed the bedpost as her hand gently stroked him. She touched and kissed, her lips warm and wet, till the groan rumbling in his chest erupted with a low moan of pure pleasure.

His fragile control snapped at the touch of her knowing mouth, and a feeling of release bloomed in him like a rose. He'd held back for too long. With her name on his lips he shuddered, and reaching down, he grasped Shasta by the arms and lifted her. Burying his hands in her delicate curls, he tilted her face and pulled her mouth to his for a slow and loving kiss. His tongue searched the moist sweet cavern, leisurely drinking the offered nectar.

Shasta took his hand and guided him to the bed. Playfully she pushed him backward, then followed him down, collapsing across his chest. Suddenly hesitant of her role as the aggressor, she wriggled in indecision, the mat of soft hair tickling her breasts and sending a rush of hot sensations through her. Her gaze met his, and she noted the sparks of light playing in his half-closed eyes, sparks that flared even brighter with her movements.

"It's your show, *chérie*." His voice was ragged with hunger as he lifted her to straddle his slim hips. She touched him, and he caught his breath. "Now, Shasta," he whispered, his muscles taut with urgency as she brought him into the warmth of her body.

Shasta looked down into his gray eyes, her heart

pounding heavily. She watched his gaze follow his hands as he caressed her thighs and stroked her hips. Fingertips moved as lingering as a kiss along her ribs to play and teasingly encircle each swollen breast. She arched her neck as he lightly strummed the dusky-rose nipples, making them harden to aching points. Shasta sighed and lowered her head, her eyes half-lidded slits of velvet brown as Kane massaged the tense muscles in her neck, then pulled her down to rest on his chest. His mouth touched hers, and his tongue traced the outline of her lips, sending a lick of fire across her skin.

Kane rolled her over and settled between her legs, his hands holding her head, his mouth clinging to hers as he set a pace designed to take her over the edge. "*Oui, mon amour.* Look at me. Look up and see what you've done."

Shasta opened her heavy lids in a haze of desire. Through the mist she saw him, and tears filled her eyes. His beautiful face was alive with expression and love. But it was his eyes that sent fat tears rolling unchecked down her cheeks. His eyes were no longer a soulless silver mirror; they shone with longing and tenderness, and a certain vulnerability.

He was free at last. Her heart sang as she held her arms open and he accepted the comfort of her embrace. Her legs wrapped around his hips, and he reveled in this prison.

"*Mon ange de feu.* My angel of fire," he crooned softly, then began to whisper endearments to her in his native tongue.

Though she was unable to understand all he said, the resonant sound of his deep voice talking to her of love was almost more than she could bare. She moved in unison with him and he loved her more. The culmination of their joining was so intense they were staggered by its depths. Too spent to move they lay cradled lovingly in each other's arms.

Finally their breathing quieted, and Kane levered himself on his elbows and stared down into Shasta's smiling face. "*Je t'aime toujours,* mouse."

Shasta touched the perfect arch of his eyebrow with the tip of her finger, then traced the bridge of his nose to his lips. "Ah, I know what that means. When will you teach me the rest?"

"Anytime or place you say." He grinned, then frowned. "Am I crushing you? You're turning the most peculiar shade of blue." Shasta laughed. "I forget how small you are, but that's understandable, you're such a fierce little thing." He attacked her neck with his lips, and as she struggled to avoid his tickling kisses, he eased his weight off her. Lying side by side, he covered his eyes with a forearm and let the silence of the room seep into his bones, bringing a peace he'd never known existed.

All his life he'd searched for this inner serenity. He thought of the years he'd spent running away from love, believing as his parents had that love was a burden. He'd vowed never to expose himself to such agony as theirs. At the back of his mind there had always been a nagging voice telling him he'd inherited the worst qualities of both his parents. Seeing the outcome of their union, he'd feared emotional involvement, despising it as a weakness. But now he knew that his father and mother had never loved each other. Max had married a young, flighty French heiress to gain entry into the European social set. And his mother, Jacqueline, had been fascinated by the older, rough-edged Texan.

Kane now recognized the bitterness and loneliness that must have slowly destroyed his parents' relationship. It was inevitable that their marriage would end, but they refused to give up gracefully. Instead they used Kane as a tool to vent their anger and frustrations, and in the process they had turned him into a cynical young man.

He wanted to believe he'd been wrong all those years and that Shasta's love for him was enough to erase the past. But was it? For a brief second he turned his head and studied her serene expression. She was so unlike any woman he'd ever met, so quiet and sure after their love-making. She needed no reassurances as to her abilities, no words of comfort. But his feelings were so new to him and he was still unsure. *Where do we go from here,* he asked himself. The question began gnawing at him. What did she expect of him now that he'd admitted his love? What did he expect of himself? He voiced his question and waited. "Where do we go from here, Shasta?"

Intuitively she knew the direction his mind was taking, but she refused to lay all her dreams and hopes on the table at one time. Her grandfather had taught her better than that. "Why, we find out who killed the professor and decide what to do with the synthetic-fuel formula."

The tranquility of the room shattered with her statement. She felt Kane stiffen beside her and she frowned at the ceiling, refusing to turn her head and look at him. She had a feeling the truth was about to come crashing down around her. Her breath hung suspended painfully in her chest, and then he spoke.

"There is no formula."

It was a long time before she could take sufficient air into her lungs to yell, and when she did Kane winced. "What did you say!"

"There's no. . . ."

"I heard you the first time." She sat upright. The sheet fell to her waist but she ignored it, glaring at Kane. "Are we all to play your fool, Mr. Stone? Me, Jeff, Julie, the government and U.S.A. Oil.'' She rubbed her forehead. "I don't understand you. I try to figure you out, and every time I think I have, you turn around and pull something like this.''

"I know the feeling, believe me, mouse.''

She scowled. "Why? Why would you put everyone through this elaborate charade if you have nothing to bargain with?'' Before he could open his mouth the answer hit her. "Of course, how stupid of me. It's the only way to force the issue. But have you thought about what they'll do to you—hell, us—if they find out there's no formula. What if they're willing to trade and you have nothing to give them? As smart as you've been, you can't manufacture a formula out of thin air.''

Kane leaned back, his mouth a tight line. "You think I can't pull it off? Remember, they don't know, Shasta, and I have enough leverage to keep them running around in circles. Besides, if push comes to shove, I have enough of the formula to make them salivate.''

"Wait a minute. Just wait.'' She snatched the sheet to cover herself and scooted back against the headboard. "Tell me everything from the beginning—from the first meeting with the professor till his death.'' She glowered at him, anger in every line of her body. "And don't give me that evasive look, either. This time I want it *all*, the whole story.''

"It's long and complicated.''

"We have all night.''

Kane swung his bare legs over the side of the high bed and pulled the silver champagne stand closer. He popped the cork and poured the bubbly wine into two fluted glasses, handing one to Shasta before slipping back into bed.

"Why are you so reluctant to talk about the professor?" With a sinking heart she watched his expression become distant and withdrawn. Then he began to speak, and she sat very still so she wouldn't distract him in any way.

"I guess because the funny little man came closest to my expectations of what a father should be." Kane closed his eyes. "In the year I knew him he pried more out of me than I realized. We examined life together, and he had the strangest habit of calling me son. He would even introduce me to the locals as his son."

Shasta touched his arm, her fingers lightly stroking the tense muscles. "Start from the beginning. How did you meet the professor?"

"Have you ever been in Barbizon, France?"

"No."

"I have an estate there, one I use infrequently—only when I need to get away from everything and everybody and rest. About a year ago I broke my leg skiing at St. Moritz and went home to recuperate. You can imagine my surprise and anger to find that my father, in his typical high-handed manner, had commandeered the carriage house and turned it into a laboratory for a scientist to work on his synthetic-fuel formula. Hell, Max didn't even have the guts to hang around and explain. He left it up to Melvin. Then, Max had the nerve to call and tell me that since I was going to be staying for a while he would call off his guards and let me keep an eye on his new acquisition—acquisition!" Kane snorted. "That's my old dad for you, everything is a possession."

He picked up the champagne bottle and refilled their empty glasses. "I was furious and hadn't decided whether to kick Melvin out or just throw in the towel and leave, but the professor convinced me he really did need a guard and friend. It seems he'd been working for U.S.A. Oil for the past ten years, trying to come up with an alternate solution to the oil problems, when he realized he could possibly have the beginnings of a synthetic fuel. He took his discoveries to the executives of the company, who were encouraging but not overly enthusiastic. So he quit in disgust and took his proposition to Max— U.S.A.'s biggest competitor."

Kane sat up and stared fixedly into space. "When Melvin described his experiments I began to get as excited as he was." He turned to Shasta, reached out and pulled her to his side, absently stroking the skin along her hip. "Can you imagine a cheap fuel to run this country? Better still, a means of breaking the stranglehold the Middle East has on the world? It was a heady prospect that could tip the scales of power back in our favor, preventing more wars and destruction. "Hell," he said, laughing, "I got so caught up I started hanging over his shoulder like some eager college student."

Shasta grinned at the image of a wild-eyed scientist in his laboratory with Kane at his heels. He caught her smile, kissed her cheek resoundingly and laughed, as if reading her mind.

"Barbizon's a quaint town with one main street and the feel of an old-fashioned village. I guess it hasn't changed much since 1830. There was a bistro the professor particularly liked, and every evening we'd walk there, sip calvados, and discuss the world and its problems. It wasn't till he got closer and closer to finishing the formula that I noticed the change. He began to drink more and argue harder and louder. His hope for world peace with the new fuel had diminished and he'd become cynical. I was on the verge of calling a doctor when he stopped drinking and going to the bar altogether. He spent twenty-four hours a day in that damned laboratory.''

Kane stopped talking, the memories painful as he recalled his helplessness at watching his friend waste away with work and worry. ''I tried—God, how I tried—to get him to open up. Then one evening I went to the laboratory, found it locked and realized Melvin was gone.'' Kane swallowed hard and Shasta hugged him close, her hands riding the rise and fall of his chest in a slow rhythmic caress. ''I was scared. There'd been men snooping around and inquiries made in town. But I finally found him in the bistro with bag and baggage, and he was the drunkest I'd ever seen him. He said he'd finished the formula and was celebrating.''

Shasta squeezed her eyes shut at the clipped emotionless tone of Kane's voice.

''We argued because he hadn't let me in on its completion. He was furious, but not with me. I could tell that. He seemed weighed down by some problem and it kept preying on his mind.'' Kane lay back, dragging her down beside him, and covered his eyes with his arm. ''Melvin walked out on our fight. Right in the middle, up he gets, grabs his bag and staggers out. I was so mad I just sat there for a few minutes like a hurt child and let him go. When I finally did follow, I remember how surprised I was to see how far down the street he had gone.'' He paused, his lips a grim line in his pale face. ''Shasta, the Rue de Fleury is a long main street and you can see down both ends for quite a distance. But the car came roaring out of the darkness—out of nowhere—with its headlights a bright beam heading directly for Melvin.''

Shasta felt a chill creep over her skin as she remembered another evening and another car racing out of the darkness. She now understood Kane's desperation that night.

"I called out to warn him, but I don't know if he was too drunk to hear or if he was too ridden with his own demons to care anymore. The next thing I recalled was holding his broken, bleeding body all the way to the hospital, and later after they'd done what they could, I held his hand."

Kane cleared his throat and dropped his arm from across his eyes. He hugged Shasta closer to him in an effort to ward off the sudden chill seeping across his flesh. "Melvin regained consciousness once during the night. He talked to me as coherently as I'm talking to you now. But he was possessed with the formula and kept repeating over and over that he didn't want Max or anyone else to have it. He said he'd done what he had to do and explained that the formula would only corrupt whoever had it, that it could be turned into the ultimate weapon of power and no one could resist the allure. I remember his last words as they were burned into my brain—'Money can turn men into whores, but great power corrodes the soul, and even you, Kane, with all your wealth, can be corrupted by power.'"

Kane shivered and pulled the covers over them. He rolled onto his side and faced Shasta for the first time since he'd begun his story. "And he was right, Shasta! He knew—he knew the oil companies would destroy the formula to save their profits, the government would use it as a weapon against other countries, and he knew I could be seduced with the knowledge of what kind of power that formula could bring."

"Kane—"

"No, listen and let me finish, because I never intend to repeat all this again as long as I live. After Melvin died, I drove home thinking of what I could do with the formula—the good I might try to accomplish. But good has its evil side, and as Melvin said, power, not money, is the root of evil. He was right. When I got back to the estate I went immediately to the laboratory and forced open the lock, thinking I'd simply retrieve the ledger and lock it up for safekeeping." Kane chuckled. "You should have seen the place. Old Melvin destroyed every scrap of paper dealing with the formula. There wasn't anything left of his notes and books but a pile of ashes. That's when it hit me that he *was* right, and no one should be able to wield that much power."

Shasta touched his brow, wanting to smooth away the deep lines and erase the pain from his eyes. "What about the men who ran the professor down? How did you trace them to U.S.A. Oil, or are you only making a wild assumption?"

"Part fact, part guesswork. But they do seem to be extremely nervous, don't they?"

She had only one or two more questions to clear everything up. "What about the government men, Kane? Why are they holding back?"

"That I don't know, Shasta. It's definitely not like them to be so coy when they want something. I think, like Tramble, the government doesn't know if I have the formula—they're only assuming I do. But once they're convinced they'll step in and make an offer I won't dare refuse."

"But, Kane, there's no formula."

"That's the sticky part." He smiled recklessly. "All this maneuvering with Tramble to make him believe I have the formula will convince the government, also. Of course, their presence has helped to step up Tramble's efforts, you can be sure of that. We might be in for some fast talking to the government later but it will be worth the trouble.''

Shasta snuggled closer. She'd had enough of formulas and agents. Her fingers played in the soft hair on his chest. ''You sleepy?'' she questioned, looking at him through her lashes, a recognizable spark in her dark eyes.

Kane removed her champagne glass, which she'd left balancing on his stomach, and set it aside. Her hand moved lower. ''If I was, I'd be wide awake now, wouldn't I?'' His lips took away her answer.

''I'm sorry about Melvin, Kane,'' she whispered against his mouth.

''I know you are. Now hush.'' And he kept her awake till the sun began to creep between the lace curtains to announce a new day.

JULIUS MET THEM at the back door, his bushy eyebrows a straight line of disapproval. He held out scraps of paper for both of them and slapped them into their outstretched hands. ''I ain't your personal answering service. I got better things to do with my time.'' Wheeling around, he stomped over to the stove, checking the progress of his quiche. ''Breakfast's about ready—sit.''

Shasta grinned at the gruff old man, mischief dancing in her eyes. ''Pandora sends her love and told me to be sure and tell you that she misses you. I didn't know you were seeing her.'' The back of Julie's neck turned beet red, and Shasta tried to hide her grin. ''By the way, how did you know when we would get here?''

''Pandora called.'' Julius thumped a plate of homemade blueberry muffins and buttermilk biscuits on the table. ''I was getting worried.''

Baskerville butted Shasta's knee for attention, and she

absently began to scratch behind his ear. "Why would you worry about me?"

"Wasn't you I was thinking of."

Kane ducked his head to hide his grin at Shasta's outraged expression. He quickly scanned the telephone messages, discarding ones from friends who had managed to trace him to Shasta's house. "I could have used a warning, Julie. A Deux Inn isn't for the fainthearted." He looked up when he heard Shasta's muffled laughter. She pointed to Baskerville and his eyes widened. The huge animal was stretched out full-length on the kitchen floor, making low whimpers as his oversized paws, one by one, pulled him across the cold surface. With a loud sigh and a last pitiful groan, he rested his massive head on the rim of his empty bowl and closed his eyes.

Shasta wiped the tears from her cheeks, looked at Kane's bewildered expression and broke up all over again. "Julie," she choked. "Have you been starving my dog?"

"Damn ham," Julius grumbled good-naturedly. "Always putting on a show." He grabbed a couple of blueberry muffins, cut a large wedge of quiche and dumped them into Baskerville's bowl.

Still laughing, Kane reared back in his chair as he glanced down at the last two messages in his hand. The amusement in his eyes hardened and the smile froze, leaving his skin pale and taut across his high cheekbones. Abruptly he excused himself and left the room.

"Kane!" Shasta was out of her chair immediately, but Julius grasped her arm firmly and held her back. "What's wrong?" she demanded, pulling free and glaring at Julie.

"Don't give me that look, kid. You still ain't too old for me to turn over my knee. Now sit down and let the man take care of his business."

"You seem to forget, Julie," Shasta's voice turned cold, "that Kane's business is our business. I have to know what's happening."

"Don't you use that tone on me, either, miss."

Shasta grinned sheepishly and slumped down in the nearest chair. "I'm overprotective, aren't I?" She gnawed at her bottom lip.

"It's okay." He patted her shoulder. "This love business is all new to you, takes a while to get the hang." He pulled up another chair and sat down. "But we got troubles, kid. Old Max Stone was beaten up in England last night. That was one of Kane's messages. The other was a call this morning from Tramble Baldwin, the president and chairman of the board of U.S.A. Oil."

Shasta whistled loud and long, and Julius nodded his head in full agreement.

"That ain't all. *We* got problems—big ones. There's G-men crawling all over Masters. Your brother's being held and interrogated there. J.T.'s fit to be tied. He says if you two brats don't clear this mess up real quick like, he's going to come down here and see for himself what's going on." He propped his elbows on his knees. "J.T. ain't a happy man. Seems he's been getting telephone calls all night about the Houston branch of Masters."

Shasta shivered at the thought of her grandfather's intervention. She'd witnessed too many situations in which he had to take over, and there wasn't anyone around who escaped the stiletto edge of his tongue. "But what are government men doing at Masters? What has Jeff done?"

"Well, now...." Julius sat up and smiled. "The boy got carried away searching codes and information on Kane. You know how he is with that damn computer. Once he gets going he forgets everything—he just went too far. But that ain't what worries me, he'll fast-talk his way out. What does concern me is the government's insistence to see the Stone file."

Shasta's face lost some of its color, then her cheeks flared an angry red. "They can't do that."

"They can do anything they damn well please and you know it. But don't fret. Margret has the file in a safe place, and she and Jeff are denying its existence."

"And Rena?" she questioned.

Julius chuckled. "She's playing the dumb blonde to the hilt."

Shasta sighed with relief. "I think it would be a wise move if Kane and I spent some time together alone." She grinned conspiratorially at Julie. "Away from the city—say at the family lake house?"

Julius winked. "Yeah, Kane looked a little peaked. A couple days' rest and fishing will do him a world of good. Want me to set it up?"

She nodded, then looked up as Kane walked in and sat down. "How's Max?"

"Bruised, but nothing broken. He doesn't have any idea who did it, and they never asked any questions. But it was a very professional job."

"A warning, Kane?"

He raised his head, his eyes blazing with anger. "I'd say so, especially when Tramble follows it up with a personal phone call." He cut himself a generous slice of quiche, poured some coffee and picked up his fork.

"How can you eat at a time like this?"

His silver eyes darkened momentarily and a suggestive smile touched his lips. "I have to keep up my strength. After all, I didn't get much sustenance last night. By the way, Tramble offered me two million for the formula."

She rested her chin in her hands and smiled. "And what did you tell him?"

"I wouldn't want to sully your delicate ears by repeating it, but I did tell him we might have a deal if he could locate the man who killed Melvin." Kane paused, broke open a hot, fluffy muffin and spread it with butter. "Of course he blustered about how sorry he was to hear of Melvin's death and that he'd do all he could to help. Lying old bastard." Kane's teeth snapped together around half of the muffin and his eyes glinted. "I'd like... never mind." He poured himself more coffee and cut another wedge of quiche.

"Do you always eat this way when you're upset?" she asked, awed by the amount of food he was consuming.

"Sometimes."

"What else did you tell Tramble?"

"I told him to think my proposal over for a couple of days and I'd do the same."

Shasta shivered at the wolfish grin on Kane's lips. "So we're back to the war of nerves again?"

Kane wiped his mouth, refolded the napkin, set his fork on his plate, then gazed up. She didn't like the look in his eyes. They were completely expressionless.

"Whatever you're thinking you're not going to do it without me."

"Now listen, Shasta!"

"No, you listen. You said I was in this as deep as you, so don't start trying to cut me out to protect me."

"They think I have the formula with me and know the government has more than a passing interest in us. They're getting desperate, and desperate men are unpredictable."

"Ah, now they're going to start playing rough." Excitement shone in her eyes. "Why don't we throw them all off balance by disappearing for a few days and give them time to think?''

Kane tried to frown at her suggestion but couldn't manage with her eager gaze on him. Hell, he thought, not only was she a mind reader, taking the very words out of his mouth, but she could just smile and twist him around her finger. He felt the first twinge of unease at her power over him, but a few days alone together were too tempting to pass up.

Shasta held her breath, and when he answered her with a smile she exhaled slowly. ''We can escape to our family vacation home on Lake Livingston. Julie said he would help us, and no one will find us until we want to be found.''

''Seems you've already planned this—'' The explosive slamming of the front door froze every muscle in Kane's body. He didn't relax until he heard a female voice call for Shasta.

''Rena!'' Shasta was halfway out of her seat when her sister-in-law bolted through the door, quickly grabbed the nearest chair and sat down. She was laughing so hard it took Shasta a few minutes to calm her down.

''Here.'' Rena yanked a thick manila file from the folds of Lizzie's worn and ragged blanket. ''I've turned your niece into a criminal. There are government men all over the office hunting for this.'' She tapped the file. ''Jeff is absolutely wild. I've never seen him so animated, not even on our honeymoon. You should hear the silver-tongued lies tripping out of his mouth to save his ass.'' Rena shifted her bright gaze to the other occupant of the table, and her next words choked in the back of her throat.

Shasta bit back a smile. She knew only too well the effect Kane had on women, but this morning he seemed

bent on causing complete havoc and smiled his most be-
guiling smile at Rena. Shasta leaned across the table and
gently tapped her sister-in-law's mouth shut. "You have
yours, Rena. This one's mine."

"What?"

"Kane, if you haven't figured it out yet, this is my
sister-in-law. Rena, meet Kane." Shasta shook her head.
Never had she seen Rena's composure slip like this. She
snapped her fingers before Rena's glazed eyes, and while
her sister-in-law composed herself, Shasta quickly told
Kane of the government men visiting Masters. "Rena,
Kane and I are going to the lake for a couple of days.
Julie will fill you in, but no one's to know."

"What?"

"Rena! Look at my lips when I talk." Exasperated,
she started to repeat what she'd said when she caught
the gleam of devilment in Rena's eyes. "You've had
your fun. You've gawked at Kane, you've delivered the
file—now go home."

Rena obediently stood up. She held out her hand to
Kane, then yanked it back and tapped her fingers to her
forehead. "How stupid! I almost forgot. Boston called
me about thirty minutes ago. Samantha went into labor,
and he rushed her to the hospital."

"She's not due for another month," Kane said,
glancing from one woman to the other. "I don't know
much about these things, but I do know Boston said the
doctor wanted her to go the full nine months to ensure a
healthy delivery for all the babies. What happened?" he
demanded fiercely of Rena.

Rena retreated a step at the accusing look he turned
on her. "I promise you, when we went shopping yesterday she was fine. I didn't let her overdo it, either.
Boston gave me a long lecture on her condition." Rena

picked up her purse to leave. "When Boston called he was so distraught. I told him I'd call you two, then meet him at the hospital." She was gone in a flash, Kane's hard gaze following her.

"Kane." Shasta laid her small hand on his arm. "Don't blame Rena."

"I don't, Shasta. I was just thinking how fragile life is. Besides, I know Samantha and how bullheaded she can be, but she'd never do anything to endanger her babies." He was quiet for a moment. "If anything happens to her, Boston will never recover. He worships her. We'd better clean up and get over there. He might need me." It scared him to think that Shasta's thoughts might be on babies— theirs. He hugged her briefly, wondering if she'd try to tie him down with a home and children.

He might be ready to admit he loved her, but anything else sent a chill of dread down his spine. Surely he'd suffocate and die in the daily routine of domestic life. A deep feeling of dread crept into his heart. He felt the weight of responsibility of Shasta's love and at the same time wondered if he was worthy of the gift. Could he change at this late date and accept the inevitable? What he needed was a stiff drink and a long overdue talk with Shasta.

CHAPTER TWELVE

WHO WOULD HAVE THOUGHT the birth of quadruplets would totally disrupt an efficiently run hospital? Shasta chuckled to herself, shifted the Porsche into low gear and switched lanes. Kane's fingers gripped his knee, and the smile she'd been holding back blossomed as he turned his tousled head toward her. Briefly she glanced at her own reflection in his sunglasses. She knew the darkened lenses hid red-rimmed eyes and the pained expression of a hangover. "Does your head still hurt?"

"Hmm."

"You're sure you don't want to drive?" He'd meekly slipped into the passenger side that morning without a single complaint.

"No."

"Are you able to talk intelligently yet?"

"Barely, and only if it's important."

Shasta ignored the slightly pleading note in his voice and plunged on. "Samantha looks wonderful considering what she's gone through. I was surprised they allowed her to have visitors this morning." Out of the corner of her eye she saw Kane sag a little lower in the seat. Poor man, he really had a bad headache. But his condition was understandable. Yesterday had been a day filled with tension.

They had arrived at the hospital forty-five minutes after Rena's departure. The entire time Shasta was trying to dress, Kane had followed her around, complaining about her slowness, arguing that Boston was alone, and would she please put her behind into fast gear. When they finally arrived they found the maternity waiting room filled with people—all men except for Rena, and the awe-struck nurses who had used every excuse they could to stroll by. Shasta sighed. She would have done the same thing if she'd seen all those good-looking men in one small area. Samantha's brothers had turned out en masse—all six, plus her father and Uncle George. The eight men, all with bright-red hair identical to Saman-tha's, alternated between pacing the floor and arguing among themselves.

Boston sat calmly, his hands welded together, totally oblivious to the commotion around him. Hours later the head nurse smiled her way through a sea of bodies and told Boston he was the father of quadruplets—all fine, healthy boys. Boston stood slowly, shakily, then fainted into Kane's waiting arms.

"What was Lucas DeSalva doing there? I didn't know he was close friends with Boston." Shasta asked.

Kane ripped his sunglasses down and eyed her glassily over the rim. "He's not. Samantha's family breeds and raises quarter horses, so does Lucas. They've all been friends for years." He pushed the dark glasses back to shield his sensitive eyes from the early-morning sunlight bouncing off the hood of the car. "You seem to be in tight with him."

Shasta disregarded the question, remembering Lucas's concern at her association with Kane the previous day, and then the laughter in his face at her panic when she realized the men were going to take Boston out to cele-brate the birth of his sons. She'd been forced to tell Lucas of her job as Kane's bodyguard, omitting the particulars of the case, and discreetly asked him not to let Kane out of his sight. Before she'd let Kane walk out of the hospital, she wrung a sworn promise from him that he wouldn't do anything more foolish than drink too much. Shasta weaved the little car in and out of traffic, changing lanes with a motion that brought a groan from her passenger.

"Must you, Shasta?"

"Yes, our followers are getting too close and it's important to keep them at the right distance."

"Could we stop this mad dash long enough to get a hot cup of coffee? I know I'd feel better." Shasta shook her head. "Ruthless damn female," he muttered, and closed his eyes.

"I'm truly sorry, Kane, but Julie's meeting us and I have to keep to the time we agreed on. If you hadn't—"

"Don't say it!" he groaned again, and slumped down.

Later, as the car began to slow down, Kane opened one eye to check his surroundings. "Shasta, why are we turning into the Sam Houston National Forest?" His head might feel the size of a basketball, but he still had enough sense to know that a person couldn't build a vacation home on federal land.

"I told you, Kane! We're meeting Julie and switching cars."

"Just when did you tell me all this?"

She laughed and slowed the low-slung car to a crawl as she drove over the deeply rutted road. "While I was putting you to bed this morning."

"Ah, I see. Would you please repeat the reason now that I'm in a more receptive frame of mind?"

"We're meeting Julie and changing cars in hopes that our friends behind us will continue to tail my car and get lost, then we'll be on our way to the lake house."

They passed picnic and camping areas in shaded

groves. Cars and campers lined one side of the road as
Shasta drove on, leaving the civilized world behind.
Giant pines so fragrant their scent penetrated the closed
confines of the car towered over them, and thick vegetation and vines scraped the doors as she maneuvered the
narrow lane, jarring Kane's aching body. He was about
to comment when they rounded a bend in the road and he
spotted Julie standing beside a dilapidated army jeep. He
groaned loudly this time, fighting the urge to demand if
Shasta had deliberately picked this mode of transporta-
tion to aggravate his hangover. He'd been in too many
similar vehicles and well remembered the rough treat-
ment they inflicted on the human body. And this old relic
with its worn camouflaged paint and rust spots looked as
if it had refined the arts of torture. He opened his mouth
to protest, but his words were cut off as Julie swung the
passenger door wide and the aroma of hot coffee filled
the car.

"Drink it fast, man. She's not about to stop the fun
now."

Kane gulped down the scalding brew and followed
Julie to the jeep. He leaned against a tall pine, silently
blessing the shade it afforded, and ignored the conversation going on around him. But his serenity was shattered
by the ear-splitting blare of the horn and Baskerville's
urgent barking.

Julius eased the empty mug from Kane's tight grip and
led him to his side of the jeep. "Cheer up. You're only
about thirty minutes from the house and a nice comfortable bed."

Shasta took off at a gear-grinding, bone-jarring pace
that snapped Kane's head back with a jerk. The rusty
springs of the bucket seats squeaked till he thought his
head would burst with the sound. "Stop!" he yelled.

The jeep bounced to a halt. Kane yanked off his sunglasses and glared at Shasta. They stared at each other for such a long moment that Baskerville, sitting on the floor between them, began to swing his head from one side to the other in puzzlement.

"Enough," Kane growled. "You want to tell me what's eating you? You seem bent on taking out your foul mood on me in the cruelest way possible. Now spit it out and let's be done with it."

Shasta frowned, her nose crinkling, but her eyes wide and blank. "Nothing's bothering me," she hedged as she ground the gears into low and eased the jeep around another mammoth hole in the dirt road.

"Don't go all female on me, mouse. I don't have the patience this morning to cope." Women, he thought irritably, could pick the most inopportune time to play coy. "Now what's the matter?"

She steered the jeep off the road and into a stand of thick trees. "We need to wait here until our followers pass." Pointing through the trees to the paved road beyond, she settled back comfortably, while Kane waited. "I received a call from Tramble Baldwin last night. He made me an excessively generous offer if I would turn over the formula. Of course your name wasn't mentioned in sharing the deal. This, he said, was just a little on the side."

Kane snorted and Baskerville growled in agreement. "What did you tell him?"

Shasta grinned, mischief dancing in her eyes. "That I'd think it over and get back to him. He dwelled on the importance of the discovery to America and reminded me that though you are a citizen you're more French than American."

Forgetting his throbbing temples, Kane laughed long

218 CHARADE

and hard. "The bastard's slick, I'll have to hand him that. He covers all the bases." Kane relaxed against the worn, squeaking cushion and rested his hand on a brown paper bag propped between the two seats. A huge paw slapped down on his hand, holding him immobile, and he stared directly into Baskerville's snarling face. "Shasta," he whispered, "Shasta, what have I done now?"

"You have your hand on his beer," Shasta laughed, as she watched man and beast glare at each other.

Kane jerked his hand free and frowned at Baskerville. "I wasn't trying to steal it, boy... ah, hell," he said disgustedly. "Why am I explaining myself to a damn dog?"

"There they go." Shasta watched the second car drive slowly by and started the engine.

A few minutes later they were once again speeding down the highway, but this time the wind was whipping around them and tearing at their clothes. Talk was impossible. The air sucked the words away as fast as they were spoken. Kane shouted, then shook his head and gave up. He realized his head had ceased to pound, and he almost laughed out loud. His body must have figured it didn't need to add to his troubles; he had plenty dealing with the Mastersons.

Kane turned to look at Shasta and couldn't help but smile as he noticed that her head barely cleared the steering wheel of the old jeep. His amusement increased when he saw that she was pressing the gas pedal with the tip of her toe.

Shasta caught Kane's smile and relaxed her shoulders a fraction. They hadn't gotten off to a very good start, and she prayed it wasn't an omen of a disastrous vacation. Her plans required an atmosphere devoid of worry and tension for her to convince Kane she'd make an ideal lifetime partner.

Her hands grasped the steering wheel, the skin pulling taut across her knuckles as she realized the enormity of her task. Kane still wasn't ready to totally accept his new-found emotions, and he'd made it only too clear that he didn't even consider a permanent commitment to be a part of his future. She could understand his distaste for the institution of marriage, though she didn't agree. But he'd never been in love before, and a change was definitely in order. He had so much love and tenderness bottled up inside that it would be a shock even to him when he discovered how deeply he could care for another person.

She'd studied every angle of their situation and decided against offering to live with him. Such an arrangement would have been too easy to walk away from if things got rough. She wasn't fool enough to think they would or could live in happy harmony forever; they both enjoyed a good fight too much.

Marriage was the only answer. But how did you propose to a man and make him think it was his idea? Shasta groaned to herself. She should have had a long talk with Rena or Samantha before she left town. If there were two women who knew how to get what they wanted from a man, it was those two.

Shasta pulled up to the four-way-stop sign at the main intersection in Coldspring, checked the traffic both ways and turned to the right. The quaint town was a step back in time, a place where people waved to strangers and stopped to chat in the town square on a busy Saturday morning. It was a place where a smile was sincere and a handshake was your word of honor.

An old brick courthouse and gazebo stood proudly among huge shade trees in the center of town, luring passersby to rest a spell and remember the past. The shops and stores surrounding the square had been remodeled with high, false clapboard fronts that teased the imagination with visions of a more leisurely yesteryear.

Shasta drove slowly around the town as she saw Kane's interest peak. People waved and nodded in friendly hellos and Kane waved back. She turned into a parking lot and cut the engine. How do you like it so far?''

"What a lovely place. It reminds me of the small villages in Europe where people still take pride in their homes and town. But why are we stopping here?''

Shasta grinned. "Did you think the lake house stocked itself with food?''

"I see." He read the distaste in her expression correctly. "Your aversion to shopping extends to supermarkets, am I right?''

"Right."

"You want me to do it?''

"No, no." She kept a straight face. "Julie called ahead and ordered our supplies. I just wanted to get several things out in the open before we continue on our way. This is as good a place as any." She cleared her throat. "Julie meant it when he told you I can't cook, so it's up to you whether we eat or starve. Of course, we can come into town for every meal, but that's so inconvenient."

Shaking his head, Kane crawled out of the jeep. He'd never understand this woman. Turning to Shasta, he was pleased to see the blush creep into her cheeks. "We won't starve. I'm an excellent cook."

By the time they reached the turnoff to the lake house the sun had risen to its zenith and was beating down unrelentingly. Shasta carefully maneuvered through a narrow gate, then around a curved bend that brought them out onto a sloping lawn thick with blooming shrubs and manicured flower beds. The Mastersons' vacation home was not the small weekend cottage he'd envisioned, and he smiled in appreciation of the beauty before him.

Amid towering pines and live oaks sprawled a large split-level cedar house built on high stilts. Kane could make out a sluggishly moving creek running in front of the house and the bright blue of Lake Livingston beyond. Shasta seemed to read his mind and answered his question before he asked it.

"We're not actually on the lake but the creek. There's a boathouse built on the lakeside that houses a boat for skiing and one for bass fishing. She pulled to a stop and jumped out, heading for the flight of stairs and the back door. Baskerville bounded out, barking and running around with his nose to the ground.

Kane followed more slowly, his body suffering the combined effects of his hangover and the bumpy ride. By the time he climbed the stairs, which seemed to go on forever, he heard Shasta mumbling and cursing softly to herself.

"Shasta, don't tell me you don't have the keys?"

"Just a minute." She sat on the cedar step and emptied out the contents of her purse, rummaging through the items frantically. Looking up, she smiled wryly. "I forgot them, but—"

"Wonderful. We have six bags of groceries, a cooler full of Julie's goodies. . . ." He sat down beside her and began to laugh. "What the hell? I couldn't care less about food. We'll just kill ourselves making love." He hauled her onto his lap and kissed her long and deep.

Her arms creeped around his neck, and she returned the slow movement of his tongue with her own. Pulling back, her breath coming fast, she grinned and held a small black leather case before his eyes. "There's one advantage in having a lover who's an expert with locks."

"Shasta, those are burglar tools and illegal to carry."
He studied the stainless-steel instruments, which resembled a dainty manicure set. His frown deepened.

She flashed him an impish smile. "Don't preach! J.T.
searches my purse every time we're together. I can't tell
you how many sets I go through." Her nose crinkled enchantingly. "My contact is threatening to go up on his
price. He's accusing me of reselling them for a higher
profit."

Kane watched in fascination as she worked, and in a
matter of seconds the lock clicked and the door swung
open.

"I'm impressed—I shouldn't be, but I am." His eyes
began to dance with laughter. "How long would it take
to teach someone the art?"

"Oh, years and years of intense study to be as good as
me." She leaned over and kissed him lingeringly on the
lips. "And we can start anytime you say."

SHASTA STRETCHED LAZILY on the dock, lulled by its
swaying motion. Between half-closed eyelids she studied
Kane, who was lying beside her. His broad chest, slick
with sweat, rose and fell in shallow even breaths that
told her he was sound asleep. For the past four days
theirs had been an idyllic existence, and as if by an unspoken mutual agreement, they refused to discuss
U.S.A. Oil, the professor, the formula or anything re-
motely related to it. Instead they made love, sunbathed
in the nude, and when they felt the necessity to talk,
they told stories about their past, funny tales that kept
them laughing for hours later. Kane told her of all the
places he'd seen, and Shasta talked about her job and
some of the crazy stunts she'd pulled during her career.
She also told him of her sideline designing locks, ex-

plaining that the sale of the designs enabled her to indulge her passion for fast foreign cars.

But even in the tender moments they shared, Shasta sensed a tension in Kane. There was an uneasiness that lurked behind his darkened eyes and a wariness that warred with the gentleness of his voice. For the past few hours the warning tingling at the base of her neck had made her more alert to his moods. Though he was trying his best to hide it, she sensed that something was terribly wrong.

The dock dipped precariously as Kane rolled over and sat up. He rubbed his face in his hands briskly, then stared off into space before he asked, "Why did you put your top back on?" Reaching out, he ran the tip of his finger down the wet valley between her breasts.

"I was beginning to get burned in the wrong place. I didn't want to deprive you of any of your pleasures."

"Me? You're the one who enjoys it so."

Shasta tugged at her brief yellow bikini top and sent him a scowl belied by her sparkling eyes. "I might ask you the same question." She slipped her fingers into the waistband of the scrap of fabric that covered him. "Why are you wearing these?"

"I wanted to get some sun on my front but didn't want to incapacitate myself and spoil your fun!"

"Touché." She grinned and lay back down. Kane did the same, bringing the palm of her hand to his lips and kissing her lingeringly. "What's wrong, Kane?" The question had been haunting her for hours.

Kane was silent for a long time, going over and over in his mind what he must say. The fickle sun dipped behind another dense white cloud, and he shivered as the air cooled his wet skin. He'd been dreading this moment for days, and he felt like a coward. He'd become so caught up in the wonder of loving that he'd blocked out the consequences. But last night as they'd cuddled together on the deck, gazing at the stars, he'd realized they'd come too far. He shivered again, remembering.

Dusk was slow in coming in the country—or so it seemed to Kane. They had spent the day out on the lake, fishing, enjoying the sun and just being lazy. As the afternoon lengthened, they went back to the lake house and cleaned up, and Kane cooked a simple meal of steaks and baked potatoes. Then they retired to the cedar deck with a bottle of wine to watch the darkness overtake the day. Stargazing had become a nightly ritual, one he had come to look forward to. The soporific drone of cicadas, the erratic flight of fireflies and the sound of the wind rustling through the tall trees brought a timeless peace that soothed away all the intruding yesterdays. They had been sitting quietly, listening to the approaching night, when the breeze brought the baying of dogs from across the creek.

Kane had felt Shasta tense as the barking animals began an earnest pursuit of their prey. Then suddenly there came a high-pitched scream, and the night grew still with death. Shasta hadn't spoken of the incident, but he knew she hurt and wept inside for the helpless animal. He could read her body and mind now, just as she could read his. They were one, and he felt the burden of that special gift. He would share her pain, and it scared him. She was too softhearted, too sensitive, and so very vulnerable now. It was then that he had faced the reality of what he'd allowed to happen and what he must do.

He wasn't good enough for her—she deserved better. He'd never measure up to her dreams and expectations, and the thought of the hurt and disappointment in those big dark eyes was more than he could handle. He knew if she ever found out of his past activities she would reject him. Better to put an end to their love now than let it be battered to death when the truth came out.

He turned to look over at Shasta now. "I asked you once before, where do we go from here, and you neatly evaded my question. I think you'd better answer it."

"Where would you like to go?" Shasta's heart pounded in her ears, and her palms began to sweat. She had sensed a feeling of doom all day, and now she knew it was upon her.

"To be honest, right now I'd like to be anywhere but here, having to go through this."

"I'll go where you go." She tried to interject a teasing note to her voice, but her throat ached and the words came out a hoarse whisper.

"You'd lead my life?" He snorted. "Come on, Shasta. You despise the way I live. But I do it for a reason—not very noble, but it does have its compensations. If you went with me, what would you do?"

"The same as you. Don't you think the World Security Agency would take me on if you tell them we're a team?"

Kane shrugged noncommittally. He knew for a fact that the WSA would be ecstatic to have her talents. "I don't know, but that's not the issue here, or an answer."

Shasta closed her eyes tightly and asked softly, "Is marriage out of the question?"

"Yes," he said harshly, and immediately regretted the curt tone. He tried to soften his reply with an explanation. "I told you once I was too old for you—that I had too many miles on me. I've done things that would sicken you." His face hardened. "I'm not good enough for you, Shasta. I'd corrupt your life and hurt you, then I could never live with myself."

Shasta's eyes shot open. "That's crazy!" She twisted

sideways, rocking the dock and sending waves of water over the sides. "I know what and who you are. . . ."

Kane laughed, and the savage sound made Shasta wince. "Don't be naive." He began to tell her the things the frivolous, vain and bored rich did for excitement, and he tried to convince her that he was exactly like the people she'd met. "Shasta, there's *nothing* I haven't done or tried."

"But—"

"No, really think about what I just said. Remember all the things you were taught were wrong, and then picture me doing them. I'm just like those friends of mine you despise so."

"Stop! We've gone through this before, and I didn't believe you then and won't believe you now. I've done a few reprehensible things myself." She began to gather her towel and get up, but Kane grabbed her arm and held her down.

"What you've done is child's play."

"I don't want to hear anymore."

"But you will, Shasta. You'll listen to every dirty little detail till I'm through."

She sat powerless in his verbal grip, torn between her love to shut his words out and a kind of fascination to know every facet of his life. Her face a stoic mask, she listened as he poured out his past. Her complexion alternated between a bloodless white and bright red, and every now and then she would flinch. The back of her eyes stung with unshed tears. She wanted to cry for him, for the devastating loneliness he must have endured.

When he had finished, Kane stared at her, his eyes depthless mirrors once again, his beautiful features expressionless except for the pale circle around his tightly held mouth. Shasta met his look squarely with an understanding smile that promised the world.

"Are you through trying to shock me? I don't give a damn about your past. It's the future I'm concerned about. I love you, Kane. You can't take that away or change my feelings."

"And your love washes the slate clean?" he yelled, exasperated at her stubbornness, yet deep down the tight knot relaxed its hold on his heart. She hadn't turned away from him in revulsion.... But it still wouldn't work. "I'm not the man for you. Even my work for the government is a sham—a way to assuage the boredom."

"Liar!" She came to her knees and faced him, rocking the dock so violently that water curled halfway across the wide platform. "Liar. You believe in good and right and your country."

Kane brought his furious face close to hers and bellowed, "You need a husband with a nine-to-five job who'll come home every evening to you and your children. I can't fill that dream."

Shasta flinched with each of his statements as if he had slapped her. She doubled her small fist and drew back without giving a second thought to what she was doing as she clipped him soundly on the chin. His head snapped backward a fraction, and he stared at her. His shocked expression would have been comical at any other time, but Shasta was so indignantly angry she could barely speak.

"You fool," she snarled. "Blind, self-centered...."

"Damn it, Shasta," he interrupted her tirade, rubbing his stinging chin. "That hurt."

Her eyes filled with tears, which she rapidly blinked away. "What would I do with a nine-to-five husband. I don't even work regular hours! After all I've tried to do and show you, you've never really seen me at all. You didn't listen to me. You—" she poked at his naked chest with a sharp fingernail "—don't know me at all. Damn you! I don't want a home. I can't take care of the one I bought. I never wanted—'' Her words trailed off and she cocked her head, listening to the tone of Baskerville's vicious growls in the distance.

Shasta leaped to her feet and sprinted up the wooden steps, running with an urgency that set Kane in motion. He yelled a warning and followed, but she'd been too quick, and her head start had given her the advantage. As he cleared the top of the slope his heart stopped, and for a split second he froze at the scene before him. Baskerville had a man by the leg, his massive head shaking his prize back and forth.

The stranger yelled and cursed as he tried to aim his gun at the huge animal's head. But Baskerville kept jerking him around in circles, his razor-sharp teeth biting deeper as he pulled and tugged.

Kane felt as if he was moving in slow motion; his feet seemed to weigh a hundred pounds. Each step made him gasp for breath, and he thought his pounding heart would burst from his chest. In his mind he saw what was coming, and a scream ripped from his throat. The stranger had spotted Shasta flying up the grassy slope and raised his arm to fire.

Kane's line of vision narrowed into a long tunnel and all he could see at the same instant the gun fired was Shasta's graceful leap into the air. Her body arched high then tucked together in a ball as she flipped and landed on the ground in a rolling motion that brought her to her feet, giving her the advantage of surprise as she threw her body against Baskerville's prisoner and brought them tumbling to the ground.

The invisible hold on Kane was released and he charged the remaining distance, kicked the fallen gun out of reach and set his bare foot across the struggling man's neck.

"Shasta, are you all right?"

"I'm fine." She glanced up at him, her eyes sparkling with excitement and anticipation.

Kane shook his head and smiled, but the smile disappeared as he looked down. "Hello, Willie. What dark hole did you crawl out of?" The little man, no taller than Shasta, twisted his ferret face in a grimace. He opened his long thin mouth to speak, but Kane applied more pressure against his throat, choking off his words.

Shasta sat back on her heels stroking Baskerville, trying to persuade him to let go of the man's leg. Her head jerked up when she realized Kane knew the fellow, but she didn't have time to ask any questions. She caught sight of a moving figure over his shoulder and screamed, "Kane, behind you!"

Everything happened at once, but Shasta only had time to marvel at Kane and his expertise in an art she'd never mastered. He pivoted on one leg, as supple and fluid as a ballet dancer, while the other leg swung out and to the side like a sledgehammer as it connected with his assailant's middle, dropping him to his knees. Kane delivered a hand-chop to the back of the man's head that knocked him out cold. Shasta could watch no longer; her captive was attempting to grab her and his fallen gun at the same time.

Shasta dived across the little man, her fingers busily touching nerve points on his body. The man grunted and spewed out foul names as his arm lost its feeling. Frantically she grabbed Willie's hand and drew his arm forcefully between his legs. As she eased the pressure, she warned him, "You make one more move like the last and I'll ruin you for life. Baskerville, back off," she ordered sternly.

"My bloodthirsty mouse, that hurts me just to watch.

Please let him go." Kane dropped the ropes he'd retrieved from the garage and quickly tied up the two assailants. "Go call the local law and ask them to come pick these men up. Then pack—we're getting out of here."

He stomped off, leaving the two men trussed up on the lawn with Baskerville standing guard. Shasta chased after him, grabbed his arm and swung him around. "We're not leaving here till we settle a few things, Kane. I won't let you end—"

"Listen to me, Shasta." His hands clamped down on her shoulders, and he gave her a tiny shake. "Willie over there is an ex-agent, a renegade for hire to anyone willing to pay his price. His fee is high, Shasta, because he's an expert at his job—extracting information." Kane crushed her to his bare chest. "Willie tortures people. I told you it was going to get dirty and dangerous, but I never envisioned a man of Tramble's stature hiring scum like Willie." He held her at arm's length, then let go and walked away. "The one drawback to employing a man of Willie's talents is that his victims never seem to live through his questioning. They meant to get the formula then kill us, Shasta. Now get moving. I want to have a talk with our two *friends* here before they're carted off."

Shasta did as she was told, her hands trembling as she dialed the number of the sheriff's office. She would follow his orders this time because she knew he was right to want to get back to the city. But if he thought he was going to get rid of her so easily, he was in for a big surprise.

CHAPTER THIRTEEN

THE RETURN TO HOUSTON was considerably rougher and faster than the original trip. The wind beat at them from all directions, making conversation impossible. Shasta had long since stopped asking Kane to slow down; her requests only met with grim silence as he pushed the jeep harder. Even Baskerville was out of sorts. He usually loved to ride in an open car with the breeze in his face, but he couldn't stand the stinging air whipping at his ears. He grumbled and growled at Kane's back, then finally gave up and stretched out on the floor in the rear of the jeep.

Shasta sighed with relief as Houston's city limits came into sight, and Kane was forced by law and traffic to decrease his speed. She shook her head a few times to clear away the lingering roar of the highway. Her appearance, she thought grimly, didn't bear thinking about. She knew her hair was in a wild tangle, and as she touched her hot, windburned cheeks she winced. She felt angered at the unjust turn of events. How could everything fall apart so quickly, she wondered. She wanted nothing more right now than a cool shower, a cold drink, and a quiet place to think. Kane pulled into the driveway, and Shasta climbed out and stomped up the back steps. Baskerville and Kane followed at a safer distance.

Julius's laughter greeted her as she marched in the kitchen.

"Who pulled you through the bushes feetfirst?" At

her murderous glare he tried to adopt a somber expression, but he couldn't restrain his chuckles.

Kane tried to ease past Shasta in a manner that set Julius off again. "Oh, you're both hopeless," she muttered. "Kane! Stop right there, we need to talk."

"Later. Shasta, I want to get to the hospital and see Samantha." Kane turned away and she grabbed his arm. He gave her a piercing look filled with determination. "I won't change my mind."

"You at least owe me a few minutes of your time."

"I don't know what's wrong between the two of you," Julius interrupted, "but before you square off for battle you best let me pass on these here messages. Kane, you're to call Boston, the decorators finished with your dad's house and Tramble Baldwin called." Julius checked his list, then glanced up. "Shasta, Jeff's gone to Dallas to meet J.T. He left at your grandfather's request of course."

"Oh, dear." Shasta backed out of the kitchen, leading Kane with her.

"You're also to call J.T., Samantha Grey and Rena." Julius looked up, his expression full of curiosity and surprise when he saw that Shasta was taking Kane to her private room. His woolly eyebrows rose in shock as she opened the door, pulled Kane inside and quickly shut them in. "Well! Don't that beat all? You see that, you dumb mutt?"

Baskerville collapsed on the cool kitchen floor and closed his eyes.

Shasta leaned against the door. "How's your chin?"

"Fine. A little touchy."

"I won't apologize for hitting you."

"Hmm." Kane studied the room with genuine surprise. Julie had warned him earlier that this was Shasta's haven and no one was allowed. For some reason he'd pictured overstuffed furniture and walls lined with books, but what he saw came as a shock. There were bookshelves all right, but instead of the bound leather editions he'd expected, there were hundreds of locks in all sizes, colors and fashion filling every spare inch of spare. A drafting table and tall stool were the only other furnishings.

"I can see I've caught you off guard again. This is where I design the locks that help support my foreign-car addiction. Damn it, Kane! Did you even try to see the real me?" She yanked a large ring of keys from his hand and put it back on the shelf with a bang.

"This isn't going to do us any good. I've made up my mind." He began to roam the small room.

Her heart sank like a stone in her breast. She blinked rapidly, telling herself she wasn't going to lose her temper, she was going to deal with this like an intelligent, sophisticated woman. "I'd like to sock you again," she yelled. "Put that down." She snatched a brass double-bolt lock from his hands and dropped it on the floor with a crash. "How can you possibly think I want roots and children? I want to be free—can't you see that?" She spread her arms wide. "Take a good look around you, Kane. I didn't want this house, I didn't decorate it, I don't cook, shop or clean. Nor do I want to—that should be obvious to anyone. And when did I ever say anything about babies? This might come as a shock to your male-chauvinist brain, but I don't want children, not for a long time, maybe never." She inhaled deeply and rocked back on her heels, glaring up at his beautiful, insolent face. "Can't you see *me*? I'm you, Kane."

He grimaced, and his skin lost some of its color.

"It's true. I'm a female version of you. I thrive on excitement and danger. I want my freedom just as you do, but that doesn't mean I can't love and have a husband." Gazing into his cool eyes, she wanted to scream. He was the most stubborn man she'd ever met. "I love you, Kane. No—don't go."

"Shasta, I wouldn't be good for you. Hush." He laid his fingers across her lips. "You're upset—"

"Of course I'm upset," she mumbled around his fingers.

"We'll talk about it later when things have settled down some."

"You bet we will," she muttered. "You just bet we will." She followed him to the door and up the stairs. "What about the professor, Kane? You haven't said a word about what Willie and his partner had to say. And don't give me that look. You were alone with them for twenty minutes while I called the sheriff and threw our clothes together."

Kane turned and faced her, his expression taut. "It's useless, Shasta, I can see that now. My whole plan was a pipe dream from the start. I thought if Tramble wanted the formula bad enough, he'd make arrangements to turn over the killer. He's the type to bribe the man into giving himself up—with monetary compensations, of course. Remember, the tragic *accident*—and that's what Tramble's lawyer will call it—took place in France, not America. I doubt, with Tramble's money, the man would even have been extradited. So you see, it's over." He cupped her curved cheek, tenderly stroking its softness with his fingers. Then, suddenly aware of his actions, he jerked his hand away as if her flesh burned. "I don't want anyone else hurt or another death on my conscience, so I've had to face the reality that in this case there will be no justice—though heaven knows it makes me sick to my stomach. Now I really have to clean up and get to the hospital.'' He walked into his room and shut the door.

Shasta stood staring at the closed door, her eyes narrowing with suspicion. His downtrodden act was not at all characteristic, and giving up wasn't his way. There was a sly glint in his eyes. It was all a bald-faced lie. Kane Stone would never retreat so meekly, no matter the danger to him or anyone else. But why did he find it necessary to make up such a story?

''Going to the hospital, like hell,'' she grumbled, and sprinted down the stairs. ''Julie.'' She bounded into the kitchen, startling both man and dog. ''Kane's up to something and I need you to follow him.'' She stopped to catch her breath. ''And this time don't let him see you.'' Looking down at herself, she frowned. ''I wish I could go, but it's going to take me hours to be presentable again. Will you do it? Please.''

Julius wiped his hands on a dish towel and tugged off his apron. ''Sure, kid. I could use some excitement and exercise myself. Want to tell me what's wrong?''

She kissed his lined cheek, and as quickly as possible told him of their two assailants and Kane's decision that he wasn't good enough for her.

''Well, he ain't.''

''Julie!''

''No man's going to be good enough for you, kid. Not where me and your grandpappy's concerned. But Kane's as good as you're going to catch, so you better think of something to change his mind.'' He patted her shoulder awkwardly. ''I better get moving.''

A COOL SHOWER and a good long cry helped soothe Shasta's jangled nerves. She fluffed her hair one last time, then leaned closer to her reflection, inspecting her

still-red nose. Why couldn't she cry prettily instead of
looking like Bozo the clown? Even a generous application of makeup hadn't hidden the bright tip of her nose
or the apple redness of her windburned cheeks. Her eyes
filled with tears of self-pity, and she fought to hold
them back. She should have remembered her grandfather's advice. He'd told her repeatedly that a person
could map out his work, his life and a vacation, but
never try to plan the course of love. And if you did,
don't be surprised when it backfired in your scheming
face. She was all out of ideas, strategies and maneuvers.
Now she'd have to ride out the storm on intuition alone.

Shasta sniffed and surged to her feet. Action was
what she needed to pull her out of the doldrums. Squaring her shoulders, she straightened the bodice of her
pink-and-gray striped sundress and slipped her feet into
a pair of wheat-colored sling-back pumps. As soon as
Kane returned, they'd sit down and work out *his* problem. All they needed, she told herself fiercely, was to
talk. And what if that didn't work and Kane was still
determined to abide by his decision? Shasta dismissed
the question, unwilling to face the heartache of the
answer.

She wandered downstairs and into the kitchen, where
Baskerville lay sleeping and unresponsive to her chatter.
She even tried the magic word "beer," but still he slept
on. "You're a wonderful watchdog, Baskerville," she
said loudly, and only received a twitch of one ear in
reply.

The house had an emptiness about it that she'd never
noticed before when she was alone. Roaming from
room to room, she touched familiar objects that now
seemed strange to her. Even her workroom didn't calm
her tension. All she could see was her life coming apart

at the seams. She had to find a way to make Kane understand that he was wrong and his crazy idea that he wasn't good enough for her was ridiculous.

When the doorbell rang, Shasta almost fell over herself in her rush to have someone to talk to, even a salesman. She swung open the door with a bright smile of welcome that slowly died on her lips as she inspected the government badges held out to her.

"Miss Masterson, I'm Gill Ham and these two men are Richard Brown and Sam Willis. We're with the FBI and would like to speak with Kane Stone."

"He's not here." She was about to close the door, but one of the agents already had his body halfway inside. Shasta opened the door wider. "Do come in," she said sarcastically.

"We really do need to talk with Mr. Stone and would like to wait." All three were inside and edging their way toward the living room. "May we?" Before she could reply they made themselves comfortable around her coffee table.

Shasta had to bite back a grin at their audacity. She'd often used the same ploy. "I've no idea when Kane will be returning."

"We'll wait."

She smiled, not at their determination but the fact that she could have spotted them as agents on any crowded street. The government, she thought disgustedly, didn't have any imagination. In an attempt to be nondescript, the agents reeked of their profession. Her smile widened dangerously, and she decided to have some fun. Maybe a good laugh would help.

"Baskerville!" she yelled, injecting just enough anxiety in her voice to bring the huge dog at a run. She ordered him to sit, and he planted himself in the center

of the doorway, his fathomless eyes alert to every move
and gesture the men made.

"Now, Miss Masterson, there's no need for him."

"Well, Mr. Ham, a girl just can't be too careful these
days, can she?" Besides, she didn't want to give the
agents free access to her house. There was going to be
trouble enough as it was without one of them talking to
Kane before she had time to warn him.

"You're right," the agent agreed, and tried to ignore
the fixed stare from the animal across the room.
"Would it be too much to ask for a cup of coffee?"

"Yes, it would. I'm afraid I don't know how to make
it."

The agent sighed. "Miss Masterson, let's stop dancing around the issue, shall we? You could be a great help
to us and your country."

Shasta's big eyes opened wide. "Oh. How?"

"You know, of course, that Kane has a synthetic-fuel
formula?" Shasta nodded eagerly. "We don't know if
he's trying to sell the formula on the open market or to
an individual."

"The formula's not for sale to anyone, Mr. Ham."

"Fine, fine. By that I take it he hasn't made any decision?"

She shrugged, her eyes beginning to flash with anger.

"You're a loyal American, Miss Masterson. You and
your family have an impeccable reputation, and a scandal could seriously damage your good name."

"What scandal?" she asked softly. Baskerville recognized the danger signal in her low voice, and his lips
curled over his teeth in a soundless snarl.

"Why, the one Kane's liable to bring down on your
head if he decided to sell." He held up his hand. "I
know you said the formula wasn't being marketed, but

look at it logically. If the formula works, it could cause untold damage in the world economy. Even a rumor of such an alternative in oil resources could cause an all-out war. The Middle East would lose its revenue and set off a disastrous chain reaction if they began to pull their investments out of banks and call in loans. Miss Masterson, they wouldn't begin with us—America. They would start with our allies. Do you have any idea how much the Middle East has invested in the British pound sterling? The chaos it would cause if they dumped their investments would put the pressure on our government and make us answerable to the world. You do see that to let such a potential weapon be controlled by one individual is unthinkable? The discovery could be as explosive an issue as the bomb.''

"I still don't see what this has to do with Masters."

"Why, Miss Masterson." He looked shocked at her ignorance. "If Kane decides to keep the formula for private enterprise, then Washington would have to step in, not only for the safety of the formula but Kane's personal protection. You know the leaks and false stories the papers are always printing. Your name would be linked with Kane's, your private investigator's license revoked and suspicion thrown on Masters' ethics." His big white teeth flashed in a grin that reminded her of Baskerville's.

"With your help we could avoid any possible misunderstandings. If you would talk to Kane, I'm sure he would listen to *you*."

The innuendo in his voice wasn't lost on Shasta, and her hand balled into a tight fist. "I see."

"We knew you would. You're an intelligent young woman. Brains and beauty, a resourceful combination."

"Yes." Shasta returned his smile. "If you'll excuse me, please." She didn't wait a second longer but marched out of the room, pausing only long enough to give Baskerville a hand order to stay.

A few seconds later she was standing in the middle of the kitchen, spinning around slowly, hunting for something to throw. She snatched up an oval platter from the counter and with a satisfied smirk on her lips held it firmly in both hands, raised it aloft, then froze. A picture snapped in her head, a scene of another throwing spree, after which Julie had made her pick up every sliver of glass then scrub the kitchen floor on hands and knees. She shivered with revulsion and gently returned the platter safely to the counter. But the inactivity didn't help her steaming temper, so she opened the pantry door, stepped inside and yelled, "Of all the unmitigated gall! Blackmail, coercion, threats. Wait till J.T. hears about this!"

She opened the door and stepped out, feeling a little better as she picked up the telephone and began to punch J.T.'s telephone number. It was time the game ended. Nothing could be done to catch the killer of the professor. She'd agreed with Kane on that. But she was sick of the three-way tug-of-war going on between Kane, U.S.A. Oil and the government. Besides, the turmoil was complicating her love life. She cleared the line and pushed a different set of numbers.

"U.S.A. Oil, Mr. Baldwin's office," the disembodied voice said.

"Tramble Baldwin, please."

"I'm sorry, but Mr. Baldwin is in a board meeting. May I take a message?"

"No, lady, you go get him. Tell him Shasta Masterson's on the line, he'll come." She waited, tapping her foot impatiently.

"Shasta, honey. Good to hear your lovely voice. What may I do for you today, sweetheart?"

Tramble's whisky-and-tobacco voice, laced with endearments, made her stomach lurch. She thought of Willie and his methods of extracting information.

"Nothing," she replied. "It's what I can do for you. If you want to know about the formula, be at my house in one hour." She hung up before he could ask any questions. Now all she had to do was wait and pray that Kane would be back soon. She sat down in the nearest chair and stared as if mesmerized by the wallpaper across the room. What had she done? Kane was going to kill her with his bare hands for interfering.

But the lies and evasion had to stop, now, before they went so far that no one would believe there wasn't a formula after all. If a false story concerning the formula were to leak to other interested parties they'd never be free; there would always be the threat of some foreign government believing the falsehood and coming after Kane. The agent was right; Kane would truly need someone's protection then. But all her rational thoughts didn't make facing Kane any easier. He'd warned her repeatedly to stop meddling. Maybe she was wrong. The problem was, she just couldn't keep an interest in a nonexistent fuel formula when her personal life was falling apart. She'd worried and fretted all day, fearing Kane wouldn't come back, then dreading having to face him again. She'd never felt as far away from Kane as she did now, all the while one thought kept running through her head—what if she couldn't convince him they belonged together?

Shasta didn't know how long she sat there, her mind grappling with her growing mountain of problems. The insistent ringing of the telephone finally jolted her out of her stupor. "Yes?"

"Shasta, Kane's just now pulling into the hospital parking lot."

"Julie, where have you been?" She mentally thanked her grandfather for his insistence that every family member have a mobile phone in their car. "Where are you?"

"In the car behind Kane. Don't ask questions, kid. It ain't easy keeping up with this slippery eel. Listen—when Kane left the house he stopped at a pay phone and made a call. Then, twenty minutes later I was following him across town. Shasta, he met Jason Leroy at the zoo, and they talked for a good hour." He paused to let his information sink in before continuing. "I think after the hospital he'll be heading home. If not, I'll call you."

Julius hung up before Shasta could say anything, and in any case her voice seemed to have deserted her completely. Jason Leroy, she mouthed silently. The name clanged in her head like a giant bell. Jason Leroy was a well-known electronics expert with a questionable past. He'd been accused many times of using illegal wiretaps and planting listening devices, but charges against him never seemed to stick, since the victims, usually large corporations, were unwilling to bring him to justice and expose themselves and their secrets. Shasta frowned fiercely in growing fear. What was Kane up to? But she knew. He was going to try one more time to trap Tramble Baldwin and to hell with the legalities.

SHASTA SIGHED, rested her elbows on the table and propped her chin on her folded hands—waiting was unbearable. She checked her watch and sighed again, deeper this time. It had been an hour and twenty minutes since Julie's call.

"Shasta. Honey! Could you call your dog off, sweetheart? I'd like to come out and talk to you."

A sly grin curved her lips as she listened to Tramble's pleas. "'Fraid not, Tramble. But I'm sure that Misters Ham, Brown and Willis would be willing to listen to anything you have to say. The four of you have so much in common." She chuckled as she heard the grumble of curses and Baskerville's sharp bark.

Tramble had arrived blustering and oozing cordiality. From the minute he contaminated her threshold she'd been offended by his "good ole boy" act and his self-assurance that she was willing to hand over the formula. But she'd had her own small revenge in the look on his face when he realized his meeting included three government agents and a dog determined to hold him prisoner till Kane showed up.

The distinctive purr of an engine pulling into the driveway and the sound of a car door slamming sent Shasta flying to meet Kane. As he stepped into the kitchen she wrapped her arms around his neck and tugged his mouth down to hers. "Thank heaven you're home."

Kane could no more resist the full lips than he could stop breathing, so he closed his eyes and savored her warmth. Just one more time, he told himself, and gathered her into his arms, feeling her pliant body melt into his as he deepened the kiss. She was so small and soft he wanted to go on holding her forever. His hands slid down her back to her hips and settled her against him. "Hey." He broke away, his breath coming a little faster. "That's some welcome."

The back door opened and Kane glanced up in time to catch the look that passed between Shasta and Julie. "Ahh." He released Shasta and retreated a few steps so he could watch them both. "You're a better tracker than I gave you credit for, Julie. I never knew you were there today."

Julius frowned, his brow pleating into deep grooves. "I can be darn near invisible if I ain't watching my back as well as the front." Then he did something that shocked Shasta—he apologized. "I was under orders, you understand?"

Kane nodded, his gaze shifting back and forth between the two people. "Did you follow me to the zoo?" Julius smiled. "And you knew the man I met?"

"Yep."

"From Shasta's expression, I guess you called her?" Julius nodded and Kane shrugged.

"I want to talk to you, Kane." Shasta looked around, trying to figure out where she could achieve total privacy and still keep her four visitors from interfering. She reached around behind Kane, opened the pantry door, and gently pushed Kane backward.

Kane found a hanging cord and pulled it. A harsh light illuminated shelves of cans, bottles and jars. "I'll have to hand it to you, mouse. This is a strange place to hold a conversation." He began to laugh, then sobered when she refused to see the humor. "You're upset?"

"You can't do it, Kane! Jason Leroy is a criminal."

"Not true." He inspected the labels at eye level, feigning a disinterest that didn't fool Shasta. "Leroy's never been behind bars."

"A mere technicality. He's an industrial Peeping Tom."

"Shasta, stay out of this." He stopped his detailed inventory of the shelves and turned his blazing eyes on her. "I'm no longer your concern." She snorted. "Where's your other earring?"

"Wha...what?"

"You're only wearing one earring. Where's the other?"

Shasta frowned, her hands automatically searching the copious pockets of her sundress. "Here." She held up a small gold loop and he took it from her, turning her sideways to the light. "I won't let you hire Leroy, Kane."

"Be still." He inserted the minute piece of metal into her pierced ear and fastened it. "Now, turn all the way around."

She did as she was told, and he fastened the two center buttons at the back of her dress, which she'd been unable to reach.

"I wasn't hiring Jason, Shasta. I was buying merchandise." With his hands on her shoulders he spun her around.

"You were going to plant bugs in Tramble's office yourself?"

"And his home," he added. Leaning down, he whispered, "Now that you know, wouldn't you like to come along? Think of it, Shasta. You'd be pulling a job for real. No more playacting or pretending you're a cat burglar."

She stared up at him, a silly smile of longing on her lips and her eyes wide with excitement at the thought of the thrill and danger. But her good judgment intervened and her eyes hardened.

"No, Kane, and I'll stop you if you try."

Kane sighed. He knew his plan was doomed the moment Shasta was on to him. He had only wanted to see that look of pure joy light her face one more time. "Okay, no Leroy."

Her gaze narrowed on his face. "The truth?"

"Yes."

Shasta grinned. Then her lips twisted as she remembered the four waiting men. "Ah, Kane. . . ." She stopped and swallowed. "I've done something I know you won't be pleased about."

"What?"

"Actually, pleased is the wrong word. I guess you'll be quite angry, really."

He grinned. "You're hedging, Shasta."

"Yes, I know." She looked up and smiled her most brilliant smile. "We have company—four men."

"Mouse. . . ."

"Three government agents."

"You've left one out."

"And Tramble Baldwin."

Kane cursed long and low in several languages, and Shasta was thankful she couldn't understand what he was saying. "I know you're mad that I've interfered, but—"

"That's an understatement." He leaned against a shelf and crossed his arms over his chest to keep from reaching out and strangling her. "How did this menagerie of misfits come to be in your living room?"

Shasta told him as quickly as possible, then asked, "Why are the agents making their move now, Kane, after all these weeks of watching our every move?" His face, set in hard lines, wrenched at her heart. She wanted to caress away the deeply etched lines on his forehead and kiss his taut lips.

Kane shrugged. "Who knows, Shasta. But you can bet their following us was not the only ongoing investigation in this case. They could probably tell us a few things." He sighed. "For whatever reason, I'm suddenly glad they've finally showed their hand. I was beginning to get nervous with them always at our backs."

Shasta remembered something one of the agents had said concerning personal safety. "Kane, do you think they could have been protecting us all this time?"

"I wouldn't discount that theory altogether." He was thoughtful for a moment. "I think they're somehow wise to Tramble and felt his escalating efforts to obtain the formula for himself weren't healthy for anyone concerned. More than likely they've stepped in at this point to make sure I hadn't been coerced into making a deal." He scowled down at her. "Now I'm forced to face them and Tramble and explain that there's no deal in the making."

"All you have to do, Kane, is go in there and tell them you don't have the formula."

"You think it will be that easy, and they'll believe me?" he sneered.

"Yes, I do. After all, it's only Tramble you've been leading down the garden path."

"And what about Melvin, Shasta?" he asked softly.

Shasta shivered at the sudden drop of temperature in the pantry. His words were so frigid she could have hung icicles from them. For the first time she truly realized how angry and disappointed Kane was at having his plans altered. Though he had faced the fact that Tramble would get off free, he'd still hoped for justice. The sadness in his eyes made her want to cry at his loss and her interference. She took a deep breath, swallowing her misgivings for what she'd done, and forged ahead.

"I think I've figured out a way to get Tramble, Kane." She placed her hands on his crossed arms, but he stood stone still. "Kane, there's nothing we can do for Melvin. You've admitted and accepted that fact. But Tramble's a different story. We can make him pay if you'll just give it time."

"That's something I have plenty of. Go on."

"Tramble and your father are just alike. What's the most important thing in their life?"

"Their business—oil."

"Right. So, if U.S.A. Oil is Tramble's life, you take it away from him in slow torturous degrees. You do it in such a way that he's helpless to fight back." Shasta tightened her hold on his arms as she felt him stiffen. "You have the money to do it, Kane," she said excitedly as she saw her words begin to take hold and his features relax.

"Go on," he urged with genuine interest in his voice.

"A stock takeover. You buy up all U.S.A. Oil's stock and take the company."

"There's not enough stock on the open market to get controlling interest. Tramble made sure of that a long time ago."

"No, not on the open market. I know something that isn't public information. JoBeth Huntley is Tramble's niece. You remember JoBeth, don't you? She's good friends with the DeSalvas and is always hanging around them."

Kane nodded, picturing the tall, pretty blonde, who made the society pages with her fabulous parties.

"JoBeth's mother and Tramble were brother and sister. When JoBeth's mother got married, Tramble refused to acknowledge or accept the man. He wouldn't have anything to do with his sister again, but when she died he could do nothing about her will leaving the stock to JoBeth. Kane, JoBeth Huntley holds forty percent of voting stock, and she despises her uncle." She smiled into his animated face, marveling at the change. "With a little help from Brandon DeSalva we could discuss a deal with her."

"Why you Machiavellian-minded, crafty little witch." He cupped her glowing face in his hands and kissed her lingeringly. "Shall we go face our adversaries and put our dragon to rest?"

For the next hour Shasta was amazed by Kane's firm but eloquent denial of a synthetic-fuel formula. Cold, precise, his eyes never leaving Tramble's disbelieving face, he told them of the burned ashes of the professor's papers.

Though Tramble couldn't openly dispute Kane's statement with the agents present, he did manage to inject a skepticism as to Kane's honesty.

"You doubt me, Tramble? Why would I lie?" Kane leaned his shoulders against the fireplace mantel, enjoying the choked sounds coming from the older man's throat.

"To make a fortune for yourself, that's why, and you damn well know it."

Kane smiled. "I already have a fortune. What would I do with two?"

Shasta's attention swung back and forth between the two combatants. The agents, she realized, seemed content to allow Kane and Tramble to fight it out, while she held her breath waiting for Kane's cool facade to explode. But he kept calm and politely turned Tramble's every insult aside. She listened, stunned and unbelieving, as Kane apologized to both Tramble and the agents for leading them astray.

"You understand I was directing my own investigation, don't you?" He glanced over at Tramble, his message clear as to whom he held responsible for the professor's death.

When at last everyone seemed to be satisfied that there was no synthetic-fuel formula, the meeting began to break up. The agents left with a promise from Kane that he'd travel to Washington for a special meeting with some concerned parties.

Tramble hung back as the agents said their goodbyes,

and as the front door closed he turned to Kane. "You better be telling the truth, Kane—" he looked pointedly at Shasta, "—because Willie didn't spend very long in that hick-town jail." He leaned closer, his florid face as close to Kane's as his short height would allow, and his gravelly voice held anger and suspicion. "If that formula's not ashes as you say, and it turns up...." He paused dramatically, and Shasta held her breath, her hand squeezing Kane's arm hard.

Tramble's cold blue eyes stared at Kane. "Accidents can happen and you could end up like old Melvin." He ignored Shasta's gasp and, shoving his Stetson on his head, sauntered out of the house.

"My God! Kane, he did it, he had Melvin killed."

Kane turned around, his face a stone mask. "I never doubted it for a second." Then he smiled, a smile that sent a shiver up and down Shasta's spine. "There *will* be a reckoning and retribution, though. I promise you that with your plan I'll make Tramble Baldwin pay—slowly, painfully. We'll have our justice, and he'll account for his sins here on earth."

Shasta collapsed into her chair. Closing her eyes, she again saw the look of menace and hate on Tramble's face. Yes, she thought, Kane would eventually have his justice. Men like Tramble didn't deserve anything less.

"All things considered, that went well, don't you think?" Kane poured himself a small amount of whisky and tossed it back in one swallow.

"You were wonderful—and surprising!"

"How so?" He added another splash of liquor into his glass and sat on the arm of her chair.

Shasta grinned. "You missed your calling. You should have been a snake-oil salesman." She began to chuckle. "The way you handled Tramble was brilliant.

Did you see the joy on his face when he really began to believe that the formula had been destroyed? And his anger when you reminded him that if one old man could discover and develop a new fuel alternative, then someone else would eventually follow in Melvin's footsteps.''

Kane smiled, but the humor didn't reach his eyes. He picked up her small hand and studied it for a long moment before turning it over and kissing the palm. "Shasta, I'm leaving—moving back to Max's house today. No, don't look like that. I told you this couldn't go on, that I wouldn't let it continue this way."

"Damn. I don't understand you." She snatched her hand from his and jumped up. "You're so hung up on your past. Haven't I made it plain enough that I don't care! It's done with—over—exactly where it belongs, in the past."

Kane rose slowly to his feet as if the weight of the world hovered around his shoulders. "And *you* don't see what I'm saying at all. The past has a way of resurfacing, and I don't know if I can change, Shasta."

She took a step toward him, then stopped. "I never wanted to change you," she whispered. "I love you just as you are—past and all."

Kane shook his head and walked out of the room, leaving his heart behind as he climbed the stairs to retrieve his packed suitcases. He had pulled Julie aside earlier and out of Shasta's hearing had asked the tight-lipped old man to drive him to his father's house. Now that he was at the back door, luggage in hand and Shasta following him down the steps, he wondered for the hundredth time if he was wrong. He stiffened his spine and kept moving, determined not to look back. But as he opened the car door to get in, his gaze swung automatically to the steps, where Shasta and Baskerville stood silently watching him leave. He hardened what was left of his heart to the tears on her cheeks, stumbled into the seat and slammed the door, keeping his eyes straight ahead.

As they drove off, Shasta's legs gave way and she sat down, her arm slung around Baskerville's neck. She couldn't believe he was really gone, that she hadn't been able to make him stay. "Stop it." She moved her head away as a wet tongue tried to wipe away her tears. "I'm all right. We'll just give him a couple of days alone, revise our plans and show up on his doorstep." She tried to force a note of optimism into her voice, but the enthusiasm was gone from her, and only a dull, hollow ache remained. "I can't have lost him, Baskerville. Mastersons are notorious for always getting their men—or women." But, she thought grimly, she was different from the rest of her family, the black sheep so to speak, and maybe their luck hadn't rubbed off on her. "Don't worry," she reassured the whining dog. "Somehow, someway, we'll get him back."

CHAPTER FOURTEEN

"SHASTA, YOU HAVE TO pull yourself together." Rena draped her body across Shasta's desk and snapped her fingers before her sister-in-law's fixed stare. "Margret's worried about you, and frankly so am I."

"I'm fine."

"No, you're not, and you're breaking my heart. I wish Jeff was here, he'd think of something. Oh," she growled, "I'd like to ring Kane Stone's neck."

"So would I." Shasta's lips twisted in a mockery of a smile. "So would I," she whispered. The past three days without him had been hell, and to make it worse she was alone. Her grandfather had finally ordered Julie to return to Dallas so they could accompany Jeff to Washington. It seemed that Jeff's fast talking hadn't soothed all the feathers he'd ruffled. Now J.T., both angry and amused at his grandson's plight, had had to step in and help him out of a sticky situation.

"Why don't you just go see him?"

Shasta slammed her fist on the desk and leaped to her feet. "Because, damn it, I haven't thought out a plan of action yet." Her once fruitful mind had dried up like a parched desert.

"Stop being so calculating, Shasta—just go over there."

Shasta dropped down in her chair, her body limp with

indecision and lack of sleep. "I don't know if he's still there."

"Oh, he's there all right." Rena spun away quickly to keep Shasta's alert gaze from seeing the sudden uncertainty in her own eyes.

"Did you know that I had to dress *twice* this morning before I got my clothes right?" She turned worried brown eyes on Rena. "I know I'm forgetful and lax, but I've never done that before. Do you think I'm losing my mind? I mean, does love make you crazy?"

Rena almost choked with laughter. After all this time Shasta was finally beginning to show some interest in her appearance. Maybe there was hope for her after all. "No, Shasta, as usual you have a lot on your mind. I'm just a little surprised you noticed it at all."

Shasta grinned. "I think I'll go to the hospital and see Samantha and the boys. Maybe she's heard from Kane."

She had indeed. Samantha's accusing words hit Shasta like a blast the minute she stepped into the hospital room.

"What have you done to Kane?"

The two new friends glared at each other. Samantha was the first to break the tension as she took in the fatigue and hurt in Shasta's face. "Let me rephrase that question. What are you and Kane doing to each other? He looks terrible but you look even worse."

"You've seen him then? When?"

"He came by this morning," she said, and pointed to the nearest chair, motioning for Shasta to sit down. "You're ready to fall. What's happened between you two? I tried to pry some answers out of Kane, but he was as reticent as ever. Infuriating man! And Boston's no different. He knows but refuses to talk. Just looks at me with that smug smile of his. Here I am stuck in this hospital while my friends need me to help straighten out their problems, and he just laughs and gloats like some damn sultan." Her blue eyes flashed in anger. "Sorry," she said sheepishly, "but I'm going stir crazy."

Shasta smiled. Samantha's temper had become legend, but it was balanced by intelligence, beauty and a good sense of humor. She was the perfect match for Boston. Thinking of the two of them, Shasta felt her insecurities resurface, hammering away at her dreams of her and Kane together. After all, Boston and Sammy complemented each other, and she certainly couldn't say that of Kane and herself. They were too much alike.

"Kane's miserable, Shasta." Samantha tried again to prod some free information.

"So am I, and it's all his fault." Hesitant at first, she began to tell Samantha of Kane's conviction that he wasn't good enough for her, that he was using his past as a barrier.

"Do you know anything of his past, Shasta?"

The deep male voice made Shasta jump. Boston leaned against the door, his long body relaxed, but his black eyes were smoky with hidden secrets.

"Kane told me."

Boston pushed away from his lounging position. "I doubt he's told you all." He leaned down and kissed Samantha, then settled on the edge of her bed. "Kane's led a rather...adventurous life."

"Adventurous!" she sneered, and gave an unladylike snort. "He told me everything he possibly could to shock me."

Boston studied her for a long moment, and something he saw in her face must have convinced him that Kane had indeed spilled out his notorious past in detail and that Shasta didn't hold it against him. She watched as husband and wife exchanged meaningful glances, as if giving their final stamp of approval on her relationship with Kane.

"Did you know he's been partying nonstop since he left your home?" She shook her head, and Boston went on. "It's been in the society papers all week."

Shasta scowled. She hadn't seen a newspaper in three days. As a matter of fact, she thought grimly, the papers at home and at the office had mysteriously disappeared lately. Then it hit her. Rena, the early riser, had been coming by her house and stealing the newspaper off her front steps, and she had conspired with Margret to hide the office copy. Her plans for retaliation were interrupted by Boston's next statement.

"Kane leaves for Washington tomorrow morning, and after his meeting he's going to New York, then back to Europe." He watched dismay settle over Shasta's features. "He's also throwing a farewell party tonight."

Shasta's breath hung painfully in the back of her throat. Europe. She knew that if he left the country she'd never see him again, never be able to convince him that he was wrong to leave her behind. She gathered up her purse and stood.

"I have to go. Million things to do. Thank you, Boston," she babbled, then took a deep gulp of air. "I know by telling me he's leaving you've broken a confidence, and I appreciate it. Samantha, I'll call you later." She was at the door when she realized how rude she'd been. "I'm sorry. How are the babies and when do you get to take them home?"

Samantha laughed, a sound destined to lighten anyone's spirits. "They're wonderful, and I'd be even more ecstatic if Boston and I could agree on names." She reached out and pinched her husband's side. "As for taking them home...." She shrugged. "They need to gain at least a pound each before that happy event." Her expression brightened. "But I get to go home tomorrow, so call me there. Now go before I really start to bore you with parental pride."

Shasta waved, stepped out into the hospital hallway and squeezed her eyes shut. Kane leaving. Did he plan to go and never contact her again? A slow burning anger began to build at the injustice of it all. She was helpless, but she'd be damned if she would make it easy for him. What was the old saying about "Hell hath no fury like a woman scorned"? Well, he'd burned her, and she was determined that if he left he would carry a few more scars than he'd started out with. Her shoulders slumped, and she punched the elevator button. Who was she fooling? The torment would be all hers. She didn't want to inflict any more pain on Kane. But, heaven help her, she was going to see him one more time. Just once more she was going to try to make him see he was wrong. She glanced at her watch—three-thirty. She had at least four hours till she could crash his party.

ONCE HOME, Shasta paced the floor. What was she going to do with herself between now and the party? She wasn't used to waiting or sitting at home with idle time on her hands. She wondered what other women did all day. The answer came as she looked in the mirror. Her hair needed shampooing, her eyes were puffy from crying and circled in shadows from sleepless nights. Time to take herself in hand. A nap would help if she could stop the memories of Kane flashing through her head in a never-ending reel. It hurt to think those memories might be all she would have left.

When the doorbell woke her three hours later, Shasta groggily groped for her robe and struggled to get it on as she staggered down the stairs.

"Miss Shasta Masterson?"

"Yes," she said, her voice husky with sleep.

"Would you sign here please?"

She accepted the small package, tucked it under her arm and scrawled her signature across the receipt. "Thank you." The door closed with a snap, and belatedly she realized she'd forgotten to tip the young man. Who, she wondered, could be sending her something from Cartier's? She unwrapped the package and stared with dread at the embossed box. The tip of her finger outlined the monogrammed name tentatively, then with a sick feeling she flipped the hinged top open and gasped. On a bed of white satin lay a diamond-and-black-onyx panther-headed bracelet. The two meeting heads winked wickedly at her with emerald eyes when she touched the bauble. They seemed to be daring her to pick up the formal, cream-colored card and read it.

Shasta didn't know how long she stood there looking at the bracelet, but she quickly realized that she hated it on sight, and she snatched the card up to confirm what she already suspected. It was from Kane, and as she read, a red mist seemed to drop like a veil over her eyes. Closing them tightly, she wished she were back in bed and this was all a horrible nightmare. She couldn't believe this was happening to her as she reread the note.

This gift is only a small insignificant object, but the only way I know to say "thank you." Also, I believe that if a woman doesn't have a handsome man on her arm, she should adorn herself with precious jewels.

I shall never forget,
Kane

Bastard! If she didn't have a handsome man! "I'll kill him," she yelled, then stopped, her breathing hard and fast. "No. I'll make him beg. I'll bring him to his knees." Fantasies were wonderful, but reality struck with the force of a sledgehammer. As far as Kane was concerned their affair was over. Was it worth the chance of more hurt and pain to confront him one last time? Her answer was yes. No matter what, she had to be the one to swallow her pride and give it another try.

An hour later she checked her appearance in the full-length mirror and smiled in satisfaction. For a brief second her gaze wandered from her reflection to the room behind her and she flinched. A rainbow of colors had spilled across the floor and her bed as she tried on outfit after outfit, discarding each in her frantic search to find the right dress. She'd finally settled on a two-piece Valentino silk. The dress was deceptively sexy with its strapless chemise of red dots on black and fingertip-length silk jacket in a reverse design of black dots on red. It was slinky yet innocent, sophisticated but naughty as it clung to her body, revealing only enough to tantalize. The barely black stockings added chic and mystery to her long legs. She was a little awed that she'd managed hair, makeup and clothes by herself. There was hope for her after all. Without another thought of the consequences she fled the house.

The night was clear and warm, the stars shining bright in the sky and the scent of the sea in the air. Shasta maneuvered her car down the street and turned into Max Stone's long graveled driveway. Bentleys, Cadillacs, Mercedes, Jaguars, several Porsches and a Rolls-Royce or two were lined respectfully together, bumper to bumper. Kane was indeed throwing a party. Judging by the glaring light streaming from every window and the blare of music, it was a farewell party to be long remembered. He was back among his so-called set and flying high.

She parked her car in the center of the driveway, slipped out and slammed the door. She took a deep breath as her steps faltered and her courage failed. All the way there she'd kept preparing herself for Kane's reaction to what she was going to do. Though he'd never been cruel to her, she knew he was capable of it. Rude, abrasive, sharp, he could be a cold-blooded savage with his words, and she knew he could devastate her in a second. Bracing herself, she ran up the steps and walked through the open door.

Tina Turner's soulful voice was pleading for everyone to stay together while people danced, milled around, laughing and talking, and Shasta was able to enter the room unnoticed. Her eyes scanned the crowd, then she turned abruptly to check out the other rooms when she didn't spot Kane among the guests.

"Shasta, Shasta Masterson."

The masculine voice was welcomingly familiar and she swung around in a quick circle to find its owner. "Lucas. Brandon." She waved, and they weaved their way toward one another.

"What are you doing here?" they all demanded in unison, then laughed.

"JoBeth dragged us. Said we were turning into a bunch of workaholics." Lucas grinned, his usually stern features lightening as Brandon groaned behind him. "The reason my gallant brother is sulking and dodging around is that there's a society columnist here trying to get his picture. Go away, Brandon."

"Maybe Shasta will allow me to hide behind her skirt?" Bright-blue eyes full of laughter and a spark of sensuality roamed over Shasta slowly. "Such a dainty little thing, isn't she, brother?"

Shasta was used to Brandon's teasing, but tonight was the first time she'd noticed the male interest in his eyes. "I'm looking for Kane. Have you seen him?"

Lucas scowled and shook his head. Brandon answered before his brother could stop him. "Last time I saw him he was upstairs in Max's private library."

She thanked them, excused herself and hurried up the long curved stairway. As she rounded the bend out of sight of Lucas and Brandon, her dread slowed her steps to a snail's pace. The husky tones of a woman's voice reached her as she neared the doorway. She stood there, feeling like an intruder and eavesdropper, though she didn't hear a word they said as her eyes devoured Kane. Dressed with his usual casual elegance in gray pleated slacks and a matching linen shirt tucked neatly in at his narrow waist, he was male personified. Shasta swallowed hard. Even with the world-weary lines etched deeper in his face and the cynical curve of his mouth twisted a little higher, he was still beautiful.

"Hello, Kane," she said softly. Shasta's gaze never wavered to the blonde draped across one corner of the big desk. She could only stare at Kane as he lounged gracefully near the woman.

Kane straightened, his surprise genuine, and for a brief second his expression lightened before the mask fell into place. "How are you?"

"I'd like to talk to you...alone, please." For the first time since she'd entered she looked pointedly at the other woman.

"I'll check with you later, Kane." The blond woman made to slip off the edge of the desk, but Kane stopped her with a motion of his hand.

"Stay, Karen, she won't be here long."

Karen settled back with a smug smile, and her hand moved intimately up and down Kane's arm.

"You want a stranger to hear what I have to say?"

"If it's going to be a personal conversation, maybe you'd better wait till tomorrow." He waved his hand around the array of scattered glasses, overflowing ashtrays and half-empty whisky bottles. "As you can see, I'm having a party."

Shasta leaned back against the doorframe as casually as possible, while inside she shook with weakness and dread. "But then you won't be here tomorrow, will you, Kane? You'll be in Washington." She reached in the pocket of the silk jacket and pulled out the unmistakable box. "I didn't want to believe this when I received it." How could he be so cool, standing before her with that damn woman touching him? She wanted to scream at her to go away and leave them alone. Instead she stared into bright-silver eyes that broke her heart with their icy depths. "I don't think I deserve to be treated this way."

"You didn't like my gift?"

"No, Kane." She took a step forward then stopped. "Kane, are you sure you want to do this? You know I don't care about your past."

"I think I made my position very clear," he said.

"You want to end our affair?"

"Hey," Karen interrupted. "I'd better leave."

"No," Kane ordered again, his voice harsh.

Shasta swallowed all her pride. "You don't want me anymore, Kane?"

He shook his head slowly. "No."

"What about love? I still love you." She persisted, determined, even if it killed her, that she would make him tell her exactly how he felt. If this was truly the end, then he was going to have to destroy the love she had for him.

"Love's overrated. You were different, you amused me."

She closed her eyes, wanting only to die. "Don't do this to us, Kane."

"There's no us, there never will be."

His words hurt beyond belief, but it was the tone that devastated her. She'd come prepared for his cruelty, and though his eyes were as cold as a winter moon, his words were spoken softly, full of understanding. How she wished to hear him call her Shasta, mouse; even baby, would be preferable to no name at all. The very omission was more insulting than if he'd slapped her face. Her fingers tightened around the forgotten jeweler's box in her hand till she threatened to crush it. There was an ache in her throat, and it hurt to breathe too deeply. He meant it when he said it was over, and no amount of talking was going to change his mind. She released her grip on her lifeline. "You'd better take this back. It offends me and would only remind me of what a fool I've been."

She pitched the box directly to him, but Kane didn't even make a move to catch it. Instead, he brought his glass to his lips and took a long drink of whisky. The box fell to the floor, and as it hit the clasp gave way and the bracelet spun on the floor, showering sparkles as the light caught and flashed the richness of the panther heads. The blond woman sucked in a ragged breath at its beauty.

"I guess this is goodbye then." She blinked rapidly, wanting only to get out of this room, but her feet seemed to have taken up a permanent relationship with the wood flooring.

"Goodbye, Shasta."

It was the use of her name that released her; the gentleness of each drawn out syllable was nearly her undoing. She whirled around and walked out, only to stop outside the door as she heard Karen gushing over *her* bracelet.

"Kane, honey, it's absolutely gorgeous. May I wear it?"

The gall, Shasta thought, and cocked her head to hear Kane's reply.

"Sure, baby. Keep it. I've no use for it anymore."

She hadn't realized she'd been holding her breath, waiting for his answer, hoping deep down that he would snatch the bracelet from the woman's hands and come after her, begging her forgiveness. But wishes don't always come true in the real world, she'd just found that out the hard way, and love was a fantasy she hoped she'd never experience again. The hurt was too damn painful. Straightening her shoulders, she continued on her way, seeing only what was before her; everything else was a haze of color, sounds and smells. She even missed the man lounging against the door, another eavesdropper whose rugged face was a study in puzzlement and anger.

KANE IGNORED THE CHATTERING WOMAN beside him and walked over to the window, looking out on the driveway below. He deliberately blanked out his thoughts and tilted the glass up to drain the contents, trying to numb his body as well as his mind. His fixed stare caught movement below, and he edged closer to the window. There she was, walking slowly, carefully down the front steps. *It's best this way, mouse. You'll see and someday forgive me.* She reached her car and was opening the door. His knuckles whitened around the heavy crystal glass as he watched her make her way down the long drive. Standing there with bleak eyes, he followed her till the taillights disappeared out of the gates and turned onto the street. "Goodbye love," he whispered.

"Come on, Kane, let's party!"

He was startled from his stupor by a woman's shrill voice, and he turned savagely on her. "Get out of here, you stupid, greedy bitch."

"But, honey?"

"Out!" he yelled, and left the window to pour himself another drink. He'd done the right thing; he knew he had. So why did the feeling persist that he'd just ruined his life and nothing would ever be good again? Returning to the window, he gazed out, seeing only the bleakness of what was to come.

"You're a fool and an ass."

Kane turned his head, his eyes following Lucas DeSalva as he moved across the room in that peculiar soundless way of his. He frowned, irritation stamped clearly across his brow at the intrusion. "Back off, Lucas. This isn't your concern."

"Maybe, maybe not. But it looks as if I'm going to interfere all the same, doesn't it? I'll repeat, you're a fool to let her go."

Kane's gaze returned to the window and the dark night beyond.

"She's worth fighting for." Lucas sat on the corner of the desk, his foot swinging back and forth.

"You don't know what you're talking about—it's over."

"Is it?" Lucas pushed off the desk and walked slowly to the door. He stopped and turned. "Is it over when you'll see her everywhere you go? She loves you desperately, Kane, but she's a strong woman. She'll eventually get over you. Can you say the same? And late at night when you're unable to sleep, will you picture Shasta in bed with another man?" The color drained from Kane's face. "Can you accept the reality of another man making love to her? Shasta's a hell of a woman and not so easily dismissed."

"But not your type, Lucas?"

Lucas paused thoughtfully for a long moment. "No, not my style." He saw Kane's tense shoulders sag a fraction in relief. "She's too untamed for my taste, too much like you Kane. But she's Brandon's type." He let his words soak in, then went on. "He'd been sniffing around before you showed up." Lucas shrugged and lit a cigarette, watching Kane over the flame, grinning to himself at the other man's clenched jaw and the flash of anger in his unusual eyes. "I imagine after a little time passes she'll be receptive to his offer to help her forget. After all, Brandon can be damn amusing, and I'm also told from numerous sources that he's a strong, imaginative lover." He wheeled around, letting his last words float over his shoulder as he left the room.

Kane's brooding gaze followed Lucas's departure, the threat still hanging heavily in the air long after he'd gone. Hell, why shouldn't she have lovers? He didn't plan to remain celibate. But the thought of her with another man sent a chill through him, and he knew he'd never be warm again. Laughing brown eyes full of mischief haunted him. He picked up the nearest bottle of liquor, wrenched off the cap, put it to his lips and took several long swallows. The burning liquid didn't set the fire in his gut he'd hoped for; instead it seemed to freeze there like a lump of ice. Why couldn't he take what was offered? She didn't care about his past or what he was; she loved him just the same. He set the bottle to his lips and turned it up. Why?

The voice in his head that had told him repeatedly he wasn't good enough was strangely quiet. Kane upended the bottle once more and asked himself the question again. Why? Only silence and a kind of peace came in reply, and he suddenly realized that he'd forgiven himself for his unspeakable behavior in the past. He'd accepted responsibly for what he'd done to his life and others and was granted freedom from his own imprisonment.

The bottle dropped to the floor, its contents spilling in a great pool as Kane sat down in the nearest chair and buried his face in his hands. He'd do it right this time—step by step. Washington was tomorrow, then he'd return and take what was his—and she was his; right or wrong he'd never let her go again. Lucas was right. He'd been the biggest kind of fool and ass, and he'd spend the rest of his life making up for the pain he'd caused.

SHASTA PULLED INTO HER DRIVEWAY, totally oblivious to the fact that she was home. She didn't even remember the drive, and it was only Baskerville's frantic barking from the house that roused her out of her dazed state. Like a robot, she entered her house and went through her nightly routine. She knew this evening would hold no rest for her, and she'd never be able to close her eyes. As if she was numb to all that had happened to her, she calmly fixed herself a Scotch and water and curled up at the end of the couch. All the way home she had tried to put the rest of her life into perspective, but her mind refused to think about her future. Instead her thoughts wanted to relive the events of the last hour, and that she absolutely refused to permit. Kane was out of her life forever. It was over.

She relaxed her tightly clenched fist, rubbing her palms together to return the circulation and smooth away the nail marks on her skin. She had her life to lead, and there were going to be some drastic changes. The hard lump in her throat threatened to choke her and she sipped her drink, grimacing at the medicinal taste. She felt hot and cold at the same time and her eyes ached with unshed tears. She'd shed bucketsful for the past three days, and now was the time to plan, not wallow in self-pity.

Her chest throbbed painfully and she placed her hand over her heart, then almost laughed hysterically. What heart? Kane had torn it out that evening, and she'd left it lying on the hardwood floor of Max's library. She cleared her throat and shook her head to dispel the maudlin thoughts. That part of her life was over. Her hand trembled as she brought the glass to her lips.

Oh God, Kane. Why? The words screamed in her mind and she almost choked on the swallow she'd taken. No! He was no longer a part of her life, her future, and she must forget his very existence. But she'd made so many plans for them together. Again she put mental brakes to her thoughts.

The idea of returning to her daily routine was disheartening. Her eyes narrowed. Maybe Kane's desertion was the catalyst she needed to spur her on to other things. Maybe it was time she broke the ties with her family and sought the life she'd always wanted. There was a whole world out there, and she was ready for some danger and excitement. And there would be men in abundance willing to help heal the wounds.

Shasta squeezed her eyes tightly together. Who was she trying to fool? What man could even compare with Kane? For the little time they had shared he'd shown her what it was to be loved. Deep down she knew she'd never find that love again. There would be no fairy-tale, happily-ever-after ending now. Almost angrily she thought that her grandfather had lied to her—she wasn't like the rest of her family after all. She buried her face in her hands and for one last time wondered what she was going to do without Kane.

CHAPTER FIFTEEN

"So it's true, the formula's gone?"

Shasta absently took a sip of tea, her eyes studying Max Stone intently over the rim of the delicate china cup. She silently questioned her sanity for coming here. It hadn't been necessary for her to hand deliver the final report and file to Max, but even after a month's absence she wasn't ready to return home and face her family. She took another sip of tea and grimaced, thinking of the phone call that had awakened her early that morning. J.T. had tracked her down and ordered her return to the States—preferably Dallas—so he could personally give her a piece of his mind. And because she'd been sleepy and disoriented, and dreadfully homesick just hearing his voice, she'd agreed.

Kane's father thumped his cup down with a clatter, rose to his impressive height and stomped across the suite's sitting room to the well-stocked bar. After a few seconds he regained his dignity and faced Shasta. "After a year of hard work and an enormous outlay of money, it all went up in ashes. What a stupid, senseless waste! You're sure the formula was destroyed?"

Shasta nodded, refusing to give voice to his question—one he had asked repeatedly since she arrived at his hotel. Instead she eyed the silver tray crowded with sandwiches and cakes. The Dorchester was famous for their high teas and her stomach growled in protest of weeks of neglect.

The soft muted sounds of pacing caught her attention, and she gritted her teeth. Max's muttering stretched her already frayed nerves to the snapping point. Not once since she had brought the twenty-page report to London had he inquired about Kane's health or whereabouts. His only concern was to establish the facts of the formula and to make absolutely certain that it might not one day surface and someone lay claim to what should have been his victory.

Max tipped the glass, draining the contents, and Shasta's throat tightened. Older and thinner than Kane, and with a thick head of salt-and-pepper hair, Max Stone fascinated and repulsed her.

"I appreciate you bringing the completed report to me in person." He smiled, but the calculating hardness in his eyes didn't soften. "The preliminary report you sent a month ago would have sufficed if Kane had bothered to tell his story."

"Kane's had other things on his mind lately. I'm sure he'll contact you soon." Why was she defending Kane, Shasta wondered.

"He's a damn fool to think he could force Tramble to do anything. Besides, dead is dead. There's nothing to gain from digging further into Kimble's death. Let the French police handle the mess."

"Mr. Stone, Kane cared deeply for the professor...."

"Bull! My son cares for nothing in this world but his own hide and his pleasures." He eyed Shasta coldly, taking in her shapely, petite form and revealing face. His gaze honed in on her changing expression, and a sly smile slid across his mouth. "Well, well. Maybe I should reread that report and pay closer attention to what's between the lines." He returned to the chair across from Shasta and continued. "You know, Shasta—" he made a

steeple with his fingers and rested his chin on it thoughtfully "—with your grandfather's reputation and your
family's wealth, I wouldn't be adverse to a merger between the Stones and the Mastersons."

"Wha...what?"

"Come now, you're not going to try and tell me that
you and Kane weren't—lovers? If you're as smart as I
think you are, you're already carrying my grandson."

Shasta sat horrified by what he was saying, but his next
words brought her up and out of her chair.

"With your family's power and prestige, and by my
pressuring Kane, we could persuade him to accept his responsibilities. At some time his mother must have taught
him about chivalry. He could be swayed into doing the
correct thing and marry you. Maybe that would give him
some purpose in life."

"Mr. Stone! I'm not pregnant, nor do I wish to marry
your son." She hurriedly gathered up her belongings and
stood. He was everything Kane said he was and more.

Max's defeat was as visible as a deflated balloon, and
he sagged in his chair.

Shasta felt a pang of sympathy as age seemed to suddenly catch up with the old devil, but before she could
voice any trite, consoling words, she hardened her soft
heart. Blood ran true to form between father and son, she
reminded herself. She felt awkward standing there with
her purse in hand and her briefcase clutched to her breast
while he stared at her. "If I don't leave now Mr. Stone,
I'll miss my flight out of Heathrow."

Her voice snapped him out of his stupor and he apologized. "I'll call my chauffeur and have him drive you."

"That's not necessary."

"I insist." He rode with her in the elevator and
together they walked out to the waiting limousine. "I'll

be returning to Houston just as soon as my business is completed here, probably in a week, so if you have anything further to add to the report, give me a call at the office.''

Stiff and correct, Shasta politely said the right things and crawled into the limousine, allowing herself to relax only when the car pulled away from the curb. For a few seconds she stared at the soothing calm of Hyde Park and the orderly greenery of trees and manicured shrubs. She leaned back against the rich leather and closed her weary eyes as the long car glided through London traffic.

She was going home. After almost a month of risk-taking and danger, she hoped she'd faced all her demons and conquered the ache in her heart. There were a few loose ends to tie up, then she would be off again. How she loved the freedom. The only thing she had to make sure of was that her work schedule would keep her out of France and Switzerland. Those two countries seemed to be Kane's favorites, and she knew that though she'd come to terms with her loss, she didn't have the strength to come face to face with him. She tightened her hold on her briefcase as memory upon memory stacked on top of one another. Dear God! Would she ever be free of his haunting image?

SHASTA'S SLOW STEPS carried her down the long corridor of the Dallas airport. Groups of people milled around the terminal juggling hand luggage and all-weather coats. Darkness had long since made its claim on the sky, bringing an unexpected nip in the air. As Shasta walked toward customs, fragments of conversations penetrated her jet-lagged state, and she smiled. The topic, of course, was the crazy Texas weather.

"Shasta, Shasta!"

She recognized Julie's husky voice before she spotted him and gave a little wave. She presented her passport to the overworked customs official and answered the necessary questions, but when he asked her to open the brown alligator briefcase she'd hand carried from London, she presented him with a small sheaf of permits and official documents.

The agent's face brightened with excitement, his black skin taking on a shine of anticipation after hours of boredom. "Mr. Lawerence is waiting for you in room two." He pointed over his shoulder with his thumb, his eyes eagerly searching for one of his co-workers to take over his position. Spotting a willing nod, he signaled and escorted Shasta to the room set aside for questioning and private business.

Shasta shot a speaking glance to a now-worried Julie, averting his uneasiness with a cock of her head and a bright smile. Ten minutes later she emerged, exhausted but relieved to be rid of her dangerous burden. A suave, fashionably dressed man now carried the brown alligator briefcase, tailed by two overdeveloped body-guards.

"Damn, kid, you look beat," grumbled Julius. "Ain't no one told you you're supposed to sleep now and then? Was that Benoit Lawerence of Lawerence Jewelers?"

"Yes."

"And you were carrying diamonds for them from London?"

"Diamonds and other stones."

Julius's bushy eyebrows drew together. He clasped her elbow firmly and led her out to the waiting Silver Cloud Rolls-Royce. Shasta's eyes didn't even widen as Julius helped her in, then slipped into the driver's seat.

She rested her head back and closed her eyes for a few seconds before she turned around. "Hello, pappy."

J. T. Masterson's heavy lids drooped farther over his eyes, concealing his concern, as he studied his granddaughter's strained face. "Burning the candle at both ends, Peewee?"

The childish nickname brought a lump to her throat and she swallowed hard before she could answer. "Looks that way, doesn't it? But I'm okay now." She forced a smile and tried to change the subject. "How's everyone?"

J.T. shook his silvery head and clucked his tongue, bringing another soft smile to Shasta's lips. She knew she was about to be reprimanded. "I taught you that maneuver, don't pull it on me."

"Yes, sir."

"And don't get sassy, either."

They were killing time and each of them knew it. They fell silent. Shasta sighed, dreading the inevitable, knowing that she was going to have to hurt her grandfather in order to have a life of her own. She let her gaze drift to the moving lights outside the car windows. The route home was one she could drive in her sleep, and when they reached the tree-lined streets of Highland Park she wondered if she would have the strength to fight her family. She was tired, emotionally and physically, and incapable of her usual logical judgment, a weakness J.T. would use to his advantage if necessary.

Julie stopped the car at the crest of the driveway and Shasta climbed out without looking at the Regency-style brick house she had called home for so many years. Dead on her feet, she dragged her lagging steps through the open door, mumbled a greeting to their butler, Sampson, and continued on her way to the living room.

She inhaled deeply, straightening her shoulders and
turned to face her adversaries. Suddenly she was eager
for this confrontation, wanting only to have it over and
done with. But as she whirled around, she caught the concern and love on the faces of her beloved men and gulped
down the harsh words she'd been about to pour out.
"Oh, pappy." She walked into his arms and reached out
for Julie's hand. "It's just a broken heart not a fatal
disease. I'll get over it." She squeezed Julie's hand and
leaned back in her grandfather's embrace.

"I best make us some hot chocolate," Julius said gruffly and left them alone.

"There's no use beating around the bush, Shasta.
Kane has made a pest of himself trying to locate you.
Something has to be done."

Shasta stiffened and turned away. "I don't want to see
him, pappy. Not now when the hurt is still fresh."

"I think you should. No, I think you must," he said
cryptically, struggling hard to hide the warring emotions
churning with each heartbeat. Should he tell her that
Kane was flying to Dallas tomorrow to meet with him? A
crafty smile touched the corners of his mouth, then immediately disappeared as he caught her staring at him.

"No, pappy. In this case I know what's best for me.
Kane will eventually get bored with his new game and
give up."

"Don't you even want to know why he's raising so
much hell looking for you?"

"Not particularly, no." But her heart contradicted her
words with a pounding roar in her ears.

Her expressionless voice sent a chill through J.T. and
he deemed it prudent to change the subject. He scowled
at Shasta and motioned for her to be seated. "You have
totally disrupted this family for a month." She opened

her mouth and he held up his hand. "No, young lady. You're going to hear me out, then we'll see if we can't come up with some solution to your problems."

Shasta sagged back in her chair and angrily crossed her arms like a petulant child. She shifted her gaze from J.T. to Julie and sighed. It was a wasted effort to try to out-maneuver these two. She eagerly accepted the steaming mug of hot chocolate, liberally laced with cherry liqueur and topped with whipped cream. "I'm sorry if I've caused you to worry."

"Not me necessarily," J.T. lied. "But your activities and the overseas jobs you took had your mother and father up in arms against Julie and me. They called at least five times a day from Washington to see if I'd heard from you. By the time I answered the other daily inquiries...." His voice trailed off as he glared fiercely at her from under his heavy eyelids.

"Pappy, I can't go back to the Houston office—I'll suffocate and die there. This isn't something that's just happened recently, and it's not all Kane's fault, either, though our situation cleared the air." She jumped up and began to pace, totally exhausting her grandfather.

"Sit down," he ordered. "Now," he said, fighting to keep his expression stern. "Julie and I have had a long discussion about this, and he's in full agreement with you."

Shasta's mouth fell open and she shot a surprised glance at Julie.

"You ain't gone and forgot that I was in prison once? I know what it's like to be caged." He glared at J.T., then hastily amended his words. "It ain't fair to keep you penned in."

"As usual, Julie's gotten right to the point, though somewhat indelicately. What we've agreed to—"

"Now wait just one minute, you two. You're doing it again, trying to run my life."

"Well, hell, kid!" Julius burst out. "Someone has to. You've made a mess of things lately what with all your running around carrying jewels and such. I ain't never heard of some of the dim-witted stunts you've pulled this past month."

Shasta scowled at Julie, knowing he was right. At times she'd even scared herself with her recklessness. Shasta was a little ashamed now, facing the two men who had taught her above all else to be careful. Her gaze dropped to the Persian rug. "Sorry. I guess I did take some rather foolish risks."

J.T. snorted in disgust. "Now are you willing to hear us out quietly before you jump to any further arguments?" Shasta nodded. "Good. First of all I never, *never* want to hear of you carrying jewels again. You and I both know those are suicide runs."

"Yes, pappy." She sipped her hot chocolate then, concentrated hard on the floating glob of melting whipped cream.

J.T. allowed himself a tiny smile, knowing the meekness she portrayed for the act it was. "Second—you may leave the Houston office. But your investment in the company must stay to keep it solvent for Jeff and Rena's sake till I can think of something. They have their dreams too, Shasta, and it's only right you do this, since you're pulling out with no forewarning."

Shasta's head shot up, her attention riveted on her grandfather as his words sent a jolt of adrenaline through her tired nervous system. Was he going to let her go without a fight?

Like a mind reader J.T. answered her unasked question. "Yes, you're free. I'm just sorry I didn't realize I was doing wrong a long time ago. This old fool—" he pointed to Julie "—tried to warn me, but I was too bull-headed to listen. Now I figure any upheaval is on my shoulders." He smiled but shook his finger at her. "However, there are some rules."

Shasta's grin grew, happiness removing the tension lines in her face. "What rules?"

"As much as I'd like to think that Julie is loyal to me, I know I'd only be lying to myself. I'd never be able to keep him here if he thought you needed him. So it's up to you two to decide what you want to do. But I would like to make one suggestion." J.T. leaned forward and became serious. "No matter how smart, experienced and tough you think you are, there are always men just one step ahead of you. It's always better to have a friend at your back, and I'd sleep a hell of a lot better if I knew that whenever you plan taking a job in Europe you'd take Julie with you. He's moped around with his feelings hurt this past month till I thought I was going to have to send him after you."

The full force of her irresponsible actions hit her, and she jumped out of her chair and wrapped her arms around Julie's shoulders. She'd forgotten for a while that he'd practically raised her. He'd given her his greatest gifts, teaching her his trade and loving her unquestionably all her life.

"Forgive me, Julie, but this past month I just need-ed. . . ." She trailed off, unsure of how to put her feelings into words.

"To put your head on straight after that man turned it around backward?" He ducked his head, blinking away the excess moisture that stung his eyes.

"Something like that," she said softly.

"If you two would quit crying all over each other I'd

like some thanks and appreciation, too." J.T.'s gruff voice made them laugh.

"Sure, pappy. Even an interfering old busybody needs a hug."

"Now don't get mushy, Shasta." He returned her embrace with a force that took her breath away. "You know how I loathe water spots on my suits." He held her at arm's length. "Will you take some jobs from Masters now and then? Do you need any money?"

"Yes and no." She laughed at his disgusted expression. "It will be strange to be free-lancing on my own." Looking her grandfather straight in the eye, she went on. "But exciting. And I think you of all people can understand that feeling."

"Don't let all this go to your head just yet. You have to face Jeff and Rena and make your peace with them."

"Tomorrow, if you'll lend me the jet and pilot so I can get to Houston early. Then I think I'll go on to Aspen to ski awhile. Julie can meet me there later."

J.T. shook his head and got up. "Not even working a job yet and she's off on vacation." He turned at the door. "Don't forget the keys to the ski lodge." Then he mumbled, "I must be getting old. She's never needed a key in her life."

"WELL, IF IT ISN'T the family renegade sneaking back in town to clear out her office before anyone can catch her stealing away into the night." Rena's voice was as cold as her blue eyes.

Shasta knew there'd be a confrontation with her brother and sister-in-law, and somewhere in the back of her mind she had thought it would be Jeff who would give her the most trouble. "Listen, Rena. . . ." She set the half-full box aside and walked toward her glaring sister-in-law.

"No, you listen, Shasta Masterson. You're making a fool of yourself. The way you're acting anyone would think you'd just lost your husband of twenty years to another woman."

"Rena!"

"Jeff's been almost out of his mind with worry." The crystalline-blue eyes turned even icier. "He blames himself for not stepping in and stopping the affair before it began. Damn you, Shasta, Kane Stone is not a god. He's only one man, and there are plenty of others in this world. Stop being a martyr and acting like you're the only one to suffer from a broken heart. Inflicting your tantrums on others is beginning to become boring!"

"Rena, please. Shut up! None of this—" she waved her hand around the office, indicating the piles of personal belongings "—none of this has anything to do with Kane."

"No?" Rena questioned, and a frown began to mar her smooth, pale forehead.

"No." Shasta smiled at her confusion. "Sit down. There are a few things you should know that even Jeff, bless his heart, doesn't know about me." She told Rena of all her destroyed dreams and the restraints that had held her back. "So you see, now's my chance."

"I didn't know you felt this way, Shasta." She was genuinely shocked, and her wide eyes and open mouth expressed her surprise more than words. "We've been friends—close friends for four years, and I never understood why you were so unhappy at times." Her eyes narrowed. "But Kane's part of this, isn't he?"

Shasta couldn't help but chuckle. Rena was as much a romantic as her brother.

"Shasta, you can't give up everything and everyone you love because of a disastrous affair."

"Rena, you're not listening to what I'm saying. Stop thinking love and romance. Think freedom. Did you know that years ago J.T. talked me out of joining the FBI and the CIA? That was only one of many shattered dreams. Now I'm going to do exactly what I want for a change."

"But Kane...."

The continued reference to Kane was getting on her nerves. With a great deal of willpower she'd deliberately forced him from her thoughts, refusing to think of what had been between them. She'd made her mind numb to any intruding memories, and Rena's constant reminders were upsetting the fragile hold she had on her overtaxed emotions.

"You say you want to be free. Free to do what?" Rena began slowly and nonchalantly unpacking the box sitting on top of Shasta's desk. "Oh, I know financially you're fixed for life whether you ever work another day or not. You're too old and set in your ways to be of any use to those government agencies." She smiled at Shasta's grimace. "Well, really, don't they like to get their recruits young and brainwash them or something? And please don't tell me you're going to continue this mad, dangerous dash you've been on lately? You'll give the entire family heart attacks."

Shasta gently removed the box from Rena's clutches and began to throw her personal belongings back in it. "I won't be so reckless anymore."

Totally exasperated, Rena pulled the box out of Shasta's hands and automatically rearranged the mess in an orderly fashion. "Are you going to continue working as an international courier?"

Shasta nodded. "I promise I'll be very careful."

"What about Julie and Baskerville?" Her voice

cracked a little as she went on. "What about Lizzie, Jeff and *me*," she wailed softly. "Will we ever see you again?"

The box was torn from Rena's hands and sent flying across the room, the contents spilling in a rolling heap on the floor. "Damn you, Rena Masterson, don't you cry." Shasta grabbed her arms and shook her hard. "I'm not going to change my name and move to another country, for heaven's sake. The way you talk you'd think I was dying or something." Rena's limp body collapsed without further assistance into a nearby chair. "Now, this time you listen to me. Julie and I have worked out a happy arrangement to our problems. As for Baskerville, he goes with me unless I'm in Europe."

She moved back to the side of the desk and with a slight hop sat on the edge. The bright smile she gave Rena should have set off warning bells in the woman's head. "You know how Lizzie loves Baskerville, and I thought that since you're the official dog sitter I'd leave him at your house in between jobs." Her smile slipped a little at Rena's blank look. "He's on the wagon now and hasn't been any trouble, has he? Rena, say something."

"Baskerville's fine—so is Lizzie, and you're right, she worships him to the point that she only rides on his back three or four times a day, now that we've explained he's not her personal pony." Her expression was still a little vague as she said absently, "That's not what's bothering me." She sighed. "I was just thinking how little I really know about you. Unfortunately, like the rest of your family, I've only seen what was on the surface or what was convenient for me to see." She slipped out of her chair and hugged Shasta. "I hope you'll be happy at whatever you decide to do, and don't worry about Jeff. I'll take care of him."

"And what, dear wife, are you planning to do to me?" Jeff asked from the open doorway. His tall good looks were marred by a distinct untidiness that was evident only when he was tied to his computer. He ran his fingers through his thick blond hair, and his eyes slid away from Shasta's steady stare. "Hi, sis."

"Jeff, Shasta was explaining—is something the matter? Are you sick?" Rena was all concern, and Jeff quickly gave her a kiss on the cheek to ward off any further questions.

"Nothing's the matter," he said, his voice a little too hardy to convince Shasta that he wasn't up to something.

"Okay, out with it," she demanded, and Jeff jumped. "What have you done?"

"Me? Listen, sis. I talked to J.T., and he's explained everything. I hate to see you leave, but if it's truly what you want then I'm all for it."

"Jeff, you're trying to evade my question. What are you up to?"

Jeff fidgeted around the office, ignoring his sister's sharp gaze and his wife's thoughtful one as he absently picked up and replaced objects off the desk and shelves. "Well, actually, there is a problem." He pulled out Shasta's chair and sat down, folding his hands together to still their nervous twitch. "The McKinneys' security system was completed yesterday, and I need you to check it out."

"But, Jeff—"

"No," he said sternly and frowned, shocking both women. "This is still part your company, and you made the McKinney commitment in good faith, so you'll stick by your word. *I* insist." He seemed proud of his firm stand, and his square chin stuck out farther.

Shasta eyed Jeff suspiciously, then leaned over the desk and kissed him on the cheek. "If I have to work tonight, I'd better go get my equipment organized." She picked up her box of personal belongings and headed for the door.

"Oh, Shasta." Rena stopped her. "You'd better call Samantha and Boston. They left for Santa Fe last week, but she's called nearly every other day wanting to know if we'd heard from you." Rena chuckled. "You know Sammy, at first she tried to hide the fact that she was also trying to find out your whereabouts for Kane. Then out of guilt, I guess, she confessed her duplicity. She's afraid that when you find out you'll think she was only calling to help Kane and not truly concerned about you. So please call her if only to ease her conscience."

Shasta agreed. She gave one last glance around her office and prepared to leave, but she still couldn't take her gaze from Jeff's guilty expression. Why, she asked herself, did she have a funny feeling in the pit of her stomach and that familiar tingling at the back of her neck? The warning signs were all there, and why did Jeff's nervousness bring with it the strange sensation that her grandfather had something to do with his discomfort? She shrugged. After all, there was nothing her grandfather could do to interfere with her life now!

CHAPTER SIXTEEN

KANE STOOD at the long line of windows in the lobby of
the Adolphus hotel, heedless of the opulent grandeur
around him. Limousines, taxis and expensive cars loaded and unloaded their elegant passengers as he watched,
searching each elderly man for something familiar in a
face, a hint of Shasta in the coloring or the flash of a
smile.

He rubbed his damp palms along his pant leg and
gave a bark of laughter. Anyone who saw him and
noticed the perspiration that gathered periodically
across his forehead would think it was a blistering day
and that the hotel's air conditioning wasn't working.
Actually a blue norther had hit Dallas and the temperature was dropping steadily. What Kane was feeling was
raw fear.

It had been a month since the night of his party. A
month of trying to track Shasta down, but to no avail.
He scowled, the signs of fatigue and worry biting deeper
into the hollow caverns of his face. In his own conceit
and arrogance it had never once crossed his mind that
when he returned to Houston she wouldn't be waiting
for him. All his life women had fallen at his feet, but he
should have remembered that Shasta was an original.
With his usual insolence he hadn't even considered her
disappearing and leaving him flat. Why hadn't he gone
straight to her that night? Because, he derided himself,

he was a pompous boor whose easy conquests had gone to
his head and impaired his judgment. He'd made mistakes
in his life, but underrating Shasta was the worst of them
all.

Now he'd come begging to her grandfather, J. T.
Masterson. He, who had never felt it necessary to explain his actions, was in for a rough time. Shasta's entire family was aware of his search. He'd seen to that
with all the hell he'd raised, but his demands had only
met with stony expressions, vicious tongue lashings and
threats that if he didn't stay out of her life, his own
wouldn't be worth living.

How could he have been so stupid as to leave Houston without going to Shasta's? He berated himself over
and over with the same question. The only answer he
could think of shamed him deeper than any event in his
past. If he'd gone to Shasta that night she would have
won, and he couldn't accept losing control of his situation. To hell with male pride! When he'd realized his
own motives he was even more outraged. He thought
he'd learned to behave like a modern, intelligent man,
and it rankled to know that he was a throwback to the
primitive Neanderthal, dragging his woman around by
her hair. Shasta certainly had her work cut out to
straighten him up—if he ever found her.

He was sweating again. The thought of dealing with
Shasta's grandfather sent a shudder through his body.
Over the past month he'd heard enough about J.T., the
shark, to last a lifetime and then some. Kane quickly unbuttoned his vest, shifted his shoulders beneath the confines of his coat and grimaced. The conservative gray
pin-striped suit ill suited his finicky taste. His tailor at
London's Turnbull & Asser would have hysterics if he
knew he'd bought off the rack. He rebuttoned the vest

and shoved his hands in his slacks pocket, then pulled them out again to check the time. The old devil had kept him cooling his heels for twenty-six and a half minutes.

Kane began scanning the traffic outside again when he froze, a feeling of hope and dread coursing through him as a vintage Silver Cloud Rolls-Royce glided to the entrance of the hotel. Porters and doormen snapped to attention as the luxurious car pulled to a stop. As he watched, the back door swung open and Julie stepped out. He turned, his hand extended to assist the passenger, and Kane grinned as the helpful offer was declined with a whack across Julie's palm by a thin gold-tipped cane. Then his attention focused on the silver-haired old man who descended from the car and straightened to his full height; he cut an impressive figure, and there was enough hauteur in his expression to shrivel the strongest of men.

Kane's head began to ache, his lips were dry and his eyes felt like a pound of sand had been poured into them. His palms were as sweaty as a teenager's on his first date. With a flash of wry humor he thought he might faint, his heart was pounding so hard in his chest. But he pulled himself together as he watched the two men entering the hotel's glass portals, and he moved to meet them.

"Mr. Masterson." He stuck out his hand to receive the older man's firm shake and a once-over, lightning glance from those disconcerting cobalt-blue eyes. "Julie, it's good to see you again." He looked back at J.T. "Thank you for seeing me."

The old man shrugged and pointed with his cane to a nearby table. "Shall we sit over there out of the way of prying eyes and big ears?" At Kane's raised eyebrow, J.T. laughed. "Shasta's cousins have been checking you

out, seems they're better at the game than I thought."
He turned to Julie. "Remind me to give the boys a
bonus."

Kane should have known he was being watched, but
his mind was distracted by more important things, and
he plunged into his prepared speech. "Mr. Masterson...."

"Might as well call me J.T." He lowered himself
slowly into an antique French chair, placed his cane between his legs and folded his hands over the crooked
handle.

"J.T., I have to know where Shasta is. I've exhausted
all means of finding her, and everywhere I turn I meet
stone walls. Even her father doesn't know, or else he's
not telling."

"My son is going to run for Congress and can't be
bothered with his daughter's problems at the moment.
And you needn't clench your jaw at that, young man.
I'm the one who can control Shasta and my son's wise
enough to be aware of that fact, so he's left it to me to
settle this mess." He leaned forward, studying Kane.
"We're a close family, and what hurts one hurts us all.
You've managed to cause us a great deal of pain lately."

Kane wondered if he would get a chance to explain or
if every time he tried he was going to be interrupted. He
looked at Julie, caught the laughter in his eyes and
frowned. He could find no humor in the situation. "Believe me, J.T., from the very beginning I've been aware
of the problems I've caused. I tried to explain this to
Shasta, but she wouldn't listen. Now I want to make up
for all the hurt, but how can I do that if I can't find
Shasta. Where is she?" He was fast losing patience. A
month of worry and wanting had taken its toll. He refused to play a cat-and-mouse game with this old man

any longer. "Where is she?" he demanded once again, his eyes flashing with determination.

"I'd like to establish a few facts before I tell you—if I tell," he corrected himself and smiled.

"No, sir," Kane shot back. "I'll tell you nothing. What's between Shasta and me is private, and until *we* settle our problems it's our affair."

J. T. Masterson had never been talked back to like this and it didn't sit well. He sent a grinning Julie a murderous look. "You find this amusing. You set me up, didn't you? Told me Kane would come crawling on his hands and knees and I could have some fun." Julius threw back his head and laughed. "You keep it up, you old goat, my day will come." He returned his attention to Kane and quickly stuck out his cane as he saw the young man rising to leave. "No, stay. I apologize, but I'm an old man with little to entertain myself with these days, and Julie and I are always pulling tricks on each other. I'm sorry you're the brunt of one of his jokes."

"If you won't tell me where Shasta is, then tell me where she's been and I'll pick up the trail from there." He couldn't believe what was happening to him. Here he was fighting for his life, and two overgrown jokers were having fun at his expense.

"For the past month she's been working on her own." Shasta's grandfather frowned fiercely at Kane. "She was moving from place to place like a person possessed."

"Where is she?" Kane demanded.

J.T. studied Kane more carefully this time and saw the haggardness in his face. "She was working as a special courier carrying merchandise from Antwerp to Tel Aviv and Lisbon for a while."

Kane's face lost all color, leaving his skin a pasty

white. The Antwerp route could only mean the diamond market and the most dangerous run any courier could make. He bolted out of his chair, but Julie's next words stopped him.

"She ain't working over there no more, Kane. She's going free-lance and will be hopping around all over the place soon."

Kane's heart resumed its normal beat and he sat down. "Where," he said hoarsely, "is she now?" Then he did something he'd never done in his life, he begged. "Please!"

J.T. pulled out a business card, turned it over and wrote something on the back. He held it between two fingers, ready to tear it up if he didn't receive the answer he wanted. "I can only assume by this urgency to see me and your reaction to what she's been up to that you care a great deal for my granddaughter. But I want to hear it from your lips before I hand her over to you."

Kane swallowed his pride and his anger. "I love Shasta, Mr. Masterson, and I'll do anything I can to get her back." J.T. handed him the card and Kane memorized the address before he looked up. "I've hurt Shasta deeply and for that I'm truly sorry, but at the time I thought I was doing the best thing for her."

The older men shook Kane's hand, and as he turned to leave, Julius stopped him. "There's something you better know that J.T. ain't told you." He shot an irksome glance at his friend and employer, his bushy eyebrows a straight line over his eyes. "Early tomorrow morning Shasta leaves for Colorado, so don't put off talking to her. Good luck." He clasped Kane on the shoulder and smiled tightly. "You're going to need it."

292   CHARADE

A BLUE NORTHER swept over Houston as the sun was sinking deeper into the sky. The crisp air could set teeth to chattering in the unprepared, those doubters who didn't believe that in a matter of minutes Houston's balmy temperatures could drop to near freezing.

Shasta was a believer. Bundled in light down-padded clothes and leather jacket, she sat on the edge of a red tiled roof, cursing the tangle of ropes in her hands. Her salty vocabulary grew even spicier as the chill wind bit at her nose and exposed cheeks.

"If it isn't just like Jeff to insist on a systems check on a night like this!" she grumbled out loud, her words forming a puffy white cloud before her. But then, she conceded, it wasn't Jeff's fault at all. Who could predict Texas weather? "I should have listened to the forecast. At least the local weatherman came close to the facts."

She shook her head and pulled the knit cap farther down on her head. In the past month she'd begun talking to herself. Kane's fault. She could lay a number of other strange changes at his feet. His desertion had almost been her undoing, but she'd managed to pull herself together. To learn that he was trying to find her infuriated her beyond belief. To face him again, then have him walk away a second time would have been too much to bear.

Shasta snapped the stiff rope in her hands in a quick movement that dislodged Kane's image from her mind. There was work to be done, and if she didn't want to become a frozen fixture on the rooftop, she'd best get busy. Jumping to her feet, she caught her balance on the chimney and gazed upward. The change in weather had cleared the sky and left the stars glittering like diamonds and the full moon glowing like translucent pearl. She shivered with a sudden feeling of déjà vu. There'd been another night when she'd been on a rooftop beneath a bright full moon. A tormented laugh filled the air and echoed off in the darkness. It was ironic, but from where she stood she could just make out Kane's father's house. Her eyes stung sharply behind the lids, and she stomped her cold foot in anger and frustration, then had to grab the edge of the chimney to keep from sliding forward.

Carefully, methodically, she buckled the harness around her waist, attached the iron hook into the loop on the belt and adjusted the ropes on the small block pulley secured around the chimney. Backing away from the stationary anchor, she slowly let the rope play out between her fingers. When her heels touched the edge of the big glass skylight, she squatted and pulled out her burglar tools, rapidly working the lock open and propping the glass panel securely back. She fished out a tiny flashlight with a high-intensity beam, flashed it around the darkened bedroom below and chuckled.

Jeff truly thought he had her this time. Besides the usual security system he'd installed hidden sensors that reacted to weight and vibrations. Her cunning brother had secured the little devices under the carpet, so that if anything over the weight of two pounds touched them they would send off a whole orchestra of alarms that would blast the peaceful night apart. She had to admit he was a genius, except for one thing. He'd designed his system from the original blueprints of the house, and studying them with him later, she'd seen what he hadn't. While making a tour of the house several months earlier she'd realized that Jeff's blueprints were not complete. The lady of the house had changed her mind at a later date and a skylight had been added to the master bedroom.

Shasta lowered herself down into the yawning hole, stopping midway to allow her vision to become accustomed to the darkness. The first thing her eyes discerned was the shape of the massive king-size bed below. She fished out her tiny flashlight from its special case clipped to her jacket pocket, and a thin stream of light sliced through the blackness. Mentally measuring the space she had to traverse, she returned the flashlight to its holder. Pulling on the ropes, she lowered herself down farther and aligned her body over the middle of the bed—directly across from the huge oil painting hanging above the headboard.

With one powerful move she tipped her body down so that she hung suspended horizontally over the silk covers. Now all she had to do was swing like a pendulum till the momentum carried her to the painting, where she could anchor herself to the frame and open the safe on the other side. She began to wave her arms back and forth, the motion widening the swing of her body.

"Come on," she huffed, the leather harness digging deeper into her stomach and ribs. This was harder than she'd envisioned, and she should have practiced it a few more times before venturing out. "Come on, come on," she muttered again as her fingers barely missed the edge of the ornate frame and she was carried backward. She took one more lunge, her body curved into a half circle, and with all the momentum she could muster she arched outward. But this time she didn't budge an inch. Instead, the snap of the ropes made her lose the rigid control she had on her muscles and she sagged like a rag doll.

"What the hell!" she exclaimed, hanging doubled over at the waist. She took a strangled breath of air and swung herself back into a vertical position, her hands grabbing the ropes in front of her.

"Hello, mouse."

Shasta threw back her head, her eyes riveted to the shadowed outline of the man above her. The numbness she'd tried so hard to hold on to had begun to fail her, and in the past few hours more and more memories of Kane kept creeping into her thoughts. She'd argued and scolded and fought a mental battle with herself, but still the heartache kept rushing back at her like a gushing river overflowing its banks. Now to look up and see him, to hear his voice—she squeezed her eyes tightly shut for a second in pain.

Kane shook the ropes playfully, shaking Shasta back and forth. She mumbled a few choice words under her breath.

"What did you say? Come up here."

"I said go away, Kane. I'm not moving from here till you leave. We have nothing to say to each other, so go away."

"It's cold up here, Shasta, and I have to talk to you." Without another word he stood, and with the aid of the pulley began to haul her now limp body upward. He groaned at her dead weight. "You could help some."

"I'm going to kill you, Kane," she yelled. "How dare you show up here after running out on me. You're a coward, Kane Stone, and I don't want anything to do with you."

"Oh, I dare, mouse. I dare a damn lot lately." He remembered the month he'd spent worrying about her, trying to find her, as he grimly pulled on the ropes. With one last gut-straining tug, he pulled her out of the black hole she'd been dangling in. His breath came in great foggy puffs as he slid down the side of the chimney to sit on the cold tiles. "I think I just gave myself a hernia," he moaned.

Shasta hooked a leg on the sill and crawled over the edge of the skylight, her eyes never leaving Kane's face. She sat down cross-legged just out of his reach, yanked off her knit cap and glared at him, her eyes snapping with temper and a hidden excitement she wasn't prepared to admit. "How did you get past Baskerville?"

Kane caught sight of Shasta's feet and smiled tenderly—she was wearing one black sock and one white one. He sobered his expression immediately as he met her angry glare. She was out for her pound of flesh. "I could have gotten past Baskerville without the beer bribe I brought. He was very happy to see me."

"Of course," said Shasta sarcastically. "You were always sneaking him food and giving him extra bowls of beer. He got fat so I put him on a diet and what happens? He sees his easy touch return and forgets he's supposed to be guarding my back. Traitor!" she yelled into the night, and received an answering whine.

"He's right, Shasta. I am easy." Kane took several deep breaths. "I love you and want you back."

"Don't you dare say that to me! Never again, do you hear me?" She glared at him, her soft full mouth a tight line. "You love only one person—yourself."

"That's not true." He leaned forward in an eager attempt to convince her, but Shasta scooted back, keeping herself out of his reach. Sighing, Kane leaned back as casually as possible. "Didn't they tell you I came back for you?"

She laughed, a hurt sound that wrenched at his heart.

"Oh yes, they told me. And you had your nerve after what you said to me."

"Damn it, Shasta. I made a mistake. Believe me, I realized it almost the instant I sent you away."

"You definitely made a mistake," she agreed. "And coming here is just another to add to your list. I don't want you." She stuck out her chin, her eyes mere slits. "You were different, you amused me, but not anymore. And don't think for one minute that you're the only man in the world for me. There are plenty out there willing to help a girl forget." Her poison arrow hit its mark, and she watched Kane flinch. Why then didn't she feel elated that she'd managed to penetrate his thick hide and return a little of the pain she'd suffered?

"No, mouse," he said softly, "your love couldn't have been so shallow that you're over me this quickly. I know you."

"Know *me*?" she whispered back. "When did you ever try? Every time I showed you who I was, you turned a blind eye. You kept comparing me to other women and your standards for them. You never saw me."

"I did, Shasta. But it's hard to admit that a woman can be so much like a man and still remain loving and feminine." He sent up silent thanks that she was willing to talk and not just throw him off the roof. Shifting his weight, he edged a fraction of an inch closer. If he could only get her into his arms. "Someone told me recently that I was a fool and an ass. He...."

"Was right."

"Yes, he was." Kane moved another inch. "Believe me, I've suffered this last month never knowing where you were or who you might be with." He didn't mention his wild jealousy at the thought of her making love to another man. "Come on, Shasta, forgive me," he wheedled, and smiled a smile destined to bring women to their knees.

"No," she pouted. "Why should I?" She was no different than the rest of the women falling victim to his charms, she realized. Faced with the power of his sensual magnetism, she felt her anger begin to drain away. She rubbed her hand across her eyes. He'd become so much a part of her life—of herself—that at first she hadn't been able to believe it was truly over. There were times when the very air would stand still and she would hear a French accent or see a man who resembled Kane. She would smell his after-shave in the middle of the night and reach for him, only to realize that the fragrance was coming through an open window. He had haunted her like a shadow, never leaving her but only disappearing with the light of day. But she knew she was strong, and as long as she didn't come face to face with him she could make it. She rubbed her hand across her eyes once more as if the action would make him vanish.

Kane had caught the change in her voice and moved a little closer. "Forgive me because I love you."

"No. When you hurt, Kane, you go for the throat. I don't ever want to go through that again."

Kane realized in that instant that Shasta thought he was only coming back for a short while, then would leave her again. He lunged toward her, caught her arms in an unbreakable grip and pulled her, fighting and struggling, across his body, forcing her to straddle his lap and tuck her legs on either side of his hips. He wrapped his arms around her, crushing her small frame to him to stop her escape.

"No, no, no," she wailed. His warmth and strength were her undoing, and a month of holding back broke free as her shoulders began to shake with deep sobs.

"Don't, Shasta. Please, mouse." Awkwardly he patted her back as she cried into the curve of his neck. "Please. Your waterworks are going to freeze my ear off." He received a watery chuckle and squeezed harder.

Shasta drew back and wiped her eyes with the sleeve of her jacket, then turned her liquid brown eyes on Kane. "Why did you do that?"

"What?" Kane smiled as her nose crinkled in distaste when she realized her leather jacket wasn't absorbent. He pushed up his own jacket sleeve and offered her his flannel shirt cuff.

"Why did you touch me? I could have made it if you hadn't." She clasped his hand and rubbed her freezing wet cheeks across the warm material of his shirt. "I can't go through this business of breaking up again, Kane."

He chuckled and dropped his hands to her hips. "Neither can I."

Suddenly aware of how intimately they were touching, Shasta wiggled.

Kane grinned. "Feel how much I've missed you. No, don't say anything, just listen and stop moving around." He closed his eyes for a second, savoring the warmth of her next to him, and when his lids opened, the moonlight showed how dark with desire his silver eyes had become. "I can't believe I'm in this condition sitting on a rooftop in the middle of a norther." Shasta tried again to shift her weight off his lap, but he stopped her. "Don't. No matter how much I complain it feels good just to have you so close."

"Kane, please let me go." His condition was beginning to affect her.

"Not till I'm through talking. Maybe having to contend with two things at once will dull that sharp brain of yours. Be still.''

''I'm cold.''

''Tough. This is the only way I could be sure we'd be alone.'' Looking at her, he couldn't help the smile that touched his lips.

''You're laughing at my red nose.'' She sensed that he was about to launch into a serious conversation, and she wanted to put it off as long as possible. What was he going to offer her this time? First a diamond bracelet to say goodbye.... Now was he going to suggest she become his mistress for as long as he wanted?

''Shasta, you're not listening to me.'' He shook her shoulders gently. ''I said that we'd better get married as soon as possible. I have this feeling that if we wait much longer, J.T. will come after us with a shotgun.''

''Married! J.T.!''

''Besides, how would it look for an up-and-coming congressman to have a daughter flaunting her freedom.''

''Congressman.''

''Who's been feeding you birdseed? You sound like a parrot repeating everything I say.''

''Daddy?''

''You didn't know?''

She shook her head, then for the first time truly realized what he was saying. ''Marriage. You want to marry me?'' She flung herself against his chest and lay there, laughing and crying as she tried to soak it all in. He told her of his meeting with her grandfather and Julie. ''Marriage? You're sure?'' Snuggling further into his embrace, she began to nibble the warm skin above his collar, her lips edging slowly to his ear. She took his cold lobe in her mouth and warmed it with her tongue.

"You didn't—" he sucked in a breath "—give me an answer."

"To what?" she asked, planting tiny kisses along his jaw.

"Shasta, it's too cold out here for these games." He jumped as her hand slipped between their bodies.

"My fingers are cold." Her innocent gaze met his.

"I want you to say—yes."

"Yes," she repeated, and slid her other hand down farther to the warm haven where their bodies touched.

"Stop that." His long, planned speech melted away at her touch. He pulled her hands out. "You'll marry me?" he persisted, wanting a clear answer to the first proposal of marriage he'd ever made.

"Hmm." Shasta licked her cold lips and his eyes followed the movement hungrily. "What happened in Washington?"

It took Kane a long confused moment to realize that she'd changed the subject. "Devil. The meeting went fine. I had to convince certain interested parties that I didn't have a formula for synthetic fuel."

Slanting a look at him from under long lashes, she asked, "Do you think that WSA will allow me to work with you?"

"That's taken care of."

She immediately bristled. "Oh, is it? Just when did you fix things up? And I'd like to know another thing, why the sudden change of heart? When you left for Washington, marriage was the furthest thing from your mind." She was angry all over again and tried to move, but Kane held her securely in place.

"I realized that nothing I've done in the past could compare to the stupidity of giving you up." He wasn't ready to tell her of the hell he'd gone through. This love business was still too new for him to completely reveal his vulnerability to her. It would take time for him to learn to share every part of his life with another person. Openness was not his strong suit, and he'd have to start taking her into his confidence. But he loved her, and love was something he'd never envisioned for himself. Everything else would fall into place with time. He grabbed a handful of delicate curls and pulled her mouth to his. "I'll answer anything you want, but first answer me this." He studied her lovely face and swallowed. "Tell me there were no men in your life this past month."

He was jealous. She could see it in his darkened eyes. "No one, Kane. I just said that to hurt you."

Kane closed his eyes for a brief second in relief. "Now what questions must I answer before we can get off this damn rooftop and into a warm bed?"

Shasta smiled then threw her head back and laughed, a tinkling sound that went straight through him. "Just a few more." She struggled with her expression, then finally gave in and continued smiling at him. "Are you going to buy my clothes?" He frowned. "You know I don't have any taste or knowledge of fashion."

"Okay, agreed."

She snuggled against him, crinkled her nose and touched the cold tip to his. While he was being so magnanimous, she went on, "I've always wanted a Lamborghini."

"Absolutely not. No! Don't do that." He squirmed away from her hands. "No, Shasta. I will not buy you a car for you to kill yourself in. I have you now, and I'm not going to lose you."

Shasta jumped up, held out her hand to him. "Come on, Kane. We have a job to finish."

"That's not funny, Shasta. We're going to your house, crawl between warm covers and make love till dawn." He looked at his watch. "Well, maybe midnight—I've had a rough time this past month."

Shasta ignored him and, whistling began to refasten the leather belt around her waist. "Straighten out those ropes, will you?"

"Now you listen here Shasta Masterson...." But she was already over the edge of the skylight, and he felt the jerk of the rope in his hands. He held it firmly and yanked backward bringing Shasta's head up. Brown eyes aglow with excitement peered at him over the windowsill and he was lost. Like a thief in the night she had stolen his heart with that look. He sighed, if nothing else, life was going to be fun—and, by the looks of it, busy. Bracing himself, he began to play out the rope.

Shasta disappeared into the darkness, then her head popped back up again, a smile flashing bright and loving. "I love you."

HARLEQUIN
PREMIERE AUTHOR EDITIONS

6 EXCITING HARLEQUIN AUTHORS —6 OF THEIR BEST BOOKS!

Daphne Clair
A STREAK OF GOLD

Marjorie Lewty
TO CATCH A BUTTERFLY

Anne Mather
SCORPIONS' DANCE

Jessica Steele
SPRING GIRL

Margaret Way
THE WILD SWAN

Violet Winspear
DESIRE HAS NO MERCY

Harlequin is pleased to offer these six very special titles, out of print since 1980. These authors have published over 250 titles between them. Popular demand required that we reissue each of these exciting romances in new beautifully designed covers.

Available in April wherever paperback books are sold, or through Harlequin Reader Service. Simply send your name, address and zip or postal code, with a check or money order for $2.50 for each copy ordered (includes 75¢ for postage and handling) payable to Harlequin Reader Service, to:

Harlequin Reader Service

In the U.S.
P.O. Box 52040
Phoenix, AZ 85072-2040

In Canada
P.O. Box 2800
Postal Station A
5170 Yonge Street
Willowdale, Ontario
M2N 6J3

PAE-1

EYE OF THE STORM

MAURA SEGER

A powerful
portrayal of
the events of
World War II in the
Pacific, *Eye of the Storm* is a riveting story of how love
triumphs over hatred. In this, the first of a three-book
chronicle, Army nurse Maggie Lawrence meets Marine
Sgt. Anthony Gargano. Despite military regulations
against fraternization, they resolve to face together
whatever lies ahead…. Author Maura Seger, also known
to her fans as Laurel Winslow, Sara Jennings, Anne
MacNeil and Jenny Bates, was named 1984's
Most Versatile Romance Author by *The Romantic Times*.

At your favorite bookstore in April.

EYE-D-1

Enter a uniquely exciting new world with

Harlequin American Romance T.M.

Harlequin American Romances are the first romances to explore today's love relationships. These compelling novels reach into the hearts and minds of women across America... probing the most intimate moments of romance, love and desire.

You'll follow romantic heroines and irresistible men as they boldly face confusing choices. Career first, love later? Love without marriage? Long-distance relationships? All the experiences that make love real are captured in the tender, loving pages of **Harlequin American Romances.**

What makes American women so different when it comes to love? Find out with **Harlequin American Romance!**

Send for your introductory FREE book now!

Get this book FREE!

Twice in a Lifetime
REBECCA FLANDERS

Harlequin American Romance

Mail to:

Harlequin Reader Service

In the U.S.
2504 West Southern Ave.
Tempe, AZ 85282

In Canada
P.O. Box 2800, Postal Station A
5170 Yonge St., Willowdale, Ont. M2N 5T5

YES! I want to be one of the first to discover **Harlequin American Romance.** Send me FREE and without obligation *Twice in a Lifetime*. If you do not hear from me after I have examined my FREE book, please send me the 4 new **Harlequin American Romances** each month as soon as they come off the presses. I understand that I will be billed only $2.25 for each book (total $9.00). There are no shipping or handling charges. There is no minimum number of books that I have to purchase. In fact, I may cancel this arrangement at any time. *Twice in a Lifetime* is mine to keep as a FREE gift, even if I do not buy any additional books.

Name _____ (please print)

Address _____ Apt. no.

City _____ State/Prov. _____ Zip/Postal Code

Signature (If under 18, parent or guardian must sign.)

This offer is limited to one order per household and not valid to current Harlequin American Romance subscribers. We reserve the right to exercise discretion in granting membership. If price changes are necessary, you will be notified.

154-BPA-NAZJ

AMR-SUB-2

WELCOME TO...

SUPERROMANCES

A sensational series of modern love stories
from Worldwide Library.

Written by masters of the genre, these longer,
sensual and dramatic novels are truly in keeping
with today's changing life-styles. Full of intriguing
conflicts, the heartaches and delights of true love,
SUPERROMANCES are absorbing stories —
satisfying and sophisticated reading that lovers
of romance fiction have long been waiting for.

SUPERROMANCES
Contemporary love stories for the woman of today!